THE EDINBURGH MYSTERY

AND OTHER TALES OF SCOTTISH CRIME

T0017099

THE EDINBURGH MYSTERY

AND OTHER TALES OF SCOTTISH CRIME

Edited and Introduced by
Martin Edwards

Poisoned Pen
PRESS

Selection, introduction, and notes © 2022, 2023 by Martin Edwards
Cover and internal design © 2023 by Sourcebooks
Cover illustration © NRM/Pictorial Collection/Science & Society Picture Library

Dates attributed to each story relate to first publication.
"Footsteps" © 1926 by The Estate of Robert McNair Wilson
"Madame Ville d'Aubier" © 1930 by The Estate of Elizabeth MacKintosh
"The Man on Ben Na Garve" © 1933 by The Estate of Henry Howarth
Bashford, reprinted with the permission of David Higham Associates
"The Case of the Frugal Cake" © 1955 by The Estate of Margery Lawrence,
reprinted with the permission of David Higham Associates
"Thursday's Child" © 1959 by The Estate of Alfred Clark,
reprinted with the permission of United Agents
"The Alibi Man" © 1965 by The Estate of William Knox
"The Fishermen" © 1970 by The Estate of J. I. M. Stewart, reprinted
with the permission of Peters Fraser and Dunlop
"Hand in Glove" © 1974 by The Estate of Gwendoline Butler
"The Running of the Deer" © 1974 by The Estate of P. M.
Hubbard, reprinted with the permission of United Agents

Published by Poisoned Pen Press, an imprint of Sourcebooks,
in association with the British Library
P.O. Box 4410, Naperville, Illinois 60567-4410
(630) 961-3900
sourcebooks.com

Cataloging-in-Publication Data is on file with the Library of Congress.

Printed and bound in the United States of America.
SB 10 9 8 7 6 5 4 3 2 1

Contents

Introduction

Scottish crime fiction has a long and dazzling history. This anthology celebrates Scotland's contribution to classic crime and offers a blend of stories written by Scottish authors together with short mysteries, like the title story, which are set north of the border.

These days, the phrase "Tartan Noir" is much in vogue, but as a leading Scottish author, Aline Templeton, has pointed out, there is really nothing new about "Tartan Noir" at all. A lecture she gave during the Alibis in the Archive crime fiction heritage weekend at Gladstone's Library in 2019 planted the seed of this anthology in my mind. She dated the interest of Scottish writers in the dark side of the criminal mind back to James Hogg's *The Private Memoirs and Confessions of a Justified Sinner*, an extraordinary and disturbing book first published (anonymously) in 1824.

Hogg's novel was written, as Aline Templeton says, "when the Gothic novels of Hugh Walpole and Ann Radcliffe were the height of fashion and he was influenced too by the

German legend of the doppelganger, the 'twin stranger.' It is a curious book, with the Memoirs section and the postscript claiming to have been written by an editor who alleges the Confession is a document that has happened to come his way. The tone of the Memoirs is satirical, often humorous... The Confession is different entirely. Robert Wringhim, hypocritical and deluded, is tempted by the sinister, demonic Gil-Martin to believe himself one of the 'justified' and therefore assured of salvation whatever he does... There are many layers in this book, a complex satire not only on Calvinism but on the self-satisfied disciples of the Enlightenment, but at heart it is a crime novel with murders, mysteries, and puzzles for the reader to solve."

Ian Rankin, one of the world's most successful contemporary crime writers and a prominent exponent of Tartan Noir, also acknowledges Hogg's influence in his essay "Why Crime Fiction is Good For You" in the Detection Club book *Howdunit*. Like Aline Templeton, he is an admirer of Robert Louis Stevenson, whose *Strange Case of Dr. Jekyll and Mr. Hyde* reflects, as Hogg's book does, the ambiguity that lies at the heart of much of the finest Scottish literature, even though Stevenson actually set his novella in London.

In terms of global success and long-term influence, no Scottish detective writer can match Sir Arthur Conan Doyle. Sherlock Holmes was English, but his methods of deduction were modelled on those of the Scottish surgeon and lecturer at the medical school of the University of Edinburgh, Dr. Joseph Bell. After meeting Bell in 1877, Doyle served as his clerk at Edinburgh Royal Infirmary. Bell's expertise was called upon in several real life cases, including the "Ardlamont mystery"; in that case, he gave evidence for the prosecution at the trial of Alfred John Monson for the murder of Cecil Hambrough. The outcome was a verdict of "not proven," which some thought erred on the side of generosity.

The Ardlamont case is one of the classic crimes of British legal history, and the central puzzle has intrigued generations of crime writers. The Scottish detective novelist J. J. Connington (Professor A. W. Stewart), a leading figure during the Golden Age of Murder between the world wars, used the story as raw material for his country house detective novel *The Ha-Ha Case* in 1934. Half a century later, a dramatised reconstruction of the case for BBC Television, "Open Season," was scripted by Peter May, who is today renowned as a bestselling crime novelist and author of The Lewis Trilogy and stand-alone novels, some of which are set in his native Scotland.

The name of Samuel Rutherford Crockett is perhaps not widely remembered, but in the late Victorian era he was a prominent Scottish man of letters. He was highly prolific and has been criticised for an excess of sentimentality in much of his work, but *The Azure Hand*, published posthumously, is an interesting and under-estimated detective novel.

Joseph Storer Clouston, whose first books were published as the nineteenth century drew to a close, came from a prominent Orcadian family and achieved considerable success. *Carrington's Cases*, a short story collection which appeared in 1920, was deemed by Ellery Queen to be a landmark title and was included in the "Queen's Quorum" list of the most important single-author story collections in the genre.

John Buchan, born in Perth and later created Baron

Tweedsmuir, was—by a distance—the finest British thriller writer of the first part of the twentieth century. He made splendid use of Scottish backgrounds in novels such as his famous manhunt story *The Thirty-Nine Steps*. His hero Richard Hannay finds himself embroiled in a murderous plot and flees to Galloway; as in much of his other work, rural Scotland is lovingly described.

Glasgow-born Robert McNair Wilson, a doctor who published many books under his own name was equally industrious as a detective novelist, writing as Anthony Wynne. He established a considerable reputation as a specialist in locked room mysteries and other stories about seemingly impossible crimes, in a career spanning a quarter of a century. His "Great Detective" was Dr. Eustace Hailey, "the Giant of Harley Street," who had a penchant for taking snuff.

Winifred Peck, a member of the famous Knox family, was born in England but married a Scot. Her novels include the detective story *The Warrielaw Jewel*, which is set in Edinburgh, a city she knew well. Other Scottish crime writers of the mid-twentieth century included Angus MacVicar, Allan MacKinnon (better known as a screenwriter) and the poet Ruthven Todd, who wrote a handful of detective novels under the name R. T. Campbell.

The most famous Golden Age novel with a Scottish backdrop is surely *The Five Red Herrings*, a Lord Peter Wimsey novel by Dorothy L. Sayers (who was English, but married to a Scot from Orkney), which is set in an artistic community in Galloway. The plot involves, as Sayers acknowledged, a trick used by the Scottish detective novelist J. J. Connington in *The Two Tickets Puzzle*, which she develops further.

Elizabeth MacKintosh, who wrote as Gordon Daviot and Josephine Tey, was born in Inverness and remained resolutely committed to her home patch, despite occasional ventures to England prompted by the success of her plays and her detective fiction. Her first detective novel featuring Inspector Alan Grant appeared in 1929, and Grant's final case, *The Singing Sands*, was published after his creator's tragically early death in 1952. During her lifetime she wrote a mere eight crime novels, but her reputation as a crime author remains as high as ever today, and she even features as a detective in the novels of contemporary author Nicola Upson.

Born in Edinburgh, John Innes Mackintosh Stewart was an eminent academic who wrote mainstream novels under his own name, but is today best remembered for his detective novels featuring John Appleby of Scotland Yard, for which he used the pen-name Michael Innes. One of Innes's earliest and most admired mysteries, *Lament for a Maker*, is set in the Scottish Highlands and makes interesting use of multiple narrators.

Of the Scottish writers to emerge during the 1950s, Alistair MacLean achieved the greatest commercial success thanks to a long run of action thrillers such as *The Guns of Navarone*; many of his books were filmed. MacLean encouraged a young journalist called Bill Knox to write fiction, and Knox became a prolific and highly reliable author of a wide range of crime stories as well as the presenter of a TV show about real life crime. Among the other notable Scottish crime writers of the last generation, Hugh C. Rae, Frederic Lindsay, and Alanna Knight all deserve mention, as well as Troy Kennedy Martin, who was (as was his younger brother Ian) a leading scriptwriter for television (*Z-Cars*, for instance) and film

(*The Italian Job*). Perhaps the most lauded was William McIlvanney, who published three novels about the tough cop Laidlaw. His last book, *The Dark Remains*, was completed by Ian Rankin and published in 2021.

Today, Scottish crime writers crowd the bestseller lists: Rankin, Val McDermid, Alexander McCall Smith, Stuart MacBride, and others have produced a long line of books that exert global appeal. So what is it about Scotland that gives rise to so much good crime writing?

Aline Templeton suggests that her native landscape plays an important part in fashioning the mindset of Scottish writers. The countryside is: "Dramatic, impressive, stunning in its beauty, certainly. But not exactly, well, cheerful. At the height of the Romantic period, with poets like Wordsworth and Coleridge hymning nature as their goddess, it became fashionable to travel to see the mountains of Scotland, but their majesty was so terrifying that shrieking travellers who had come to see them pulled down the blinds of the coaches to escape their menace. And before you laugh, try driving across Skye towards the west through what seem like perfectly respectable mountains until suddenly behind them, like some monster, looms up the immense, threatening bulk of the Black Cuillin, and I defy you not to gasp aloud. Travel through Glencoe, with its history of treachery and tragedy, and even on the brightest day it has a foreboding atmosphere."

The Edinburgh Mystery and Other Tales of Scottish Crime gathers together a wide range of classic Scottish crime and mystery stories. As ever with anthologies in this series, I have aimed to showcase a diverse range of settings, styles, and storylines. Once again, I'd like to express my gratitude to all those who have helped and encouraged me with this project. Particular thanks go to Aline Templeton, Jennifer Morag Henderson, Cally Wright, Jamie Sturgeon, John Cooper, Nigel Moss, and all those at the British Library who have worked on this book.

—Martin Edwards
www.martinedwardsbooks.com

A Note from the Publisher

The original novels and short stories reprinted in the British Library Crime Classics series were written and published in a period ranging, for the most part, from the 1890s to the 1960s. There are many elements of these stories which continue to entertain modern readers; however, in some cases there are also uses of language, instances of stereotyping and some attitudes expressed by narrators or characters which may not be endorsed by the publishing standards of today. We acknowledge therefore that some elements in the works selected for reprinting may continue to make uncomfortable reading for some of our audience. With this series British Library Publishing and Poisoned Pen Press aim to offer a new readership a chance to read some of the rare books of the British Library's collections in an affordable paperback format, to enjoy their merits, and to look back into the world of the twentieth century as portrayed by its writers. It is not possible to separate these stories from the history of their writing and as such the following stories are presented as they were originally published with minor edits only, made for consistency of style and sense. We welcome feedback from our readers.

Markheim

Robert Louis Stevenson

Robert Louis Stevenson (1850–94) was not a crime writer in the generally accepted sense, but crime features in much of his fiction. He exerted an important influence on the development of sensational literature, including crime writing. Although he was much admired during his lifetime, in the twentieth century his reputation faded, and he was regarded by some as essentially an exponent of children's fiction and macabre stories. Virginia Woolf was among his detractors, while G. K. Chesterton was prominent among those who appreciated the quality of his work. Today his storytelling gifts and the power of his imagination are widely recognised.

Stevenson's famous Gothic novella, *Strange Case of Dr. Jekyll and Mr. Hyde* (1886) is a masterly study of a divided personality; its influence can be seen in Hugh Walpole's chilling murder story *The Killer and the Slain* (1942) among many other books. *The Wrong Box* (1889), co-written with

Lloyd Osbourne, is an enjoyable comedy thriller about a tontine which was filmed with a starry cast in 1966. "Markheim," which blends crime, horror, and the supernatural in a distinctively Stevensonian fashion, was first published in *The Broken Shaft,* as part of *Unwin's Christmas Annual,* in 1885.

———

"YES," SAID THE DEALER, "OUR WINDFALLS ARE OF VARious kinds. Some customers are ignorant, and then I touch a dividend on my superior knowledge. Some are dishonest," and here he held up the candle, so that the light fell strongly on his visitor, "and in that case," he continued, "I profit by my virtue."

Markheim had but just entered from the daylight streets, and his eyes had not yet grown familiar with the mingled shine and darkness in the shop. At these pointed words, and before the near presence of the flame, he blinked painfully and looked aside.

The dealer chuckled. "You come to me on Christmas Day," he resumed, "when you know that I am alone in my house, put up my shutters, and make a point of refusing business. Well, you will have to pay for that; you will have to pay for my loss of time, when I should be balancing my books; you will have to pay, besides, for a kind of manner that I remark in you today very strongly. I am the essence of discretion, and ask no awkward questions; but when a customer cannot look me in the eye, he has to pay for it." The dealer once more chuckled; and then, changing to his usual business voice, though still with a note of irony, "You can give, as usual, a clear account of how you came into the possession of the object?" he continued. "Still your uncle's cabinet? A remarkable collector, sir!"

And the little pale, round-shouldered dealer stood almost on tip-toe, looking over the top of his gold spectacles, and nodding his head with every mark of disbelief. Markheim returned his gaze with one of infinite pity, and a touch of horror.

"This time," said he, "you are in error. I have not come to sell, but to buy. I have no curios to dispose of; my uncle's cabinet is bare to the wainscot; even were it still intact, I have done well on the Stock Exchange, and should more likely add to it than otherwise, and my errand today is simplicity itself. I seek a Christmas present for a lady," he continued, waxing more fluent as he struck into the speech he had prepared; "and certainly I owe you every excuse for thus disturbing you upon so small a matter. But the thing was neglected yesterday; I must produce my little compliment at dinner; and, as you very well know, a rich marriage is not a thing to be neglected."

There followed a pause, during which the dealer seemed to weigh this statement incredulously. The ticking of many clocks among the curious lumber of the shop, and the faint rushing of the cabs in a near thoroughfare, filled up the interval of silence.

"Well, sir," said the dealer, "be it so. You are an old customer after all; and if, as you say, you have the chance of a good marriage, far be it from me to be an obstacle. Here is a nice thing for a lady now," he went on, "this hand glass—fifteenth century, warranted; comes from a good collection, too; but I reserve the name, in the interests of my customer, who was just like yourself, my dear sir, the nephew and sole heir of a remarkable collector."

The dealer, while he thus ran on in his dry and biting voice, had stooped to take the object from its place; and, as he had done so, a shock had passed through Markheim, a start both of hand and foot, a sudden leap of many tumultuous passions to the face. It passed as swiftly as it came, and left no trace beyond a certain trembling of the hand that now received the glass.

"A glass," he said hoarsely, and then paused, and repeated it more clearly. "A glass? For Christmas? Surely not?"

"And why not?" cried the dealer. "Why not a glass?"

Markheim was looking upon him with an indefinable expression. "You ask me why not?" he said. "Why, look here—look in it—look at yourself! Do you like to see it? No! nor I—nor any man."

The little man had jumped back when Markheim had so suddenly confronted him with the mirror; but now, perceiving there was nothing worse on hand, he chuckled. "Your future lady, sir, must be pretty hard favoured," said he.

"I ask you," said Markheim, "for a Christmas present, and you give me this—this damned reminder of years, and sins and follies—this hand-conscience! Did you mean it? Had you a thought in your mind? Tell me. It will be better for you if you do. Come, tell me about yourself. I hazard a guess now, that you are in secret a very charitable man?"

The dealer looked closely at his companion. It was very odd, Markheim did not appear to be laughing; there was something in his face like an eager sparkle of hope, but nothing of mirth.

"What are you driving at?" the dealer asked.

"Not charitable?" returned the other, gloomily. "Not charitable; not pious; not scrupulous; unloving, unbeloved; a hand to get money, a safe to keep it. Is that all? Dear God, man, is that all?"

"I will tell you what it is," began the dealer, with some sharpness, and then broke off again into a chuckle. "But I see this is a love match of yours, and you have been drinking the lady's health."

"Ah!" cried Markheim, with a strange curiosity. "Ah, have you been in love? Tell me about that."

"I," cried the dealer. "I in love! I never had the time, nor have I the time today for all this nonsense. Will you take the glass?"

"Where is the hurry?" returned Markheim. "It is very pleasant to stand here talking; and life is so short and insecure that I would not hurry away from any pleasure—no, not even from so mild a one as this. We should rather cling, cling to what little we can get, like a man at a cliff's edge. Every second is a cliff, if you think upon it—a cliff a mile high—high enough, if we fall, to dash us out of every feature of humanity. Hence it is best to talk pleasantly. Let us talk of each other: why should we wear this mask? Let us be confidential. Who knows, we might become friends?"

"I have just one word to say to you," said the dealer. "Either make your purchase, or walk out of my shop!"

"True, true," said Markheim. "Enough fooling. To business. Show me something else."

The dealer stooped once more, this time to replace the glass upon the shelf, his thin blond hair falling over his eyes as he did so. Markheim moved a little nearer, with one hand in the pocket of his greatcoat; he drew himself up and filled his lungs; at the same time many different emotions were depicted together on his face—terror, horror, and resolve, fascination, and a physical repulsion; and through a haggard lift of his upper lip, his teeth looked out.

"This, perhaps, may suit," observed the dealer: and then, as he began to re-arise, Markheim bounded from behind upon his victim. The long, skewer-like dagger flashed and fell. The dealer struggled like a hen, striking his temple on the shelf, and then tumbled on the floor in a heap.

Time had some score of small voices in that shop, some stately and slow as was becoming to their great age; others garrulous and hurried. All these told out the seconds in an intricate chorus of tickings. Then the passage of a lad's feet, heavily running on the pavement, broke in upon these smaller voices and startled Markheim into the consciousness of his surroundings. He looked about him awfully. The candle stood on the counter, its flame solemnly wagging in a draught; and by that inconsiderable movement, the whole room was filled with noiseless bustle and kept heaving like a sea: the tall shadows nodding, the gross blots of darkness swelling and dwindling as with respiration, the faces of the portraits and the china gods changing and wavering like images in water. The inner door stood ajar, and peered into that leaguer of shadows with a long slit of daylight like a pointing finger.

From these fear-stricken rovings, Markheim's eyes returned to the body of his victim, where it lay both humped and sprawling, incredibly small and strangely meaner than in life. In these poor, miserly clothes, in that ungainly attitude, the dealer lay like so much sawdust. Markheim had feared to see it, and, lo! it was nothing. And yet, as he gazed, this bundle of old clothes and pool of blood began to find eloquent voices. There it must lie; there was none to work the cunning hinges or direct the miracle of locomotion—there it must lie till it was found. Found! ay, and then? Then would this dead flesh lift up a cry that would ring over England, and fill the world with the echoes of pursuit. Ay, dead or not, this was still the enemy. "Time was that when the brains were out," he thought; and the first word struck into his mind. Time, now that the deed was accomplished—time, which had closed for the victim, had become instant and momentous for the slayer.

The thought was yet in his mind, when, first one and then another, with every variety of pace and voice—one deep as the bell from a cathedral turret, another ringing on its treble notes the prelude of a waltz—the clocks began to strike the hour of three in the afternoon.

The sudden outbreak of so many tongues in that dumb chamber staggered him. He began to bestir himself, going to and fro with the candle, beleaguered by moving shadows, and startled to the soul by chance reflections. In many rich mirrors, some of home design, some from Venice or Amsterdam, he saw his face repeated and repeated, as it were an army of spies; his own eyes met and detected him; and the sound of his own steps, lightly as they fell, vexed the surrounding quiet. And still, as he continued to fill his pockets, his mind accused him with a sickening iteration, of the thousand faults of his design. He should have chosen a more quiet hour; he should have prepared an alibi; he should not have used a knife; he should have been more cautious, and only bound and gagged the dealer, and not killed him; he should have been more bold, and killed the servant also; he should have done all things otherwise: poignant regrets, weary, incessant toiling of the mind to change what was unchangeable, to plan what was now useless, to be the architect of the irrevocable past. Meanwhile, and behind all this activity, brute terrors, like the scurrying of rats in a deserted attic, filled the more remote chambers of his brain with riot; the hand of the constable would fall heavy on his shoulder, and his nerves would jerk like a hooked fish; or he beheld, in galloping defile, the dock, the prison, the gallows, and the black coffin.

Terror of the people in the street sat down before his mind like a besieging army. It was impossible, he thought, but that some rumour of the struggle must have reached their ears and set on edge their curiosity; and now, in all the neighbouring houses, he divined them sitting motionless and with uplifted ear—solitary people, condemned to spend Christmas dwelling alone on memories of the past, and now startlingly recalled from that tender exercise; happy family parties, struck into silence round the table, the mother still with raised finger: every degree and age and humour, but all, by their own hearths, prying and hearkening and weaving the rope that was to hang him. Sometimes it seemed to him he could not move too softly; the clink of the tall Bohemian goblets rang out loudly like a bell; and alarmed by the bigness of the ticking, he was tempted to stop the clocks. And then, again, with a swift transition of his terrors, the very silence of the place appeared a source of peril, and a thing to strike and freeze the passer-by; and he would step more boldly, and bustle aloud among the contents of the shop, and imitate, with elaborate bravado, the movements of a busy man at ease in his own house.

But he was now so pulled about by different alarms that, while one portion of his mind was still alert and cunning, another trembled on the brink of lunacy. One hallucination in particular took a strong hold on his credulity. The neighbour hearkening with white face beside his window, the passer-by arrested by a horrible surmise on the pavement—these could at worst suspect, they could not know; through the brick walls and shuttered windows only sounds could penetrate. But here, within the house, was he alone? He knew he was; he had watched the servant set forth sweet-hearting, in her poor best, "out for the day" written in every ribbon and smile. Yes, he was alone, of course; and yet, in the bulk of empty house above him, he could surely hear a stir of delicate foot-ing—he was surely conscious, inexplicably conscious of some presence. Ay, surely; to every room and corner of the house his imagination followed it; and now it was a faceless thing, and yet had eyes to see with; and again it was a shadow of himself; and yet again behold the image of the dead dealer, reinspired with cunning and hatred.

At times, with a strong effort, he would glance at the open door which still seemed to repel his eyes. The house was tall, the skylight small and dirty, the day blind with fog; and the light that filtered down to the ground storey was exceedingly faint, and showed dimly on the threshold of the shop. And yet, in that strip of doubtful brightness, did there not hang wavering a shadow?

Suddenly, from the street outside, a very jovial gentleman began to beat with a staff on the shop-door, accompanying his blows with shouts and railleries in which the dealer was continually called upon by name. Markheim, smitten into ice, glanced at the dead man. But no! he lay quite still; he was fled away far beyond earshot of these blows and shoutings; he was sunk beneath seas of silence; and his name, which would once have caught his notice above the howling of a storm, had become an empty sound. And presently the jovial gentleman desisted from his knocking and departed.

Here was a broad hint to hurry what remained to be done, to get forth from this accusing neighbourhood, to plunge into a bath of London multitudes, and to reach, on the other side of day, that haven of safety and apparent innocence—his bed. One visitor had come: at any moment another might follow and be more obstinate. To have done the deed, and yet not to reap the profit, would be too abhorrent a failure. The money, that was now Markheim's concern; and as a means to that, the keys.

He glanced over his shoulder at the open door, where the shadow was still lingering and shivering; and with no conscious repugnance of the mind, yet with a tremor of the belly, he drew near the body of his victim. The human character had quite departed. Like a suit half-stuffed with bran, the limbs lay scattered, the trunk doubled, on the floor; and yet the thing repelled him. Although so dingy and inconsiderable to the eye, he feared it might have more significance to the touch. He took the body by the shoulders, and turned it on its back. It was strangely light and supple, and the limbs, as if they had been broken, fell into the oddest postures. The face was robbed of all expression; but it was as pale as wax, and shockingly smeared with blood about one temple. That was, for Markheim, the one displeasing circumstance.

It carried him back, upon the instant, to a certain fair-day in a fishers' village: a grey day, a piping wind, a crowd upon the street, the blare of brasses, the booming of drums, the nasal voice of a ballad singer; and a boy going to and fro, buried over head in the crowd and divided between interest and fear, until, coming out upon the chief place of concourse, he beheld a booth and a great screen with pictures, dismally designed, garishly coloured: Brownrigg with her apprentice; the Mannings with their murdered guest; Weare in the death-grip of Thurtell; and a score besides of famous crimes. The thing was as clear as an illusion; he was once again that little boy; he was looking once again, and with the same sense of physical revolt, at these vile pictures; he was still stunned by the thumping of the drums. A bar of that day's music returned upon his memory; and at that, for the first time, a qualm came over him, a breath of nausea, a sudden weakness of the joints, which he must instantly resist and conquer.

He judged it more prudent to confront than to flee from these considerations; looking the more hardily in the dead face, bending his mind to realise the nature and greatness of his crime. So little a while ago that face had moved with every change of sentiment, that pale mouth had spoken, that body had been all on fire with governable energies; and now, and by his act, that piece of life had been arrested, as the horologist, with interjected finger, arrests the beating of the clock. So he reasoned in vain; he could rise to no more remorseful consciousness; the same heart which had shuddered before the painted effigies of crime, looked on its reality unmoved. At best, he felt a gleam of pity for one who had been endowed in vain with all those faculties that can make the world a garden of enchantment, one who had never lived and who was now dead. But of penitence, no, not a tremor.

With that, shaking himself clear of these considerations, he found the keys and advanced towards the open door of the shop. Outside, it had begun to rain smartly; and the sound of the shower upon the roof had banished silence. Like some dripping cavern, the chambers of the house were haunted by an incessant echoing, which filled the ear and mingled with the ticking of the clocks. And, as Markheim approached the door, he seemed to hear, in answer to his own cautious tread, the steps of another foot withdrawing up the stair. The shadow still palpitated loosely on the threshold. He threw a ton's weight of resolve upon his muscles, and drew back the door.

The faint, foggy daylight glimmered dimly on the bare floor and stairs; on the bright suit of armour posted, halbert in hand, upon the landing; and on the dark wood-carvings, and framed pictures that hung against the yellow panels of the wainscot. So loud was the beating of the rain through all the house that, in Markheim's ears, it began to be distinguished into many different sounds. Footsteps and sighs, the tread of regiments marching in the distance, the chink of money in the counting, and the creaking of doors held stealthily ajar, appeared to mingle with the patter of the drops upon the cupola and the gushing of the water in the pipes. The sense that he was not alone grew upon him to the verge of madness. On every side he was haunted and begirt by presences. He heard them moving in the upper chambers; from the shop, he heard the dead man getting to his legs; and as he began with a great effort to mount the stairs, feet fled quietly before him and followed stealthily behind. If he were but deaf, he thought, how tranquilly he would possess his soul! And then again, and hearkening with ever fresh attention, he blessed himself for that unresting sense which held the outposts and stood a trusty sentinel upon his life. His head turned continually on his neck; his eyes, which seemed starting from their orbits, scouted on every side, and on every side were half-rewarded as with the tail of something nameless vanishing. The four-and-twenty steps to the first floor were four-and-twenty agonies.

On that first storey, the doors stood ajar, three of them like three ambushes, shaking his nerves like the throats of cannon. He could never again, he felt, be sufficiently immured and fortified from men's observing eyes; he longed to be home, girt in by walls, buried among bedclothes, and invisible to all but God. And at that thought he wondered a little, recollecting tales of other murderers and the fear they were said to entertain of heavenly avengers. It was not so, at least, with him. He feared the laws of nature, lest, in their callous and immutable procedure, they should preserve some damning evidence of his crime. He feared tenfold more, with a slavish, superstitious terror, some scission in the continuity of man's experience, some wilful illegality of nature. He played a game of skill, depending on the rules, calculating consequence from cause; and what if nature, as the defeated tyrant overthrew the chess-board, should break the mould of their succession? The like had befallen Napoleon (so writers said) when the winter changed the time of its appearance. The like might befall Markheim: the solid walls might become transparent and reveal his doings like those of bees in a glass hive; the stout planks might yield under his foot like quicksands and detain him in their clutch; ay, and there were soberer accidents that might destroy him: if, for instance, the house should fall and imprison him beside the body of his victim; or the house next door should fly on fire, and the firemen invade him from all sides. These things he feared; and, in a sense, these things might be called the hands of God reached forth against sin. But about God himself he was at ease; his act was doubtless exceptional, but so were his excuses, which God knew; it was there, and not among men, that he felt sure of justice.

When he had got safe into the drawing-room, and shut the door behind him, he was aware of a respite from alarms. The room was quite dismantled, uncarpeted besides, and strewn with packing cases and incongruous furniture; several great pier-glasses, in which he beheld himself at various angles, like an actor on a stage; many pictures, framed and unframed, standing, with their faces to the wall; a fine Sheraton side-board, a cabinet of marquetry, and a great old bed, with tapestry hangings. The windows opened to the floor; but by great good fortune the lower part of the shutters had been closed, and this concealed him from the neighbours. Here, then, Markheim drew in a packing case before the cabinet, and began to search among the keys. It was a long business, for there were many; and it was irksome, besides; for, after all, there might be nothing in the cabinet, and time was on the wing. But the closeness of the occupation sobered him. With the tail of his eye he saw the door—even glanced at it from time to time directly, like a besieged commander pleased to verify the good estate of his defences. But in truth he was at peace. The rain falling in the street sounded natural and pleasant. Presently, on the other side, the notes of a piano were wakened to the music of a hymn, and the voices of many children took up the air and words. How stately, how comfortable was the melody! How fresh the youthful voices! Markheim gave ear to it smilingly, as he sorted out the keys; and his mind was thronged with answerable ideas and images; church-going children and the pealing of the high organ; children afield, bathers by the brookside, ramblers on the brambly common, kite-flyers in the windy and cloud-navigated sky; and then, at another cadence of the hymn, back again to church, and the somnolence of summer Sundays, and the high genteel voice of the parson (which he smiled a little to recall) and the painted Jacobean tombs, and the dim lettering of the Ten Commandments in the chancel.

And as he sat thus, at once busy and absent, he was startled to his feet. A flash of ice, a flash of fire, a bursting gush of blood, went over him, and then he stood transfixed and thrilling. A step mounted the stair slowly and steadily, and presently a hand was laid upon the knob, and the lock clicked, and the door opened.

Fear held Markheim in a vice. What to expect he knew not, whether the dead man walking, or the official ministers of human justice, or some chance witness blindly stumbling in to consign him to the gallows. But when a face was thrust into the aperture, glanced round the room, looked at him, nodded and smiled as if in friendly recognition, and then withdrew again, and the door closed behind it, his fear broke loose from his control in a hoarse cry. At the sound of this the visitant returned.

"Did you call me?" he asked, pleasantly, and with that he entered the room and closed the door behind him.

Markheim stood and gazed at him with all his eyes. Perhaps there was a film upon his sight, but the outlines of the new comer seemed to change and waver like those of the idols in the wavering candlelight of the shop; and at times he thought he knew him; and at times he thought he bore a likeness to himself; and always, like a lump of living terror, there lay in his bosom the conviction that this thing was not of the earth and not of God.

And yet the creature had a strange air of the commonplace, as he stood looking on Markheim with a smile; and when he added: "You are looking for the money, I believe?" it was in the tones of everyday politeness.

Markheim made no answer.

"I should warn you," resumed the other, "that the maid has left her sweetheart earlier than usual and will soon be here. If Mr. Markheim be found in this house, I need not describe to him the consequences."

"You know me?" cried the murderer.

The visitor smiled. "You have long been a favourite of mine," he said; "and I have long observed and often sought to help you."

"What are you?" cried Markheim: "the devil?"

"What I may be," returned the other, "cannot affect the service I propose to render you."

"It can," cried Markheim; "it does! Be helped by you? No, never; not by you! You do not know me yet; thank God, you do not know me!"

"I know you," replied the visitant, with a sort of kind severity or rather firmness. "I know you to the soul."

"Know me!" cried Markheim. "Who can do so? My life is but a travesty and slander on myself. I have lived to belie my nature. All men do; all men are better than this disguise that grows about and stifles them. You see each dragged away by life, like one whom bravos have seized and muffled in a cloak. If they had their own control—if you could see their faces, they would be altogether different, they would shine out for heroes and saints! I am worse than most; myself is more overlaid; my excuse is known to me and God. But, had I the time, I could disclose myself."

"To me?" inquired the visitant.

"To you before all," returned the murderer. "I supposed you were intelligent. I thought—since you exist—you would prove a reader of the heart. And yet you would propose to judge me by my acts! Think of it; my acts! I was born and I have lived in a land of giants; giants have dragged me by the wrists since I was born out of my mother—the giants of circumstance. And you would judge me by my acts! But can you not look within? Can you not understand that evil is hateful to me? Can you not see within me the clear writing of conscience, never blurred by any wilful sophistry, although too often disregarded? Can you not read me for a thing that surely must be common as humanity—the unwilling sinner?"

"All this is very feelingly expressed," was the reply, "but it regards me not. These points of consistency are beyond my province, and I care not in the least by what compulsion you may have been dragged away, so as you are but carried in the right direction. But time flies; the servant delays, looking in the faces of the crowd and at the pictures on the hoardings, but still she keeps moving nearer; and remember, it is as if the gallows itself was striding towards you through the Christmas streets! Shall I help you; I, who know all? Shall I tell you where to find the money?"

"For what price?" asked Markheim.

"I offer you the service for a Christmas gift," returned the other.

Markheim could not refrain from smiling with a kind of bitter triumph. "No," said he, "I will take nothing at your hands; if I were dying of thirst, and it was your hand that put the pitcher to my lips, I should find the courage to refuse. It may be credulous, but I will do nothing to commit myself to evil."

"I have no objection to a deathbed repentance," observed the visitant.

"Because you disbelieve their efficacy!" Markheim cried.

"I do not say so," returned the other; "but I look on these things from a different side, and when the life is done my interest falls. The man has lived to serve me, to spread black looks under colour of religion, or to sow tares in the wheat-field, as you do, in a course of weak compliance with desire. Now that he draws so near to his deliverance, he can add but one act of service—to repent, to die smiling, and thus to build up in confidence and hope the more timorous of my surviving followers. I am not so hard a master. Try me. Accept my help. Please yourself in life as you have done hitherto; please yourself more amply, spread your elbows at the board; and when the night begins to fall and the curtains to be drawn, I tell you, for your greater comfort, that you will find it even easy to compound your quarrel with your conscience, and to make a truckling peace with God. I came but now from such a deathbed, and the room was full of sincere mourners, listening to the man's last words: and when I looked into that face, which had been set as a flint against mercy, I found it smiling with hope."

"And do you, then, suppose me such a creature?" asked Markheim. "Do you think I have no more generous aspirations than to sin, and sin, and sin, and, at the last, sneak into heaven? My heart rises at the thought. Is this, then, your experience of mankind? or is it because you find me with red hands that you presume such baseness? and is this crime of murder indeed so impious as to dry up the very springs of good?"

"Murder is to me no special category," replied the other. "All sins are murder, even as all life is war. I behold your race, like starving mariners on a raft, plucking crusts out of the hands of famine and feeding on each other's lives. I follow sins beyond the moment of their acting; I find in all that the last consequence is death; and to my eyes, the pretty maid who thwarts her mother with such taking graces on a question of a ball, drips no less visibly with human gore than such a murderer as yourself. Do I say that I follow sins? I follow virtues also; they differ not by the thickness of a nail, they are both scythes for the reaping angel of Death. Evil, for which I live, consists not in action but in character. The bad man is dear to me; not the bad act, whose fruits, if we could follow them far enough down the hurtling cataract of the ages, might yet be found more blessed than those of the rarest virtues. And it is not because you have killed a dealer, but because you are Markheim, that I offer to forward your escape."

"I will lay my heart open to you," answered Markheim.

"This crime on which you find me is my last. On my way to it I have learned many lessons; itself is a lesson, a momentous lesson. Hitherto I have been driven with revolt to what I would not; I was a bond-slave to poverty, driven and scourged. There are robust virtues that can stand in these temptations; mine was not so: I had a thirst of pleasure. But today, and out of this deed, I pluck both warning and riches—both the power and a fresh resolve to be myself. I become in all things a free actor in the world; I begin to see myself all changed, these hands the agents of good, this heart at peace. Something comes over me out of the past; something of what I have dreamed on Sabbath evenings to the sound of the church organ, of what I forecast when I shed tears over noble books, or talked, an innocent child, with my mother. There lies my life; I have wandered a few years, but now I see once more my city of destination."

"You are to use this money on the Stock Exchange, I think?" remarked the visitor; "and there, if I mistake not, you have already lost some thousands?"

"Ah," said Markheim, "but this time I have a sure thing."

"This time, again, you will lose," replied the visitor quietly.

"Ah, but I keep back the half!" cried Markheim.

"That also you will lose," said the other.

The sweat started upon Markheim's brow. "Well, then, what matter?" he exclaimed. "Say it be lost, say I am plunged again in poverty, shall one part of me, and that the worse, continue until the end to override the better? Evil and good run strong in me, haling me both ways. I do not love the one thing, I love all. I can conceive great deeds, renunciations, martyrdoms; and though I be fallen to such a crime as murder, pity is no stranger to my thoughts. I pity the poor; who knows their trials better than myself? I pity and help them; I prize love, I love honest laughter; there is no good thing nor true thing on earth but I love it from my heart. And are my vices only to direct my life, and my virtues to lie without effect, like some passive lumber of the mind? Not so; good, also, is a spring of acts."

But the visitant raised his finger. "For six-and-thirty years that you have been in this world," said he, "through many changes of fortune and varieties of humour, I have watched you steadily fall. Fifteen years ago you would have started at a theft. Three years back you would have blenched at the name of murder. Is there any crime, is there any cruelty or meanness, from which you still recoil?—five years from now I shall detect you in the fact! Downward, downward, lies your way; nor can anything but death avail to stop you."

"It is true," Markheim said huskily, "I have in some degree complied with evil. But it is so with all: the very saints, in the mere exercise of living, grow less dainty, and take on the tone of their surroundings."

"I will propound to you one simple question," said the other; "and as you answer, I shall read to you your moral horoscope. You have grown in many things more lax; possibly you do right to be so; and at any account, it is the same with all men. But granting that, are you in any one particular, however trifling, more difficult to please with your own conduct, or do you go in all things with a looser rein?"

"In any one?" repeated Markheim, with an anguish of consideration. "No," he added, with despair, "in none! I have gone down in all."

"Then," said the visitor, "content yourself with what you

are, for you will never change; and the words of your part on this stage are irrevocably written down."

Markheim stood for a long while silent, and indeed it was the visitor who first broke the silence. "That being so," he said, "shall I show you the money?"

"And grace?" cried Markheim.

"Have you not tried it?" returned the other. "Two or three years ago, did I not see you on the platform of revival meetings, and was not your voice the loudest in the hymn?"

"It is true," said Markheim; "and I see clearly what remains for me by way of duty. I thank you for these lessons from my soul; my eyes are opened, and I behold myself at last for what I am."

At this moment, the sharp note of the door-bell rang through the house; and the visitant, as though this were some concerted signal for which he had been waiting, changed at once in his demeanour.

"The maid!" he cried. "She has returned, as I forewarned you, and there is now before you one more difficult passage. Her master, you must say, is ill; you must let her in, with an assured but rather serious countenance—no smiles, no overacting, and I promise you success! Once the girl within, and the door closed, the same dexterity that has already rid you of the dealer will relieve you of this last danger in your path. Thenceforward you have the whole evening—the whole night, if needful—to ransack the treasures of the house and to make good your safety. This is help that comes to you with the mask of danger. Up!" he cried; "up, friend; your life hangs trembling in the scales: up, and act!"

Markheim steadily regarded his counsellor. "If I be

condemned to evil acts," he said, "there is still one door of freedom open—I can cease from action. If my life be an ill thing, I can lay it down. Though I be, as you say truly, at the beck of every small temptation, I can yet, by one decisive gesture, place myself beyond the reach of all. My love of good is damned to barrenness; it may, and let it be! But I have still my hatred of evil; and from that, to your galling disappointment, you shall see that I can draw both energy and courage."

The features of the visitor began to undergo a wonderful and lovely change: they brightened and softened with a tender triumph, and, even as they brightened, faded and dislimned. But Markheim did not pause to watch or understand the transformation. He opened the door and went downstairs very slowly, thinking to himself. His past went soberly before him; he beheld it as it was, ugly and strenuous like a dream, random as chance-medley—a scene of defeat. Life, as he thus reviewed it, tempted him no longer; but on the further side he perceived a quiet haven for his bark. He paused in the passage, and looked into the shop, where the candle still burned by the dead body. It was strangely silent. Thoughts of the dealer swarmed into his mind, as he stood gazing. And then the bell once more broke out into impatient clamour.

He confronted the maid upon the threshold with something like a smile.

"You had better go for the police," said he: "I have killed your master."

The Field Bazaar

Arthur Conan Doyle

Surely nobody has exerted more influence on the development of detective fiction than Edinburgh-born Arthur Ignatius Conan Doyle (1859–1930). He studied medicine at the University of Edinburgh Medical School, and encountered Dr. Joseph Bell, a Scottish surgeon and lecturer. He served as Bell's clerk at the Edinburgh Royal Infirmary and the older man's powers of observation and deduction made a great impression on him. Doyle was keen to supplement his income by writing fiction and when he tried his hand at a detective story, his recollection of Bell's gifts helped him to convey the peculiar talents of the consulting detective Sherlock Holmes.

By the time Holmes made his debut in *A Study in Scarlet* (1887), Doyle was working in England, but Scotland remained close to his heart. In 1900 he stood for Parliament as a Liberal Unionist Party candidate for Edinburgh Central, but without success. He blamed his poor showing on a poster campaign denouncing him, falsely, as a Papist conspirator determined to destroy the Scottish Kirk and Covenant. "The Field Bazaar" is a pleasing curiosity, a little story which he wrote to help raise money for sports facilities for the students of Edinburgh University; it was published in the *Student* magazine on 20 November 1896.

———

"I should certainly do it," said Sherlock Holmes.

I started at the interruption, for my companion had been eating his breakfast with his attention entirely centred upon the paper which was propped up by the coffee pot. Now I looked across at him to find his eyes fastened upon me with the half-amused, half-questioning expression which he usually assumed when he felt he had made an intellectual point.

"Do what?" I asked.

He smiled as he took his slipper from the mantelpiece and drew from it enough shag tobacco to fill the old clay pipe with which he invariably rounded off his breakfast.

"A most characteristic question of yours, Watson," said he. "You will not, I am sure, be offended if I say that any reputation for sharpness which I may possess has been entirely gained by the admirable foil which you have made for me. Have I not heard of debutantes who have insisted upon plainness in their chaperones? There is a certain analogy."

Our long companionship in the Baker Street rooms had left us on those easy terms of intimacy when much may be said without offence. And yet I acknowledged that I was nettled at his remark.

"I may be very obtuse," said I, "but I confess that I am unable to see how you have managed to know that I was… I was…"

"Asked to help in the Edinburgh University Bazaar…"

"Precisely. The letter has only just come to hand, and I have not spoken to you since."

"In spite of that," said Holmes, leaning back in his chair and putting his fingertips together, "I would even venture to suggest that the object of the bazaar is to enlarge the University cricket field."

I looked at him in such bewilderment that he vibrated with silent laughter.

"The fact is, my dear Watson, that you are an excellent subject," said he. "You are never blasé. You respond instantly to any external stimulus. Your mental processes may be slow but they are never obscure, and I found during breakfast that you were easier reading than the leader in the *Times* in front of me."

"I should be glad to know how you arrived at your conclusions," said I.

"I fear that my good nature in giving explanations has seriously compromised my reputation," said Holmes. "But in this case the train of reasoning is based upon such obvious facts that no credit can be claimed for it. You entered the room with a thoughtful expression, the expression of a man who is debating some point in his mind. In your hand you held a solitary letter. Now last night you retired in the best of spirits, so it was clear that it was this letter in your hand which had caused the change in you."

"This is obvious."

"It is all obvious when it is explained to you. I naturally asked myself what the letter could contain which might have this effect upon you. As you walked you held the flap side of the envelope towards me, and I saw upon it the same shield-shaped device which I have observed upon your old college cricket cap. It was clear, then, that the request came from Edinburgh University—or from some club connected with the University. When you reached the table you laid down the letter beside your plate with the address uppermost, and you walked over to look at the framed photograph upon the left of the mantelpiece."

It amazed me to see the accuracy with which he had observed my movements. "What next?" I asked.

"I began by glancing at the address, and I could tell, even at the distance of six feet, that it was an unofficial communication. This I gathered from the use of the word 'Doctor' upon the address, to which, as a Bachelor of Medicine, you have no legal claim. I knew that University officials are pedantic in their correct use of titles, and I was thus enabled to say with certainty that your letter was unofficial. When on your return to the table you turned over your letter and allowed me to perceive that the enclosure was a printed one, the idea of a bazaar first occurred to me. I had already weighed the possibility of its being a political communication, but this seemed improbable in the present stagnant conditions of politics.

"When you returned to the table your face still retained its expression and it was evident that your examination of the photograph had not changed the current of your thoughts. In that case it must itself bear upon the subject in question.

I turned my attention to the photograph, therefore, and saw at once that it consisted of yourself as a member of the Edinburgh University Eleven, with the pavilion and cricket field in the background. My small experience of cricket clubs has taught me that next to churches and cavalry ensigns they are the most debt-laden things upon earth. When upon your return to the table I saw you take out your pencil and draw lines upon the envelope, I was convinced that you were endeavouring to realise some projected improvement which was to be brought about by a bazaar. Your face still showed some indecision, so that I was able to break in upon you with my advice that you should assist in so good an object."

I could not help smiling at the extreme simplicity of his explanation.

"Of course, it was as easy as possible," said I.

My remark appeared to nettle him.

"I may add," said he, "that the particular help which you have been asked to give was that you should write in their album, and that you have already made up your mind that the present incident will be the subject of your article."

"But how—!" I cried.

"It is as easy as possible," said he, "and I leave its solution to your own ingenuity. In the meantime," he added, raising his paper, "you will excuse me if I return to this very interesting article upon the trees of Cremona, and the exact reasons for the pre-eminence in the manufacture of violins. It is one of those small outlying problems to which I am sometimes tempted to direct my attention."

The Edinburgh Mystery

Baroness Orczy

Baroness Orczy (1865–1947) was born in Hungary and spent her later years in the wealthy enclave of Monte Carlo, and of all the authors featured in this volume, she probably had the slenderest connection with Scotland. Nevertheless, she wrote two short detective stories set in the great cities of Edinburgh and Glasgow respectively. Her full name was Emma Magdolna Rozália Mária Jozefa Borbála Orczy de Orc, but she was known to many friends as Emmuska. When she was fourteen, her family moved to Britain and after studying art, she married Montagu Barstow, the son of an English clergyman, in 1894. She achieved lasting fame thanks to her creation of the Scarlet Pimpernel, who featured in a series of dashing historical romances from 1903 onwards, but she also wrote detective fiction that achieved considerable popularity.

She created a number of detective characters, but the first and most interesting was "The Old Man in the Corner." This character, whose real name is never revealed, is an "armchair detective" who solves mysteries while sitting in a teashop. He featured in half a dozen "Mysteries of London," which appeared in the *Royal Magazine* in 1901 and was one of many detectives to emerge after Conan Doyle decided to plunge Sherlock Holmes into the Reichenbach Falls. The stories were well-received, and Orczy produced half a dozen "Mysteries of Great Cities" set around the United Kingdom in 1902. The twelve stories were collected, in slightly revised form, in a single volume, and two further collections later appeared. "The Edinburgh Mystery" featured in the BBC Radio 4 series *The Teahouse Detective*, starring Bernard Hepton, and was first broadcast in 2000.

————

THE MAN IN THE CORNER HAD NOT ENJOYED HIS LUNCH. Miss Polly Burton could see that he had something on his mind, for, even before he began to talk that morning, he was fidgeting with his bit of string, and setting all her nerves on the jar.

"Have you ever felt real sympathy with a criminal or a thief?" he asked her after a while.

"Only once, I think," she replied, "and then I am not quite sure that the unfortunate woman who did enlist my sympathies was the criminal you make her out to be."

"You mean the heroine of the York mystery?" he replied blandly. "I know that you tried very hard that time to discredit the only possible version of that mysterious murder, the version which is my own. Now, I am equally sure that you have at the present moment no more notion as to who killed and robbed poor Lady Donaldson in Charlotte Square, Edinburgh, than the police have themselves, and yet you are fully prepared to pooh-pooh my arguments, and to disbelieve my version of the mystery. Such is the lady journalist's mind."

"If you have some cock-and-bull story to explain that extraordinary case," she retorted, "of course I shall disbelieve it. Certainly, if you are going to try and enlist my sympathies on behalf of Edith Crawford, I can assure you you won't succeed."

"Well, I don't know that that is altogether my intention. I see you are interested in the case, but I dare say you don't remember all the circumstances. You must forgive me if I repeat that which you know already. If you have ever been to Edinburgh at all, you will have heard of Graham's bank, and Mr. Andrew Graham, the present head of the firm, is undoubtedly one of the most prominent notabilities of 'modern Athens.'"

The man in the corner took two or three photos from his pocket-book and placed them before the young girl; then, pointing at them with his long bony finger—

"That," he said, "is Mr. Elphinstone Graham, the eldest son, a typical young Scotchman, as you see, and this is David Graham, the second son."

Polly looked more closely at this last photo, and saw before her a young face, upon which some lasting sorrow seemed already to have left its mark. The face was delicate and thin, the features pinched, and the eyes seemed almost unnaturally large and prominent.

"He was deformed," commented the man in the corner in

answer to the girl's thoughts, "and, as such, an object of pity and even of repugnance to most of his friends. There was also a good deal of talk in Edinburgh society as to his mental condition, his mind, according to many intimate friends of the Grahams, being at times decidedly unhinged. Be that as it may, I fancy that his life must have been a very sad one; he had lost his mother when quite a baby, and his father seemed, strangely enough, to have an almost unconquerable dislike towards him.

"Every one got to know presently of David Graham's sad position in his father's own house, and also of the great affection lavished upon him by his godmother, Lady Donaldson, who was a sister of Mr. Graham's.

"She was a lady of considerable wealth, being the widow of Sir George Donaldson, the great distiller; but she seems to have been decidedly eccentric. Latterly she had astonished all her family—who were rigid Presbyterians—by announcing her intention of embracing the Roman Catholic faith, and then retiring to the convent of St. Augustine's at Newton Abbot in Devonshire.

"She had sole and absolute control of the vast fortune which a doting husband had bequeathed to her. Clearly, therefore, she was at liberty to bestow it upon a Devonshire convent if she chose. But this evidently was not altogether her intention.

"I told you how fond she was of her deformed godson, did I not? Being a bundle of eccentricities, she had many hobbies, none more pronounced than the fixed determination to see—before retiring from the world altogether—David Graham happily married.

"Now, it appears that David Graham, ugly, deformed, half-demented as he was, had fallen desperately in love with Miss Edith Crawford, daughter of the late Dr. Crawford, of Prince's Gardens. The young lady, however—very naturally, perhaps—fought shy of David Graham, who, about this time, certainly seemed very queer and morose, but Lady Donaldson, with characteristic determination, seems to have made up her mind to melt Miss Crawford's heart towards her unfortunate nephew.

"On October the 2nd last, at a family party given by Mr. Graham in his fine mansion in Charlotte Square, Lady Donaldson openly announced her intention of making over, by deed of gift, to her nephew, David Graham, certain property, money, and shares, amounting in total value to the sum of £100,000, and also her magnificent diamonds, which were worth £50,000, for the use of the said David's wife. Keith Macfinlay, a lawyer of Prince's Street, received the next day instructions for drawing up the necessary deed of gift, which she pledged herself to sign the day of her godson's wedding.

"A week later *The Scotsman* contained the following paragraph:—

"'A marriage is arranged and will shortly take place between David, younger son of Andrew Graham, Esq., of Charlotte Square, Edinburgh, and Dochnakirk, Perthshire, and Edith Lillian, only surviving daughter of the late Dr. Kenneth Crawford, of Prince's Gardens.'

"In Edinburgh society comments were loud and various upon the forthcoming marriage, and, on the whole, these comments were far from complimentary to the families concerned. I do not think that the Scotch are a particularly sentimental race, but there was such obvious buying, selling, and bargaining about this marriage that Scottish chivalry rose in revolt at the thought.

"Against that the three people most concerned seemed perfectly satisfied. David Graham was positively transformed; his moroseness was gone from him, he lost his queer ways and wild manners, and became gentle and affectionate in the midst of this great and unexpected happiness. Miss Edith Crawford ordered her trousseau, and talked of the diamonds to her friends, and Lady Donaldson was only waiting for the consummation of this marriage—her heart's desire—before she finally retired from the world, at peace with it and with herself.

"The deed of gift was ready for signature on the wedding day, which was fixed for November 7th, and Lady Donaldson took up her abode temporarily in her brother's house in Charlotte Square.

"Mr. Graham gave a large ball on October 23rd. Special interest is attached to this ball, from the fact that for this occasion Lady Donaldson insisted that David's future wife should wear the magnificent diamonds which were soon to become hers.

"They were, it seems, superb, and became Miss Crawford's stately beauty to perfection. The ball was a brilliant success, the last guest leaving at four a.m. The next day it was the universal topic of conversation, and the day after that, when Edinburgh unfolded the late editions of its morning papers, it learned with horror and dismay that Lady Donaldson had been found murdered in her room, and that the celebrated diamonds had been stolen.

"Hardly had the beautiful little city, however, recovered from this awful shock, than its newspapers had another thrilling sensation ready for their readers.

"Already all Scotch and English papers had mysteriously hinted at 'startling information' obtained by the Procurator Fiscal, and at an 'impending sensational arrest.'

"Then the announcement came, and every one in Edinburgh read, horror-struck and aghast, that the 'sensational arrest' was none other than that of Miss Edith Crawford, for murder and robbery, both so daring and horrible that reason refused to believe that a young lady, born and bred in the best social circle, could have conceived, much less executed, so heinous a crime. She had been arrested in London at the Midland Hotel, and brought to Edinburgh, where she was judicially examined, bail being refused."

"Little more than a fortnight after that, Edith Crawford was duly committed to stand her trial before the High Court of Justiciary. She had pleaded 'Not Guilty' at the pleading diet, and her defence was entrusted to Sir James Fenwick, one of the most eminent advocates at the Criminal Bar.

"Strange to say," continued the man in the corner after a while, "public opinion from the first went dead against the accused. The public is absolutely like a child, perfectly irresponsible and wholly illogical; it argued that since Miss Crawford had been ready to contract a marriage with a half-demented, deformed creature for the sake of his £100,000 she must have been equally ready to murder and rob an old lady for the sake of £50,000 worth of jewellery, without the encumbrance of so undesirable a husband.

"Perhaps the great sympathy aroused in the popular mind for David Graham had much to do with this ill-feeling against the accused. David Graham had, by this cruel and dastardly murder, lost the best—if not the only—friend he possessed. He had also lost at one fell swoop the large fortune which Lady Donaldson had been about to assign to him.

"The deed of gift had never been signed, and the old lady's vast wealth, instead of enriching her favourite nephew, was distributed—since she had made no will—amongst her heirs-at-law. And now to crown this long chapter of sorrow David Graham saw the girl he loved accused of the awful crime which had robbed him of friend and fortune.

"It was, therefore, with an unmistakable thrill of righteous satisfaction that Edinburgh society saw this 'mercenary girl' in so terrible a plight.

"I was immensely interested in the case, and journeyed down to Edinburgh in order to get a good view of the chief actors in the thrilling drama which was about to be unfolded there.

"I succeeded—I generally do—in securing one of the front seats among the audience, and was already comfortably installed in my place in court when through the trap door I saw the head of the prisoner emerge. She was very becomingly dressed in deep black, and, led by two policemen, she took her place in the dock. Sir James Fenwick shook hands with her very warmly, and I could almost hear him instilling words of comfort into her.

"The trial lasted six clear days, during which time more

than forty persons were examined for the prosecution, and as many for the defence. But the most interesting witnesses were certainly the two doctors, the maid Tremlett, Campbell, the High Street jeweller, and David Graham.

"There was, of course, a great deal of medical evidence to go through. Poor Lady Donaldson had been found with a silk scarf tied tightly round her neck, her face showing even to the inexperienced eye every symptom of strangulation.

"Then Tremlett, Lady Donaldson's confidential maid, was called. Closely examined by Crown Counsel, she gave an account of the ball at Charlotte Square on the 23rd, and the wearing of the jewels by Miss Crawford on that occasion.

"'I helped Miss Crawford on with the tiara over her hair,' she said; 'and my lady put the two necklaces round Miss Crawford's neck herself. There were also some beautiful brooches, bracelets, and earrings. At four o'clock in the morning when the ball was over, Miss Crawford brought the jewels back to my lady's room. My lady had already gone to bed, and I had put out the electric light, as I was going, too. There was only one candle left in the room, close to the bed.

"'Miss Crawford took all the jewels off, and asked Lady Donaldson for the key of the safe, so that she might put them away. My lady gave her the key and said to me, "You can go to bed, Tremlett, you must be dead tired." I was glad to go, for I could hardly stand up—I was so tired. I said "Good night!" to my lady and also to Miss Crawford, who was busy putting the jewels away. As I was going out of the room I heard Lady Donaldson saying: "Have you managed it, my dear?" Miss Crawford said: "I have put everything away very nicely."'

"In answer to Sir James Fenwick, Tremlett said that Lady Donaldson always carried the key of her jewel safe on a ribbon round her neck, and had done so the whole day preceding her death.

"'On the night of the 24th,' she continued, 'Lady Donaldson still seemed rather tired, and went up to her room directly after dinner, and while the family were still sitting in the dining-room. She made me dress her hair, then she slipped on her dressing-gown and sat in the armchair with a book. She told me that she then felt strangely uncomfortable and nervous, and could not account for it.

"'However, she did not want me to sit with her, so I thought that the best thing I could do was to tell Mr. David Graham that her ladyship did not seem very cheerful. Her ladyship was so fond of Mr. David; it always made her happy to have him with her. I then went to my room, and at half-past eight Mr. David called me. He said: "Your mistress does seem a little restless tonight. If I were you I would just go and listen at her door in about an hour's time, and if she has not gone to bed I would go in and stay with her until she has." At about ten o'clock I did as Mr. David suggested, and listened at her ladyship's door. However, all was quiet in the room, and, thinking her ladyship had gone to sleep, I went back to bed.

"'The next morning at eight o'clock, when I took in my mistress's cup of tea, I saw her lying on the floor, her poor dear face all purple and distorted. I screamed, and the other servants came rushing along. Then Mr. Graham had the door locked and sent for the doctor and the police.'

"The poor woman seemed to find it very difficult not to break down. She was closely questioned by Sir James

Fenwick, but had nothing further to say. She had last seen her mistress alive at eight o'clock on the evening of the 24th.

"'And when you listened at her door at ten o'clock,' asked Sir James, 'did you try to open it?'

"'I did, but it was locked,' she replied.

"'Did Lady Donaldson usually lock her bedroom at night?'

"'Nearly always.'

"'And in the morning when you took in the tea?'

"'The door was open. I walked straight in.'

"'You are quite sure?' insisted Sir James.

"'I swear it,' solemnly asserted the woman.

"After that we were informed by several members of Mr. Graham's establishment that Miss Crawford had been in to tea at Charlotte Square in the afternoon of the 24th, that she told every one she was going to London by the night mail, as she had some special shopping she wished to do there. It appears that Mr. Graham and David both tried to persuade her to stay to dinner, and then to go by the 9.10 p.m. from the Caledonian Station. Miss Crawford however had refused, saying she always preferred to go from the Waverley Station. It was nearer to her own rooms, and she still had a good deal of writing to do.

"In spite of this, two witnesses saw the accused in Charlotte Square later on in the evening. She was carrying a bag which seemed heavy, and was walking towards the Caledonian Railway Station.

"But the most thrilling moment in that sensational trial was reached on the second day, when David Graham, looking wretchedly ill, unkempt, and haggard, stepped into the witness-box. A murmur of sympathy went round the audience at sight of him, who was the second, perhaps, most deeply stricken victim of the Charlotte Square tragedy.

"David Graham, in answer to Crown Counsel, gave an account of his last interview with Lady Donaldson.

"'Tremlett had told me that she seemed anxious and upset, and I went to have a chat with her; she soon cheered up and…'

"There the unfortunate young man hesitated visibly, but after a while resumed with an obvious effort.

"'She spoke of my marriage, and of the gift she was about to bestow upon me. She said the diamonds would be for my wife, and after that for my daughter, if I had one. She also complained that Mr. Macfinlay had been so punctilious about preparing the deed of gift, and that it was a great pity the £100,000 could not just pass from her hands to mine without so much fuss.

"'I stayed talking with her for about half an hour; then I left her, as she seemed ready to go to bed; but I told her maid to listen at the door in about an hour's time.'

"There was deep silence in the court for a few moments, a silence which to me seemed almost electrical. It was as if, some time before it was uttered, the next question put by Crown Counsel to the witness had hovered in the air.

"'You were engaged to Miss Edith Crawford at one time, were you not?'

"One felt, rather than heard, the almost inaudible 'Yes' which escaped from David Graham's compressed lips.

"'Under what circumstances was that engagement broken off?'

"Sir James Fenwick had already risen in protest, but David Graham had been the first to speak.

"'I do not think that I need answer that question.'

"'I will put it in a different form, then,' said Crown Counsel urbanely—'one to which my learned friend cannot possibly take exception. Did you or did you not on October 27th receive a letter from the accused, in which she desired to be released from her promise of marriage to you?'

"Again David Graham would have refused to answer, and he certainly gave no audible reply to the learned counsel's question; but every one in the audience there present—aye, every member of the jury and of the bar—read upon David Graham's pale countenance and large, sorrowful eyes that ominous 'Yes!' which had failed to reach his trembling lips."

"There is no doubt," continued the man in the corner, "that what little sympathy the young girl's terrible position had aroused in the public mind had died out the moment that David Graham left the witness-box on the second day of the trial. Whether Edith Crawford was guilty of murder or not, the callous way in which she had accepted a deformed lover, and then thrown him over, had set every one's mind against her.

"It was Mr. Graham himself who had been the first to put the Procurator Fiscal in possession of the fact that the accused had written to David from London, breaking off her engagement. This information had, no doubt, directed the attention of the Fiscal to Miss Crawford, and the police soon brought forward the evidence which had led to her arrest.

"We had a final sensation on the third day, when Mr. Campbell, jeweller, of High Street, gave his evidence. He said that on October 25th a lady came to his shop and offered to sell him a pair of diamond earrings. Trade had been very bad, and he had refused the bargain, although the lady seemed ready to part with the earrings for an extraordinarily low sum, considering the beauty of the stones.

"In fact it was because of this evident desire on the lady's part to sell at *any* cost that he had looked at her more keenly than he otherwise would have done. He was now ready to swear that the lady that offered him the diamond earrings was the prisoner in the dock.

"I can assure you that as we all listened to this apparently damnatory evidence, you might have heard a pin drop amongst the audience in that crowded court. The girl alone, there in the dock, remained calm and unmoved. Remember that for two days we had heard evidence to prove that old Dr. Crawford had died leaving his daughter penniless, that having no mother she had been brought up by a maiden aunt, who had trained her to be a governess, which occupation she had followed for years, and that certainly she had never been known by any of her friends to be in possession of solitaire diamond earrings.

"The prosecution had certainly secured an ace of trumps, but Sir James Fenwick, who during the whole of that day had seemed to take little interest in the proceedings, here rose from his seat, and I knew at once that he had got a tit-bit in the way of a 'point' up his sleeve. Gaunt, and unusually tall, and with his beak-like nose, he always looks strangely impressive when he seriously tackles a witness. He did it this time with a vengeance, I can tell you. He was all over the pompous little jeweller in a moment.

"'Had Mr. Campbell made a special entry in his book, as to the visit of the lady in question?'

"'No.'

"'Had he any special means of ascertaining when that visit did actually take place?'

"'No—but—'

"'What record had he of the visit?'

"Mr. Campbell had none. In fact, after about twenty minutes of cross-examination, he had to admit that he had given but little thought to the interview with the lady at the time, and certainly not in connection with the murder of Lady Donaldson, until he had read in the papers that a young lady had been arrested.

"Then he and his clerk talked the matter over, it appears, and together they had certainly recollected that a lady had brought some beautiful earrings for sale on a day which *must have been* the very morning after the murder. If Sir James Fenwick's object was to discredit this special witness, he certainly gained his point.

"All the pomposity went out of Mr. Campbell, he became flurried, then excited, then he lost his temper. After that he was allowed to leave the court, and Sir James Fenwick resumed his seat, and waited like a vulture for its prey.

"It presented itself in the person of Mr. Campbell's clerk, who, before the Procurator Fiscal, had corroborated his employer's evidence in every respect. In Scotland no witness in any one case is present in court during the examination of another, and Mr. Macfarlane, the clerk, was, therefore, quite unprepared for the pitfalls which Sir James Fenwick had prepared for him. He tumbled into them, head foremost, and the eminent advocate turned him inside out like a glove.

"Mr. Macfarlane did not lose his temper; he was of too humble a frame of mind to do that, but he got into a hopeless quagmire of mixed recollections, and he too left the witness-box quite unprepared to swear as to the day of the interview with the lady with the diamond earrings.

"I dare say, mind you," continued the man in the corner with a chuckle, "that to most people present, Sir James Fenwick's cross-questioning seemed completely irrelevant. Both Mr. Campbell and his clerk were quite ready to swear that they had had an interview concerning some diamond earrings with a lady, of whose identity with the accused they were perfectly convinced, and to the casual observer the question as to the time or even the day when that interview took place could make but little difference in the ultimate issue.

"Now I took in, in a moment, the entire drift of Sir James Fenwick's defence of Edith Crawford. When Mr. Macfarlane left the witness-box, the second victim of the eminent advocate's caustic tongue, I could read as in a book the whole history of that crime, its investigation, and the mistakes made by the police first and the Public Prosecutor afterwards.

"Sir James Fenwick knew them, too, of course, and he placed a finger upon each one, demolishing—like a child who blows upon a house of cards—the entire scaffolding erected by the prosecution.

"Mr. Campbell's and Mr. Macfarlane's identification of the accused with the lady who, on some date—admitted to be uncertain—had tried to sell a pair of diamond earrings, was the first point. Sir James had plenty of witnesses to prove that on the 25th, the day after the murder, the accused was in London, whilst, the day before, Mr. Campbell's shop had been closed long before the family circle had seen the last of Lady Donaldson. Clearly the jeweller and his clerk must have seen some other lady, whom their vivid imagination had pictured as being identical with the accused.

"Then came the great question of time. Mr. David Graham had been evidently the last to see Lady Donaldson alive. He had spoken to her as late as 8.30 p.m. Sir James Fenwick had called two porters at the Caledonian Railway Station who testified to Miss Crawford having taken her seat in a first-class carriage of the 9.10 train, some minutes before it started.

"'Was it conceivable, therefore,' argued Sir James, 'that in the space of half an hour the accused—a young girl—could have found her way surreptitiously into the house, at a time when the entire household was still astir, that she should have strangled Lady Donaldson, forced open the safe, and made away with the jewels? A man—an experienced burglar might have done it, but I contend that the accused is physically incapable of accomplishing such a feat.

"'With regard to the broken engagement,' continued the eminent counsel with a smile, 'it may have seemed a little heartless, certainly, but heartlessness is no crime in the eyes of the law. The accused has stated in her declaration that at the time she wrote to Mr. David Graham, breaking off her engagement, she had heard nothing of the Edinburgh tragedy.

"'The London papers had reported the crime very briefly. The accused was busy shopping; she knew nothing of Mr. David Graham's altered position. In no case was the breaking off of the engagement a proof that the accused had obtained possession of the jewels by so foul a deed.'

"It is, of course, impossible for me," continued the man in the corner apologetically, "to give you any idea of the eminent advocate's eloquence and masterful logic. It struck every one, I think, just as it did me, that he chiefly directed his attention to the fact that there was absolutely no *proof* against the accused.

"Be that as it may, the result of that remarkable trial was a verdict of 'Non Proven.' The jury was absent forty minutes, and it appears that in the mind of every one of them there remained, in spite of Sir James' arguments, a firmly rooted conviction—call it instinct, if you like—that Edith Crawford had done away with Lady Donaldson in order to become possessed of those jewels, and that in spite of the pompous jeweller's many contradictions, she had offered him some of those diamonds for sale. But there was not enough proof to convict, and she was given the benefit of the doubt.

"I have heard English people argue that in England she would have been hanged. Personally I doubt that. I think that an English jury, not having the judicial loophole of 'Non Proven,' would have been bound to acquit her. What do you think?"

There was a moment's silence, for Polly did not reply immediately, and he went on making impossible knots in his bit of string. Then she said quietly—

"I think that I agree with those English people who say that an English jury would have condemned her… I have no doubt that she was guilty. She may not have committed that awful deed herself. Some one in the Charlotte Square house may have been her accomplice and killed and robbed Lady Donaldson while Edith Crawford waited outside for the jewels. David Graham left his godmother at 8.30 p.m. If the accomplice was one of the servants in the house, he or she would have had plenty of time for any amount of villainy, and Edith Crawford could have yet caught the 9.10 p.m. train from the Caledonian Station."

"Then who, in your opinion," he asked sarcastically, and cocking his funny birdlike head on one side, "tried to sell diamond earrings to Mr. Campbell, the jeweller?"

"Edith Crawford, of course," she retorted triumphantly; "he and his clerk both recognised her."

"When did she try to sell them the earrings?"

"Ah, that is what I cannot quite make out, and there to my mind lies the only mystery in this case. On the 25th she was certainly in London, and it is not very likely that she would go back to Edinburgh in order to dispose of the jewels there, where they could most easily be traced."

"Not very likely, certainly," he assented drily.

"And," added the young girl, "on the day before she left for London, Lady Donaldson was alive."

"And pray," he said suddenly, as with comic complacency he surveyed a beautiful knot he had just twisted up between his long fingers, "what has that fact got to do with it?"

"But it has everything to do with it!" she retorted.

"Ah, there you go," he sighed with comic emphasis. "My teachings don't seem to have improved your powers of reasoning. You are as bad as the police. Lady Donaldson has been robbed and murdered, and you immediately argue that she was robbed and murdered by the same person."

"But—" argued Polly.

"There is no but," he said, getting more and more excited. "See how simple it is. Edith Crawford wears the diamonds one night, then she brings them back to Lady Donaldson's room. Remember the maid's statement: 'My lady said: "Have you put them back, my dear?"'—a simple statement, utterly ignored by the prosecution. But what did it mean? That Lady Donaldson could not see for herself whether Edith Crawford had put back the jewels or not, *since she asked the question*."

"Then you argue—"

"I never argue," he interrupted excitedly; "I state undeniable facts. Edith Crawford, who wanted to steal the jewels, took them then and there, when she had the opportunity. Why in the world should she have waited? Lady Donaldson was in bed, and Tremlett, the maid, had gone.

"The next day—namely, the 25th—she tries to dispose of a pair of earrings to Mr. Campbell; she fails, and decides to go to London, where she has a better chance. Sir James Fenwick did not think it desirable to bring forward witnesses to prove what I have since ascertained is a fact, namely, that on the 27th of October, three days before her arrest, Miss Crawford crossed over to Belgium, and came back to London the next day. In Belgium, no doubt, Lady Donaldson's diamonds, taken out of their settings, calmly repose at this moment, while the money derived from their sale is safely deposited in a Belgian bank."

"But then, who murdered Lady Donaldson, and why?" gasped Polly.

"Cannot you guess?" he queried blandly. "Have I not placed the case clearly enough before you? To me it seems so simple. It was a daring, brutal murder, remember. Think of one who, not being the thief himself, would, nevertheless, have the strongest of all motives to shield the thief from the consequences of her own misdeed: aye! and the power too—since it would be absolutely illogical, nay, impossible, that he should be an accomplice."

"Surely—"

"Think of a curious nature, warped morally, as well as physically—do you know how those natures feel? A thousand times more strongly than the even, straight natures in everyday life. Then think of such a nature brought face to face with this awful problem.

"Do you think that such a nature would hesitate a moment before committing a crime to save the loved one from the consequences of that deed? Mind you, I don't assert for a moment that David Graham had any *intention* of murdering Lady Donaldson. Tremlett tells him that she seems strangely upset; he goes to her room and finds that she has discovered that she has been robbed. She naturally suspects Edith Crawford, recollects the incidents of the other night, and probably expresses her feelings to David Graham, and threatens immediate prosecution, scandal, what you will.

"I repeat it again, I dare say he had no wish to kill her. Probably he merely threatened to. A medical gentleman who spoke of sudden heart failure was no doubt right. Then imagine David Graham's remorse, his horror, and his fears. The empty safe probably is the first object that suggested to him the grim tableau of robbery and murder, which he arranges in order to ensure his own safety.

"But remember one thing: no miscreant was seen to enter or leave the house surreptitiously; the murderer left no signs of entrance, and none of exit. An armed burglar would have left some trace—*some one* would have heard *something*. Then who locked and unlocked Lady Donaldson's door that night while she herself lay dead?

"Some one in the house, I tell you—some one who left no trace—some one against whom there could be no suspicion—some one who killed without apparently the slightest premeditation, and without the slightest motive. Think of it—I know I am right—and then tell me if I have at all enlisted your sympathies in the author of the Edinburgh Mystery."

He was gone. Polly looked again at the photo of David Graham. Did a crooked mind really dwell in that crooked body, and were there in the world such crimes that were great enough to be deemed sublime?

The Honour of Israel Gow

G. K. Chesterton

Gilbert Keith Chesterton (1874–1936) was an Englishman and proud of it, but he also had a strong affinity with Scotland and the Scots. As he said in his autobiography: "my mother came of Scottish people, who were Keiths from Aberdeen; and...partly because of a certain vividness in any infusion of Scots blood or patriotism, this northern affiliation appealed strongly to my affections; and made a sort of Scottish romance in my childhood." He admired both Sir Walter Scott and Robert Louis Stevenson, and wrote a passionate defence of the latter when reviewing "perhaps the first of the rather stupid books written to belittle Stevenson." In 1927 he published a book about Stevenson which is respected to this day for its critical insight.

Chesterton's analysis of *Strange Case of Dr. Jekyll and Mr. Hyde* is characteristically illuminating: "The point of the story is not that a man can cut himself off from his conscience, but that he cannot... The reason is that there can never be equality between the evil and the good. Jekyll and Hyde are not twin brothers. They are rather, as one of them truly remarks, like father and son. After all, Jekyll created Hyde; Hyde would never have created Jekyll; he only destroyed Jekyll." In his detective fiction, Chesterton didn't often venture north of the border, but this story is an exception. It was published in the *Saturday Evening Post* on 25 March 1911 as "The Strange Justice."

———

A STORMY EVENING OF OLIVE AND SILVER WAS CLOSING in, as Father Brown, wrapped in a grey Scotch plaid, came to the end of a grey Scotch valley and beheld the strange castle of Glengyle. It stopped one end of the glen or hollow like a blind alley; and it looked like the end of the world. Rising in steep roofs and spires of seagreen slate in the manner of the old French-Scottish châteaux, it reminded an Englishman of the sinister steeple-hats of witches in fairly tales; and the pine woods that rocked round the green turrets looked, by comparison, as black as numberless flocks of ravens. This note of a dreamy, almost a sleepy devilry, was no mere fancy from the landscape. For there did rest on the place one of those clouds of pride and madness and mysterious sorrow which lie more heavily on the noble houses of Scotland than on any other of the children of men. For Scotland has a double dose of the poison called heredity; the sense of blood in the aristocrat, and the sense of doom in the Calvinist.

The priest had snatched a day from his business at

Glasgow to meet his friend Flambeau, the amateur detective, who was at Glengyle Castle with another more formal officer investigating the life and death of the late Earl of Glengyle. That mysterious person was the last representative of a race whose valour, insanity, and violent cunning had made them terrible even among the sinister nobility of their nation in the sixteenth century. None were deeper in that labyrinthine ambition, in chamber within chamber of that palace of lies that was built up around Mary Queen of Scots.

The rhyme in the countryside attested the motive and the result of their machinations candidly:

> *"As green sap to the simmer trees*
> *Is red gold to the Ogilvies."*

For many centuries there had never been a decent lord in Glengyle Castle; and with the Victorian era one would have thought that all eccentricities were exhausted. The last Glengyle, however, satisfied his tribal tradition by doing the only thing that was left for him to do; he disappeared. I do not mean that he went abroad; by all accounts he was still in the castle, if he was anywhere. But though his name was in the church register and the big red Peerage, nobody ever saw him under the sun.

If anyone saw him it was a solitary man-servant, something between a groom and a gardener. He was so deaf that the more business-like assumed him to be dumb; while the more penetrating declared him to be half-witted. A gaunt, red-haired labourer, with a dogged jaw and chin, but quite blank blue eyes, he went by the name of Israel Gow, and was the one silent servant on that deserted estate. But the energy with which he dug potatoes, and the regularity with which he disappeared into the kitchen gave people an impression that he was providing for the meals of a superior, and that the strange earl was still concealed in the castle. If society needed any further proof that he was there, the servant persistently asserted that he was not at home. One morning the provost and the minister (for the Glengyles were Presbyterian) were summoned to the castle. There they found that the gardener, groom, and cook had added to his many professions that of an undertaker, and had nailed up his noble master in a coffin. With how much or how little further inquiry this odd fact was passed, did not as yet very plainly appear; for the thing had never been legally investigated till Flambeau had gone north two or three days before. By then the body of Lord Glengyle (if it was the body) had lain for some time in the little churchyard on the hill.

As Father Brown passed through the dim garden and came under the shadow of the château, the clouds were thick and the whole air damp and thundery. Against the last stripe of the green-gold sunset he saw a black human silhouette; a man in a chimney-pot hat, with a big spade over his shoulder. The combination was queerly suggestive of a sexton; but when Brown remembered the deaf servant who dug potatoes, he thought it natural enough. He knew something of the Scotch peasant; he knew the respectability which might well feel it necessary to wear "blacks" for an official inquiry; he knew also the economy that would not lose an hour's digging for that. Even the man's start and suspicious stare as the priest went by were consonant enough with the vigilance and jealousy of such a type.

The great door was opened by Flambeau himself, who had with him a lean man with iron-grey hair and papers in his hand: Inspector Craven from Scotland Yard. The entrance hall was mostly stripped and empty; but the pale, sneering faces of one or two of the wicked Ogilvies looked down out of black periwigs and blackening canvas.

Following them into an inner room, Father Brown found that the allies had been seated at a long oak table, of which their end was covered with scribbled papers, flanked with whisky and cigars. Through the whole of its remaining length it was occupied by detached objects arranged at intervals; objects about as inexplicable as any objects could be. One looked like a small heap of glittering broken glass. Another looked like a high heap of brown dust. A third appeared to be a plain stick of wood.

"You seem to have a sort of geological museum here," he said, as he sat down, jerking his head briefly in the direction of the brown dust and the crystalline fragments.

"Not a geological museum," replied Flambeau; "say a psychological museum."

"Oh, for the Lord's sake," cried the police detective laughing, "don't let's begin with such long words."

"Don't you know what psychology means?" asked Flambeau with friendly surprise. "Psychology means being off your chump."

"Still I hardly follow," replied the official.

"Well," said Flambeau, with decision, "I mean that we've only found out one thing about Lord Glengyle. He was a maniac."

The black silhouette of Gow with his top hat and spade

passed the window, dimly outlined against the darkening sky. Father Brown stared passively at it and answered:

"I can understand there must have been something odd about the man, or he wouldn't have buried himself alive—nor been in such a hurry to bury himself dead. But what makes you think it was lunacy?"

"Well," said Flambeau, "you just listen to the list of things Mr. Craven has found in the house."

"We must get a candle," said Craven, suddenly, "A storm is getting up, and it's too dark to read."

"Have you found any candles," asked Brown smiling, "among your oddities?"

Flambeau raised a grave face, and fixed his dark eyes on his friend.

"That is curious, too," he said. "Twenty-five candles, and not a trace of a candlestick."

In the rapidly darkening room and rapidly rising wind, Brown went along the table to where a bundle of wax candles lay among the other scrappy exhibits. As he did so he bent accidentally over the heap of red-brown dust; and a sharp sneeze cracked the silence.

"Hullo!" he said, "snuff!"

He took one of the candles, lit it carefully, came back and stuck it in the neck of the whisky bottle. The unrestful night air, blowing through the crazy window, waved the long flame like a banner. And on every side of the castle they could hear the miles and miles of black pine wood seething like a black sea around a rock.

"I will read the inventory," began Craven gravely, picking up one of the papers, "the inventory of what we found loose and unexplained in the castle. You are to understand that the place generally was dismantled and neglected; but one or two rooms had plainly been inhabited in a simple but not squalid style by somebody; somebody who was not the servant Gow. The list is as follows:

"First item. A very considerable hoard of precious stones, nearly all diamonds, and all of them loose, without any setting whatever. Of course, it is natural that the Ogilvies should have family jewels; but those are exactly the jewels that are almost always set in particular articles of ornament. The Ogilvies would seem to have kept theirs loose in their pockets, like coppers.

"Second item. Heaps and heaps of loose snuff, not kept in a horn, or even a pouch, but lying in heaps on the mantelpieces, on the sideboard, on the piano, anywhere. It looks as if the old gentleman would not take the trouble to look in a pocket or lift a lid.

"Third item. Here and there about the house curious little heaps of minute pieces of metal, some like steel springs and some in the form of microscopic wheels. As if they had gutted some mechanical toy.

"Fourth item. The wax candles, which have to be stuck in bottle necks because there is nothing else to stick them in. Now I wish you to note how very much queerer all this is than anything we anticipated. For the central riddle we are prepared; we have all seen at a glance that there was something wrong about the last earl. We have come here to find out whether he really lived here, whether he really died here, whether that red-haired scarecrow who did his burying had anything to do with his dying. But suppose the worst in all this, the most lurid or melodramatic solution you like. Suppose the servant really killed the master, or suppose the master isn't really dead, or suppose the master is dressed up as the servant, or suppose the servant is buried for the master; invent what Wilkie Collins' tragedy you like, and you still have not explained a candle without a candlestick, or why an elderly gentleman of good family should habitually spill snuff on the piano. The core of the tale we could imagine; it is the fringes that are mysterious. By no stretch of fancy can the human mind connect together snuff and diamonds and wax and loose clockwork."

"I think I see the connection," said the priest. "This Glengyle was mad against the French Revolution. He was an enthusiast for the *ancien régime*, and was trying to re-enact literally the family life of the last Bourbons. He had snuff because it was the eighteenth century luxury; wax candles, because they were the eighteenth century lighting; the mechanical bits of iron represent the locksmith hobby of Louis XVI; the diamonds are for the Diamond Necklace of Marie Antoinette."

Both the other men were staring at him with round eyes. "What a perfectly extraordinary notion!" cried Flambeau. "Do you really think that is the truth?"

"I am perfectly sure it isn't," answered Father Brown, "only you said that nobody could connect snuff and diamonds and clockwork and candles. I give you that connection off-hand. The real truth, I am very sure, lies deeper."

He paused a moment and listened to the wailing of the wind in the turrets. Then he said, "The late Earl of Glengyle was a thief. He lived a second and darker life as a desperate housebreaker. He did not have any candlesticks because he only used these candles cut short in the little lantern he carried. The snuff he employed as the fiercest French criminals have used pepper: to fling it suddenly in dense masses in the face of a captor or pursuer. But the final proof is in the curious coincidence of the diamonds and the small steel wheels. Surely that makes everything plain to you? Diamonds and small steel wheels are the only two instruments with which you can cut out a pane of glass."

The bough of a broken pine tree lashed heavily in the blast against the windowpane behind them, as if in parody of a burglar, but they did not turn round. Their eyes were fastened on Father Brown.

"Diamonds and small wheels," repeated Craven ruminating. "Is that all that makes you think it the true explanation?"

"I don't think it the true explanation," replied the priest placidly; "but you said that nobody could connect the four things. The true tale, of course, is something much more humdrum. Glengyle had found, or thought he had found, precious stones on his estate. Somebody had bamboozled him with those loose brilliants, saying they were found in the castle caverns. The little wheels are some diamond-cutting affair. He had to do the thing very roughly and in a small way, with the help of a few shepherds or rude fellows on these hills. Snuff is the one great luxury of such Scotch shepherds; it's the one thing with which you can bribe them. They didn't have candlesticks because they didn't want them; they held the candles in their hands when they explored the caves."

"Is that all?" asked Flambeau after a long pause. "Have we got to the dull truth at last?"

"Oh, no," said Father Brown.

As the wind died in the most distant pine woods with a long hoot as of mockery Father Brown, with an utterly impassive face, went on:

"I only suggested that because you said one could not plausibly connect snuff with clockwork or candles with bright stones. Ten false philosophies will fit the universe; ten false theories will fit Glengyle Castle. But we want the real explanation of the castle and the universe. But are there no other exhibits?"

Craven laughed, and Flambeau rose smiling to his feet and strolled down the long table.

"Items five, six, seven, etc.," he said, "and certainly more varied than instructive. A curious collection, not of lead pencils, but of the lead out of lead pencils. A senseless stick of bamboo, with the top rather splintered. It might be the instrument of the crime. Only, there isn't any crime. The only other things are a few old missals and little Catholic pictures, which the Ogilvies kept, I suppose, from the Middle Ages— their family pride being stronger than their Puritanism. We only put them in the museum because they seem curiously cut about and defaced."

The heady tempest without drove a dreadful wrack of clouds across Glengyle and threw the long room into darkness as Father Brown picked up the little illuminated pages to examine them. He spoke before the drift of darkness had passed; but it was the voice of an utterly new man.

"Mr. Craven," said he, talking like a man ten years younger, "you have got a legal warrant, haven't you, to go up and examine that grave? The sooner we do it the better, and get to the bottom of this horrible affair. If I were you I should start now."

"Now," repeated the astonished detective, "and why now?"

"Because this is serious," answered Brown; "this is not spilt snuff or loose pebbles, that might be there for a hundred reasons. There is only one reason I know of for this being done; and the reason goes down to the roots of the world. These religious pictures are not just dirtied or torn or scrawled over, which might be done in idleness or bigotry, by children or by Protestants. These have been treated very carefully—and very queerly. In every place where the great ornamented name of God comes in the old illuminations it has been elaborately taken out. The only other thing that has been removed is the halo round the head of the Child Jesus. Therefore, I say, let us get our warrant and our spade and our hatchet, and go up and break open that coffin."

"What *do* you mean?" demanded the London officer.

"I mean," answered the little priest, and his voice seemed to rise slightly in the roar of the gale. "I mean that the great devil of the universe may be sitting on the top tower of this castle at this moment, as big as a hundred elephants, and roaring like the Apocalypse. There is black magic somewhere at the bottom of this."

"Black magic," repeated Flambeau in a low voice, for he was too enlightened a man not to know of such things; "but what can these other things mean?"

"Oh, something damnable, I suppose," replied Brown impatiently. "How should I know? How can I guess all their mazes down below? Perhaps you can make a torture out of snuff and bamboo. Perhaps lunatics lust after wax and steel filings. Perhaps there is a maddening drug made of lead pencils! Our shortest cut to the mystery is up the hill to the grave."

His comrades hardly knew that they had obeyed and followed him till a blast of the night wind nearly flung them on their faces in the garden. Nevertheless they had obeyed him like automata; for Craven found a hatchet in his hand, and the warrant in his pocket; Flambeau was carrying the heavy spade of the strange gardener; Father Brown was carrying the little gilt book from which had been torn the name of God.

The path up the hill to the churchyard was crooked but short; only under that stress of wind it seemed laborious and long. Far as the eye could see, farther and farther as they mounted the slope, were seas beyond seas of pines, now all aslope one way under the wind. And that universal gesture seemed as vain as it was vast, as vain as if that wind were whistling about some unpeopled and purposeless planet. Through all that infinite growth of grey-blue forests sang, shrill and high, that ancient sorrow that is in the heart of all heathen things. One could fancy that the voices from the under world of unfathomable foliage were cries of the lost and wandering pagan gods: gods who had gone roaming in that irrational forest, and who will never find their way back to heaven.

"You see," said Father Brown in low but easy tone, "Scotch people before Scotland existed were a curious lot. In fact, they're a curious lot still. But in the prehistoric times I fancy they really worshipped demons. That," he added genially, "is why they jumped at the Puritan theology."

"My friend," said Flambeau, turning in a kind of fury, "what does all that snuff mean?"

"My friend," replied Brown, with equal seriousness, "there is one mark of all genuine religions: materialism. Now, devil-worship is a perfectly genuine religion."

They had come up on the grassy scalp of the hill, one of the few bald spots that stood clear of the crashing and roaring pine forest. A mean enclosure, partly timber and partly wire, rattled in the tempest to tell them the border of the graveyard. But by the time Inspector Craven had come to the corner of the grave, and Flambeau had planted his spade point downwards and leaned on it, they were both almost as shaken as the shaky wood and wire. At the foot of the grave grew great tall thistles, grey and silver in their decay. Once or twice, when a ball of thistledown broke under the breeze and flew past him, Craven jumped slightly as if it had been an arrow.

Flambeau drove the blade of his spade through the whistling grass into the wet clay below. Then he seemed to stop and lean on it as on a staff.

"Go on," said the priest very gently. "We are only trying to find the truth. What are you afraid of?"

"I am afraid of finding it," said Flambeau.

The London detective spoke suddenly in a high crowing voice that was meant to be conversational and cheery. "I wonder why he really did hide himself like that. Something nasty, I suppose; was he a leper?"

"Something worse than that," said Flambeau.

"And what do you imagine," asked the other, "would be worse than a leper?"

"I don't imagine it," said Flambeau.

He dug for some dreadful minutes in silence, and then said in a choked voice, "I'm afraid of his not being the right shape."

"Nor was that piece of paper, you know," said Father Brown quietly, "and we survived even that piece of paper."

Flambeau dug on with a blind energy. But the tempest

had shouldered away the choking grey clouds that clung to the hills like smoke and revealed grey fields of faint starlight before he cleared the shape of a rude timber coffin, and somehow tipped it up upon the turf. Craven stepped forward with his axe; a thistle-top touched him, and he flinched. Then he took a firmer stride, and hacked and wrenched with an energy like Flambeau's till the lid was torn off, and all that was there lay glimmering in the grey starlight.

"Bones," said Craven; and then he added, "but it is a man," as if that were something unexpected.

"Is he," asked Flambeau in a voice that went oddly up and down, "is he all right?"

"Seems so," said the officer huskily, bending over the obscure and decaying skeleton in the box. "Wait a minute."

A vast heave went over Flambeau's huge figure. "And now I come to think of it," he cried, "why in the name of madness shouldn't he be all right? What is it gets hold of a man on these cursed cold mountains? I think it's the black, brainless repetition; all these forests, and over all an ancient horror of unconsciousness. It's like the dream of an atheist. Pine-trees and more pine-trees and millions more pine-trees—"

"God!" cried the man by the coffin, "but he hasn't got a head."

While the others stood rigid the priest, for the first time, showed a leap of startled concern.

"No head!" he repeated. "*No head?*" as if he had almost expected some other deficiency.

Half-witted visions of a headless baby born to Glengyle, of a headless youth hiding himself in the castle, of a headless man pacing those ancient halls or that gorgeous garden, passed in panorama through their minds. But even in that stiffened instant the tale took no root in them and seemed to have no reason in it. They stood listening to the loud woods and the shrieking sky quite foolishly, like exhausted animals. Thought seemed to be something enormous that had suddenly slipped out of their grasp.

"There are three headless men," said Father Brown, "standing round this open grave."

The pale detective from London opened his mouth to speak, and left it open like a yokel, while a long scream of wind tore the sky; then he looked at the axe in his hands as if it did not belong to him, and dropped it.

"Father," said Flambeau in that infantile and heavy voice he used very seldom, "what are we to do?"

His friend's reply came with the pent promptitude of a gun going off.

"Sleep!" cried Father Brown. "Sleep. We have come to the end of the ways. Do you know what sleep is? Do you know that every man who sleeps believes in God? It is a sacrament; for it is an act of faith and it is a food. And we need a sacrament, if only a natural one. Something has fallen on us that falls very seldom on men; perhaps the worst thing that can fall on them."

Craven's parted lips came together to say, "What do you mean?"

The priest had turned his face to the castle as he answered:

"We have found the truth; and the truth makes no sense."

He went down the path in front of them with a plunging and reckless step very rare with him, and when they reached the castle again he threw himself upon sleep with the simplicity of a dog.

Despite his mystic praise of slumber, Father Brown was up earlier than anyone else except the silent gardener; and was found smoking a big pipe and watching that expert at his speechless labours in the kitchen garden. Towards daybreak the rocking storm had ended in roaring rains, and the day came with a curious freshness. The gardener seemed even to have been conversing, but at sight of the detectives he planted his spade sullenly in a bed and, saying something about his breakfast, shifted along the lines of cabbages and shut himself in the kitchen. "He's a valuable man, that," said Father Brown. "He does the potatoes amazingly. Still," he added, with a dispassionate charity, "he has his faults; which of us hasn't? He doesn't dig this bank quite regularly. There, for instance," and he stamped suddenly on one spot. "I'm really very doubtful about that potato."

"And why?" asked Craven, amused with the little man's new hobby.

"I'm doubtful about it," said the other, "because old Gow was doubtful about it himself. He put his spade in methodically in every place but just this. There must be a mighty fine potato just here."

Flambeau pulled up the spade and impetuously drove it into the place. He turned up, under a load of soil, something that did not look like a potato, but rather like a monstrous, over-domed mushroom. But it struck the spade with a cold click; it rolled over like a ball, and grinned up at them.

"The Earl of Glengyle," said Brown sadly, and looked down heavily at the skull.

Then, after a momentary meditation, he plucked the spade from Flambeau, and, saying "We must hide it again," clamped the skull down in the earth. Then he leaned his little body and huge head on the great handle of the spade, that stood up stiffly in the earth, and his eyes were empty and his forehead full of wrinkles. "If one could only conceive," he muttered, "the meaning of this last monstrosity." And leaning on the large spade handle, he buried his brows in his hands, as men do in church.

All the corners of the sky were brightening into blue and silver; the birds were chattering in the tiny garden trees; so loud it seemed as if the trees themselves were talking. But the three men were silent enough.

"Well, I give it all up," said Flambeau at last boisterously. "My brain and this world don't fit each other; and there's an end of it. Snuff, spoilt Prayer Books, and the insides of musical boxes—what—"

Brown threw up his bothered brow and rapped on the spade handle with an intolerance quite unusual with him. "Oh, tut, tut, tut, tut!" he cried. "All that is as plain as a pike-staff. I understood the snuff and clockwork, and so on, when I first opened my eyes this morning. And since then I've had it out with old Gow, the gardener, who is neither so deaf nor so stupid as he pretends. There's nothing amiss about the loose items. I was wrong about the torn mass-book, too; there's no harm in that. But it's this last business. Desecrating graves and stealing dead men's heads—surely there's harm in that? Surely there's black magic still in that? That doesn't fit in to the quite simple story of the snuff and the candles." And, striding about again, he smoked moodily.

"My friend," said Flambeau, with a grim humour, "you must be careful with me and remember I was once a criminal.

The great advantage of that estate was that I always made up the story myself, and acted it as quick as I chose. This detective business of waiting about is too much for my French impatience. All my life, for good or evil, I have done things at the instant; I always fought duels the next morning; I always paid bills on the nail; I never even put off a visit to the dentist—"

Father Brown's pipe fell out of his mouth and broke into three pieces on the gravel path. He stood rolling his eyes, the exact picture of an idiot. "Lord, what a turnip I am!" he kept saying. "Lord, what a turnip!" Then, in a somewhat groggy kind of way, he began to laugh.

"The dentist!" he repeated. "Six hours in the spiritual abyss, and all because I never thought of the dentist! Such a simple, such a beautiful and peaceful thought! Friends, we have passed a night in hell; but now the sun is risen, the birds are singing, and the radiant form of the dentist consoles the world."

"I will get some sense out of this," cried Flambeau, striding forward, "if I use the tortures of the Inquisition."

Father Brown repressed what appeared to be a momentary disposition to dance on the now sunlit lawn and cried quite piteously, like a child, "Oh, let me be silly a little. You don't know how unhappy I have been. And now I know that there has been no deep sin in this business at all. Only a little lunacy, perhaps—and who minds that?"

He spun round once, then faced them with gravity.

"This is not a story of crime," he said; "rather it is the story of a strange and crooked honesty. We are dealing with the one man on earth, perhaps, who has taken no more than his due. It is a study in the savage living logic that has been the religion of this race.

"That old local rhyme about the house of Glengyle—

> "'As green sap to the simmer trees
> Is red gold to the Ogilvies'—

was literal as well as metaphorical. It did not merely mean that the Glengyles sought for wealth; it was also true that they literally gathered gold; they had a huge collection of ornaments and utensils in that metal. They were, in fact, misers whose mania took that turn. In the light of that fact, run through all the things we found in the castle. Diamonds without their gold rings; candles without their gold candlesticks; snuff without the gold snuff-boxes; pencil-leads without the gold pencil-cases; a walking stick without its gold top; clockwork without the gold clocks—or rather watches. And, mad as it sounds, because the halos and the name of God in the old missals were of real gold; these also were taken away."

The garden seemed to brighten, the grass to grow gayer in the strengthening sun, as the crazy truth was told. Flambeau lit a cigarette as his friend went on.

"Were taken away," continued Father Brown; "were taken away—but not stolen. Thieves would never have left this mystery. Thieves would have taken the gold snuff-boxes, snuff and all; the gold pencil-cases, lead and all. We have to deal with a man with a peculiar conscience, but certainly a conscience. I found that mad moralist this morning in the kitchen garden yonder, and I heard the whole story.

"The late Archibald Ogilvie was the nearest approach to a

good man ever born at Glengyle. But his bitter virtue took the turn of the misanthrope; he moped over the dishonesty of his ancestors, from which, somehow, he generalised a dishonesty of all men. More especially he distrusted philanthropy or free-giving; and he swore if he could find one man who took his exact rights he should have all the gold of Glengyle. Having delivered this defiance to humanity he shut himself up, without the smallest expectation of its being answered. One day, however, a deaf and seemingly senseless lad from a distant village brought him a belated telegram; and Glengyle, in his acrid pleasantry, gave him a new farthing. At least he thought he had done so, but when he turned over his change he found the new farthing still there and a sovereign gone. The accident offered him vistas of sneering speculation. Either way, the boy would show the greasy greed of the species. Either he would vanish, a thief stealing a coin; or he would sneak back with it virtuously, a snob seeking a reward. In the middle of that night Lord Glengyle was knocked up out of his bed—for he lived alone—and forced to open the door to the deaf idiot. The idiot brought with him, not the sovereign, but exactly nineteen shillings and eleven-pence three-farthings in change.

"Then the wild exactitude of this action took hold on the mad lord's brain like fire. He swore he was Diogenes, that had long sought an honest man, and at last had found one. He made a new will, which I have seen. He took the literal youth into his huge, neglected house, and trained him up as his solitary servant and—after an odd manner—his heir. And whatever that queer creature understands, he understood absolutely his lord's two fixed ideas: first, that the letter of right is everything; and second, that he himself was to have the gold of Glengyle. So far, that is all; and that is simple. He has stripped the house of gold, and taken not a grain that was not gold; not so much as a grain of snuff. He lifted the gold leaf off an old illumination, fully satisfied that he left the rest unspoilt. All that I understood; but I could not understand this skull business. I was really uneasy about that human head buried among the potatoes. It distressed me—till Flambeau said the word.

"It will be all right. He will put the skull back in the grave, when he has taken the gold out of the tooth."

And, indeed, when Flambeau crossed the hill that morning, he saw that strange being, the just miser, digging at the desecrated grave, the plaid round his throat thrashing out in the mountain wind; the sober top hat on his head.

A Medical Crime

J. Storer Clouston

Joseph Storer Clouston (1870–1944) came from an old Orcadian family. He was actually born in Cumberland, at a time when his father—the eminent psychiatrist Sir Thomas Clouston—was superintendent of an asylum in Carlisle, but in 1873 the family moved to Edinburgh. Storer Clouston was educated at Merchiston Castle School in the city and at Magdalen College, Oxford. He was called to the Bar, but never practised, preferring to establish himself as an author. He published his first book in 1898 and followed it up with a comic novel, *The Lunatic at Large*, which was presumably inspired by his experience of growing up in close proximity to people suffering from mental health troubles. According to legend, it was this novel that introduced the word "bonkers" to the English language. The book was so popular—its admirers included P. G. Wodehouse—that it was twice filmed and spawned three sequels. He continued to write until almost the end of his life and his titles included *A History of Orkney* and *Scotland Expects*.

Clouston's comic thriller *The Mystery of No. 49* (1912) was also filmed twice. *The Spy in Black* (1917) was set in his native territory, near Scapa Flow, and had the distinction of being filmed in 1939 by Michael Powell and Emeric Pressburger with a good cast including Conrad Veldt, Valerie Hobson, and Marius Goring. Clouston continued to dabble in espionage fiction and his final novel was *Beastmark the Spy* (1941). In the field of detective fiction, he is remembered for *Carrington's Cases* (1920), which earned the approval of authorities such as Dorothy L. Sayers and Ellery Queen, and included this story, which also appeared in *The Sphere* on 16 October 1920. F. T. Carrington is a private investigator; youngish, amiable, and shrewd. The case he describes here takes place in Clouston's beloved Scotland.

———

"ONE OF THE MOST FUTILE-LOOKING JOBS THAT EVER came my way," said Carrington, "was my trip to the royal burgh of Kinbuckie in the Kingdom of Scotland; and yet…" he paused and flicked the ash of his cigarette into the fire with a reminiscent smile.

"And yet," echoed one of his audience, "I rather suspect it wasn't as futile as it looked!"

"Why?"

"From your eye."

"I must wear an eyeglass in both eyes," he smiled, "if I'm going to give myself away like that. But I assure you it did honestly seem a pretty hopeless case when I was first asked to take it up. There had been a series of very mysterious burglaries in Kinbuckie, and the police were absolutely beaten. The provost of the town, however, was a determined gentleman, and extremely well-to-do; he had heard of me somehow or other—one's sins will find one out, don't you know—and he took it into his head to get me down at his own expense to try and clear the business up. As you'll hear in a moment, there was something particularly unpleasant about it for a man like this provost, who took a keen interest and a great deal of pride in the town, and he was quite resolved to remove the shadow somehow. So I said I'd go down and see him, and I went.

"All the way in the train, the futility of the quest struck me more and more forcibly. It was over a fortnight since the last of these crimes had been committed, and what clues would be likely to be left? Probably none. I couldn't possibly afford the time to spend more than two or three nights in the place at the outside, and it was any odds against another burglary being committed while I was there. And after that I could only advise them from London. Even if it were a provincial town in England, the difficulties of acting effectively would have been enormous, but the fact of its being away up in Scotland added to them infinitely. It wasn't a job for a man like me in the very least; or anyhow, that is what I thought on the way between King's Cross and Kinbuckie. But, as some other great thinker has probably remarked, one never knows one's luck.

"Well, at the end of a long journey I found myself in a grey-stone, seaboard town, with a small harbour, an old clock tower on the town hall, a couple of church spires, and the Lord knows how many kirks without them. At one end were quite a few modern residential villas, and there were a certain number of solid old-fashioned houses more in the heart of the town, that also looked as if they might have pickings for the enterprising burglar. But the total population was something under ten thousand, and even before I reached the provost's house, the very idea of a series of mysterious crimes in a place as small as this, where everybody must surely know everybody else, began to intrigue me. And when one gets really interested, the mind works a lot more briskly. Though at that moment, mind you, I didn't see a glimmer of how to tackle the problem.

"I found the provost to be a very shrewd sensible man, and we had a long talk together over a glass—or possibly even two glasses—of one of the best whiskies I've ever tasted. All the time I was in Kinbuckie there was a whistling east wind, a bursting grey sea, and exactly one half-hour's blink of sunshine; and with such a climate and such whiskies, why everybody in Scotland doesn't die of drink is a mystery to me.

"What the provost told me of the burglaries was also told me later by the Superintendent of Police, and I'll come to it in a moment. Meantime I'll only say that I quite saw why he was so keen to clear the thing up, and that personally I became very interested and curious indeed. But I got one very nasty jar that seemed, at the moment, to dish any slender chance I had of finding much out. He had told several people that he was getting up a detective, whereas I had counted on making my inquiries in the guise of a harmless visitor. In fact, I had brought my golf clubs as a blind, and even taken the trouble to turn into a shop on my way up from the station and buy half a dozen balls. And now here was the fat in the fire! However, as I remarked before, one never knows one's luck.

"From his house I went on to the police office, and introduced myself to Superintendent Pringle. He was a tall, stout, square-shouldered man, every inch a bobby, with a face very full below and narrowing towards the top, a red moustache, small but exceedingly alert eyes, and a manner worth a small fortune in this suspicious, credulous, competitive world. It was a manner so confidential, impressive, and genial, that one simply couldn't help feeling that with Superintendent Pringle at one's back things were bound to be all right. And my first glance round his office showed me that he was evidently an enthusiast in his profession, and studied its possibilities and finer points. For I noticed on a shelf three or four volumes of stories of crime, and the reminiscences of great detectives.

"'A most mysterious business, sir,' said he. 'Aye, five separate burglaries in a matter of as mony months. Ye've got the fac's precisely right, sir. It's nae wonder the provost's upset, poor man. There's not been such ongoings in Kinbuckie since the Police Act first came into force. I'm aware, sir, it kin' o' reflects upon me, but if ye kent all the trouble I've taken! I've suspected everybody in this town excep' the provost, and I've been gey near suspecting him!'

"'By Jove, really!' said I. 'You almost suspected the provost, did you? I say! By Jingo!'

"As I've often assured my friends, I really do need an eyeglass in my left eye, and don't in my right. I don't know that they believe me, but anyhow, a monocle comes in very handy when one wants to produce an amateurish impression, and I let the Superintendent have the benefit of it now. I was also as Anglified as possible, for I know the deep-rooted provincial Scot's contempt for the Sassenach. I wanted Mr. Pringle to be quite at his ease, you see. I knew from the provost he had a very interesting theory, and I wished to draw him well out. In a few minutes, when we had become very friendly, and he had obviously set me down as a better listener than a detective, I asked him—

"'What's this the provost tells me about a curious feature that seems to run through all these five crimes?'

"The Superintendent became even more confidential and impressive.

"'Well,' said he, 'in four o' the cases there's a very singular coincidence, and nae doot it would have been in the fifth too had the man been able to find what he found in the ither houses. Mr. Ogilvy—that's the first case—he's a sort of antiquarian gentleman, and there was a lot of auld bones and things in his library—things he'd dug up, ye understand, sir. Well, if this burglar didna tak' some o' thae bones! What was he wanting them for? I rather wondered.'

"He looked at me very wisely, and of course I asked—

"'And what did he want them for?'

"'Wait a wee minute, sir,' said he, 'and I'll tell you something else. When he broke into Mr. Thomson's he took a medical book—*Advice to Mothers*, it's called. At the Burnets' house there was an auld skull, and he took that. And mind you, sir, these were just in addition to the valuables he lifted, and no worth a brass farthing, one of them.'

"'You think, then,' said I, 'that it points to some one interested in medicine?'

"'In my deleeberate opinion, it does that, sir! And I

havena tellt you that in the fourth case—that was Mistress Lindsay's—he took anither medical book, Burton's *Anatomy*.

I opened my eyes this time pretty wide.

"'Do you mean Burton's *Anatomy of Melancholy*?'" I asked.

"'Aye, sir, that was the vera name of it.'

"Sometimes a flash of light will illuminate the dark of the mind from the impact of two things that haven't apparently a spark of luminosity in them, just as the striking of a brown-tipped splinter on a bit of roughened paper will illuminate the dark of the night. Such a flash lit my brain at that instant, but I think I may say my face showed little more evidence of intelligence than before.

"'Then, Superintendent, what is your theory?' I asked.

"He glanced round the office, as though to see that its bareness hid no eavesdroppers.

"'There is only one kind of folk that has any business to be gaun about the toon at a' hours of the night,' said he in a lowered voice. 'Folks, that's to say, sir, that the police would never think of coupling wi' criminal intent; and that's the doctors.'

"He looked at me hard as though to see how I would take this surprising suggestion, and I made no effort to hide the fact that it gave me food for very serious thought indeed. The provost had told me of this theory of the Superintendent's; and you can imagine how upset he was at the idea of the most respectable professional men in the town going in for housebreaking. He hadn't, however, told me all these details.

"'Do you suspect any doctor in particular?' I asked.

"The Superintendent became cautious.

"'Well, sir,' said he, 'there's six doctors in the town, and it's no' for me to say exac'ly which one's to be suspectit without mair positive evidence. There's Dr. Mitchell and Dr. Rattray, and Dr. Smith and Dr. Douglas, and Dr. Hills and Dr. MacTavish. That's the lot, sir.'

"He spoke with an impartial air, but I could see that there were unspoken thoughts behind his words. I lowered my voice and asked him very confidentially—

"'Now, Superintendent, honestly, what's your own private opinion of these six gentlemen?'

"'Well,' said he, 'Dr. Mitchell is a very decent auld gentleman, and it's no' vera likely to be him. Dr. Rattray is a kind o' cousin of the provost's, and they're a' vera decent folk indeed. Smith and Douglas have been in the place a long while, and it's queer if they should tak' to burgling now. But Hills, sir, is an Englishman.'

"The Superintendent looked very grave as he revealed this damning fact, and then suddenly became distinctly embarrassed as he realised that I came of the same predatory race myself.

"'I know them!' I reassured him. 'You are quite right to be suspicious. And what about the last man?'

"'MacTavish?' said the Superintendent in accents which made his opinion of the English seem comparatively flattering—'He's a Hielander.'

"He left it at that, and seemed to think no further comment was necessary. Hitherto I had always imagined that a Scot was a Scot, and that one drappie set them all quoting Robbie Burns like a Gaiety chorus. But it seems that's only when you meet them in London. Go to a Lowland town, especially anywhere near the Highland border, and ask the average inhabitant his opinion of the MacDonalds and the MacTavishes, and you'll see!

"'Have you anything more definite against Dr. Hills and Dr. MacTavish?' I ventured to ask. 'Were they out on the nights of these crimes? Are they in financial difficulties? Have you traced any of the stolen things to their possession?'

"The Superintendent was prepared with a certain number of facts. He pulled out a note-book and gave me some particulars of the movements of all the six doctors on the nights of the crimes, so far as they could be traced. He had also collected some information as to the money they owed, or were said to owe, in the town. Definite evidence connecting any of these men with the stolen property was not to hand, he admitted, but it was a fact that Dr. MacTavish had settled at least two large bills since the series of robberies began.

"'Well, Superintendent,' I said at last, 'I mean to spend the next day or two in Kinbuckie, and I shall devote my attention to these six doctors. The provost is anxious either to have them all cleared, or to find which is the black sheep and get rid of him, so I won't look outside the doctors meanwhile— especially as you don't suspect anybody else.'

"'Vera good, sir,' said he; 'I ca' that a very sensible procedure.'

"I walked out of that office very thoughtfully indeed, and I spent the next hour or two in solid thinking; and then I set to work. I had come by the night train from King's Cross and arrived at Kinbuckie in the forenoon. The rest of that day and the whole of the next I went my own way, and my next meeting with Superintendent Pringle was in the evening. He was clearly all agog to learn what I had been doing, and when I first began to tell him of my methods, I am afraid he was considerably disappointed.

"'In a case like this,' I told him, 'where there is next to no real evidence, and the scent has got cold, I depend chiefly on my judgment of the people suspected. I try to size them up and see whether they look like the criminal type; do you see?'

"The Superintendent clearly did not see, and had some difficulty in refraining from telling me what he thought of such unscientific methods.

"'I have had a good look at all the six doctors,' I went on, 'and made the acquaintance of two or three of them, and I am bound to tell you, Superintendent, that I think you have judged very shrewdly in thinking that Hills and MacTavish are the likeliest criminals.'

"At this the Superintendent manifestly quite changed his opinion, and made no effort at all to refrain from indicating his admiration of my judgment.

"'I spent some time with them both,' I said. 'Of course I went to see them professionally, with the remains of a cold for Dr. Hills and a touch of lumbago for Dr. MacTavish, and of course we started talking about the burglaries. You see, everybody knows who I am; I thought it would be a serious handicap at first, but as things turned out I made a foul wind into a fair, and took advantage of their knowing I was a detective to give them a little confidential information.'

"The Superintendent opened his eyes and shook his head at this, but I soothed him with a confidential smile.

"'Wait till you hear what I told them,' said I. 'I informed Dr. Hills in the strictest confidence that I was depending very largely on the new footprint test. It was practically impossible now, I said, for a criminal to avoid detection unless he wore rubber tennis shoes of the largest size, with ribbed soles. Of course this was a dead secret and I trusted him not to breathe a word to a soul.'

"The Superintendent was beginning to look puzzled.

"'I never heard of that test, sir,' said he.

"'Did you ever hear of the olfactory test?' I inquired.

"He shook his head. He was evidently getting extremely mystified.

"'Well,' I said, 'when I went on to see Dr. MacTavish, I told him in equal confidence that the olfactory or smelling test was the very latest thing. A criminal was nailed to an absolute certainty by means of a delicate odour-registering instrument, and the only dodge for defeating it was by burning feathers. Of course this was an equally dead secret.'

"I looked at him gravely and asked—

"'Now, Superintendent, do you mean to say you haven't heard of either of these tests before?'

"He seemed a little troubled.

"'Well, sir, not exactly…'

"'No more have I!' I said; 'but these two doctors have, and if there's another burglary in this town and you find traces of large rubber tennis shoes, you'll know the criminal is Hills, and if you find traces of burnt feathers, you'll know it's MacTavish.'

"The Superintendent tumbled to the idea.

"'Man, that's fairly champion!' he cried. 'I've read a lot o' smart stories of detectives, in fac' it's ma favourite reading, but I'm bound to say, sir, this is the best dodge I've heard of yet!'

"I warned him very solemnly not to tell a single soul about

this scheme, and we parted on the friendliest terms. To the provost I merely said I had laid a mine, which might go off and blow up something or might not, and next morning I took the early train back to town. And that was the last I saw of the burgh of Kinbuckie."

Carrington paused in his tale, and smiled upon the company.

"Well," he said, "that was a pretty good gamble, wasn't it? Fixing on two respectable professional men at sight, without a scrap of evidence against either of them, and not doing a hand's turn to detect anybody else—not much of Sherlock Holmes or Dr. Thorndyke about that; what?

"But it came off! Within a week I got a wire from Superintendent Pringle to say that a fresh burglary had been committed, and that there were the remains of several burnt feathers, and what he described as a heavy smell, and should he at once arrest Dr. MacTavish? That night the Superintendent was under lock and key himself with six separate burglary charges against him. You see, I hadn't told another living soul but him about the olfactory test!"

"How did I suspect it was the Superintendent? By his unfortunate choice of Burton's *Anatomy of Melancholy*. I realised in a flash that only an ignorant, half-educated man would mistake that classic for a medical treatise, and therefore it was obviously such a man who was clumsily trying to throw suspicion on the doctors. Besides, imagine a doctor taking the trouble to steal *Advice to Mothers*! Then my eye fell on the shelf of detective stories, and I realised further that the Superintendent had his mind well stored with criminal dodges and false clues, and all that sort of thing. Also, leaving out the doctors, whom he was ingenious enough to select as his victims, nobody but himself and his constables had the same opportunities for wandering about the town at night unsuspected. And, by the way, it was found that one of his constables was in the game with him. And finally, the man himself had his character written on his face—a low, cunning, specious, animal type.

"Inside half a minute I had made up my mind that it was a hundred to one on the burglar being Pringle himself. The only question was, how to bowl him out? And, by Jingo, I got the middle stump right enough that time!"

Footsteps

Anthony Wynne

Anthony Wynne was the pen-name under which Robert McNair Wilson (1882–1963) wrote detective fiction. McNair Wilson was born in Maryhill, Glasgow (the location of the police headquarters in the long-running TV crime series *Taggart*), and educated at Glasgow Academy and Glasgow University. He was medical correspondent of *The Times* from 1914–42. Keenly interested in politics, he stood for Parliament as a Liberal candidate on a couple of occasions in the 1920s, but without success. As his obituary in *The Times* said, "his lively and inquiring mind could not be bound to any one subject for long... A keen student of French history, he wrote books on Napoleon and the Empress Josephine, on Madame de Staël and on the women of the French Revolution. His other books included a biography of Lord Northcliffe... and *Doctor's Progress: Some Reminiscences*."

Today, he is best remembered as a detective story writer

with a specialism in "impossible crime stories." *Murder of a Lady*, with a Scottish setting, has been republished as a British Library Crime Classic, and "Footsteps" is also set in a grand but mysterious house in a distant corner of Scotland. Wynne's series detective, Dr. Eustace Hailey, the snuff-taking "Giant of Harley Street" solves the puzzle in both stories. "Footsteps" first appeared in *Flynn's Magazine* on 9 January 1926 and was collected in Wynne's *Sinners Go Secretly* the following year.

———

"THERE IT IS AGAIN!"

Lord Tarbet's face had grown tense, revealing the fact that this strange phenomenon was very definitely getting on his nerves. Doctor Hailey listened intently.

He heard the sound of footsteps which were far away in one of the dim corridors of the old castle. They hurried and came nearer. He caught his breath. The footsteps grew louder and it was evident that they were approaching the door of the room.

They came to the door, stopped, and both men stiffened involuntarily as though they expected next instant to hear the sound of the handle being turned.

But instead of that the eerie silence of a sultry West Highland night resumed its sway. The distant moaning of the sea alone disturbed it.

Lord Tarbet rose and strode to the door of the room. He flung it open.

"You see. There is nobody there."

He stood at the door gazing along the empty corridor.

Doctor Hailey got up and came beside him. The long corridor was absolutely empty and deserted. It was utterly impossible that any human being, no matter how swift-footed, could have escaped from it in so short a space of time.

The two men looked at one another.

"You will admit, my dear doctor, that I did not exaggerate," Tarbet remarked.

Doctor Hailey inclined his head. His tall, broad figure filled the doorway. His host thought that he looked in that setting, even bigger than usual. No wonder they called him the "Harley Street giant."

"No. You didn't exaggerate certainly. On the contrary, I think you understated the facts. It is certainly most extraordinary!"

"It has happened like that on five separate occasions before. Dudley Despard went after his second dose, protesting, of course, that he had promised to make a round of visits. As if any round of visits would have dragged him away from these wonderful moors on the fifteenth of August. No, the little man was scared stiff. Then Pykewood left me—after the fourth. He had the decency to send himself a telegram. I confess that I asked you to come, busy man as you are, because I couldn't have endured it alone another day. My God, there it is again!"

Lord Tarbet had gone to the room but he stood in full view of the corridor, for the door remained open. Doctor Hailey was actually leaning on the jamb of the door. They both bent forward tensely.

The footsteps approached, growing louder and louder. They came to the door. They stopped.

Lord Tarbet wiped his brow.

"I don't mind telling you, Doc," he muttered, "that I can't stand much more of it myself. It's—it's beginning to tell on me. I didn't sleep well last night. Haven't slept well, indeed, for a week. God! And I've always had such a contempt for the people who keep chattering about ghosts and haunted houses."

He moved to the fire and sat down in one of the big leather-covered armchairs which was drawn up beside it. Doctor Hailey closed the door and joined him.

"Providence," he said in calm tones, "decreed that superstition in all its forms should be left entirely out of my composition." He took his snuff-box from his pocket and extracted a pinch. As he did so a streak of lightning flashed across the window. It was followed by a thunderclap which went rolling among the hills behind the castle. Lord Tarbet breathed deeply.

"That should clear the air." He got up and crossed the room towards the windows which overlooked the sea. "The trouble is," he said in tones from which anxiety was banished with difficulty, "that this ghost has a very mysterious and ghostly history. You know perhaps that Colonel McCallien, the late laird of Ardvore committed suicide six years ago while his wife's dead body lay in this room. She died very suddenly in her sleep. The night before her funeral he disappeared and next day they found his hat on the rocks below the cliffs. These footsteps are supposed to indicate his frenzied attempts to rejoin his wife; at least that is the idea the servants have now formed, for this room was kept closed, I understand, until I arrived last week. The present Ardvore has never stayed here himself. Till this year the shoot was always let to the tenant of the next estate."

Another blaze of lightning filled the windows, causing the young man to start back involuntarily. He turned to the doctor who saw that his cold, handsome face was rather drawn, as though the strain of the experiences he had sustained was indeed beginning to tell on him.

"Did they find the poor fellow's body?" Doctor Hailey asked.

"No. Never."

Lord Tarbet turned back to watch the storm, which was becoming more severe. The doctor rose and joined him. Each new flash of lightning gave them the bold, rugged headlands of the wild coast, bare of all vegetation, save the ubiquitous heather. It revealed the sweep of the distant mountains downwards to the sea. Under the lashing rain the roof of a small building, set near the edge of the cliffs, shone like polished silver, adding somehow a weird touch to the spectacle.

"What a scene for uncanny happenings!" Lord Tarbet exclaimed in low tones.

He was bending forward, as though his eyes strained to view some distant object. Doctor Hailey thought that, in all the five years he had known him, he had never before seen him so intent or so obviously ill at ease. An inexplicable feeling that his presence was causing embarrassment made him stroll back again to the fireplace, and sit down.

Once again he wondered why it was that Tarbet should have taken this remote place and come to it with only a couple of men friends. For a recently-married man, obviously very much in love with his wife, such conduct was, to say the least of it, astonishing. He reflected that when he had got the very urgent telegram begging him to join the shooting party, he had assumed, as a matter of course, that the new Lady Tarbet would be with her husband.

"Oh, my God!"

A fresh flood of light poured through the windows. His host staggered back; holding his hand to his brow as though the flame had scorched his sight. He swung to face his companion, showing Doctor Hailey cheeks from which every drop of blood seemed to have ebbed away. A wild, new fear was staring in his eyes.

"I—I feel—unwell."

The doctor jumped up and came to his side. But Tarbet refused the help he proffered. He seemed to make a tremendous effort at self-control.

"No, no," he cried. "It's all right. Only my nerves and that lightning." He glanced round the room as if trying to collect his thoughts. "If you will excuse me for a moment; I feel a little sick."

He went staggering to the door. After he had turned the handle he looked back.

"Please don't trouble about me," he said. "I shall be all right in a minute or two."

There was a look in his eyes which implored that he should be allowed to escape without further attention. Doctor Hailey said, "All right," in tones which he tried to render casual. As the door shut he returned to his seat beside the fire. The storm seemed for a moment to have grown less violent. He heard the departing footsteps of his host quite distinctly in the unnatural silence. The thought came to him that this sound did not in the least resemble the supposed footsteps of Ardvore's "ghosts."

He lay back and closed his eyes, wondering anew what could be the explanation of that strange phenomenon. His mind, trained in the strict school of experimental science, rejected absolutely the popular interpretation. Yet he had to confess that the illusion was a very striking one—so striking that, in this old house, at the dead of night, a man had to control his nerves in order to resist the instinct of dread which it inspired.

He rose and stood in front of the fire, listening for his host's return. That, however, as he told himself, might be delayed, because some people remain unwell during the whole period of a thunderstorm. He walked across the room towards the window, but paused suddenly. The footsteps, those of the "ghost" were approaching once again!

He sprang to the door and, recalling the first principles of stethoscopy, put his ear to the woodwork of the jamb. But a great peal of thunder defeated this purpose. It was only when the last echoes had died away that he was able to hear the sounds at all. They had become loud as the "ghost" neared the door.

He started in surprise. He threw the door open and began to inspect the woodwork behind the hinges. An exclamation escaped his lips. He felt in his pocket and extracted a pen-knife. A moment later he had removed what appeared to be the lid of a small aperture in the solid beam. He stooped down, evidently following something with his eyes. Then he exclaimed again. A thin insulated wire connected the aperture with the floor.

This wire, as he now saw, ran between two of the loosely set floorboards. He rolled back the heavy rug which covered these to follow the course of the connection across the room.

"Ah!"

He bent again. The wire ended in a switch of the type used in some dining-rooms to enable the mistress of the house to summon the servants without leaving her chair. The switch was set deeply in one of the boards, yet anyone treading on it must put it into action.

He set his foot on it. Instantly in the far distance, as it seemed, the steps became audible.

He strode back to the aperture in the jamb. A tocking sound proceeded from it, a sound which, when muffled by the lid he had just removed, would exactly resemble the impact of a shoe on a wooden floor. Once again he had cause to reflect on the extreme difficulty of localising any sound. If a note, at first faint, was made to develop by slow degrees the listener always had the impression of something approaching him.

He returned to the fireplace and helped himself to snuff. The explanation of the "ghost" was complete. It had appeared, manifestly, each time that anybody happened to tread on the switch in the floor, for in that way the piece of mechanism in the jamb had been set in motion. A smile curled his lips as he anticipated the satisfaction of imparting his discovery to Lord Tarbet.

Why was the young man absent so long a time? He went back to the door of the room and listened intently. The house was as silent as the grave. It might have been utterly deserted—for the servants' quarters were far away in the wing remote from that in which he stood. He wondered if he might follow his host to his bedroom and make inquiries, but decided against that course. Tarbet had seemed so very anxious to be left undisturbed.

He sat down again and fell to wondering who had installed the ghost machine in the room. That thought, as it developed in his mind, brought a look of deepening perplexity to his face. The author of the illusion could only be the late laird of Ardvore himself because this had been his own bedroom and none of his retainers or guests would have dared to play such a trick on him. For what conceivable reason had he wished to suggest a ghostly visitor?

It was scarcely credible that his object had been the terrifying of his own wife—hardly more credible that he had desired to frighten his servants. Yet both these effects must almost certainly have been produced, because sooner or later, anyone making frequent use of the room was bound to tread on the switch. Unless, indeed, it had been permanently covered by some piece of furniture.

Doctor Hailey adjusted his eyeglass and made a quick examination of the carpet. From the marks on this he satisfied himself that the bedstead, while the room was so used, had been placed well away from the switch. Nor were there any marks near it indicative of the super-imposition of any other furnishings.

He stood with his chin in his hand, reflecting that a woman who listened to those "footsteps" at night, in this house, might well be thrown into a state of terror of the most extreme kind. In his own experience, a girl had become cataleptic and remained seemingly dead for several days as a consequence of just such an apparent manifestation of the supernatural.

He returned to the machine and was about to make a further inspection of it, when his eye encountered a new surprise. This was a round hole in the panelling of the room, a short distance from the door, a hole running at an acute angle to the surface of the woodwork. He focussed his glass on it and, as he did so, drew a sharp breath. The hole had been made, without doubt, by a revolver bullet.

A sense of uneasiness came upon him as he gazed on this fresh evidence of extraordinary happenings in the old room. He recalled vividly the story Tarbet had told him of the disappearance of the Chieftain on the eve of his wife's funeral, while her body lay in its coffin within those very walls. Was there some connection between the disappearance and this bullet-hole—between that disappearance and the ghost machine?

Doctor Hailey satisfied himself again that the bullet mark was of comparatively recent origin. Its edges had not even begun to mellow to the rich tone of the surrounding wood-work. He followed the direction in which the weapon had been fired and took up his position accordingly. So far as he could see the individual discharging it must have been standing near the foot of the bed, facing someone who had just entered or who was trying to leave the bedroom. He inclined to the former view because the bullet had gone wide of the door. Had the threatened individual been about to leave the room, and so been grasping the door handle, the hole, presuming the aim to have been moderately accurate, would have been clear to the jamb.

He drew his hand across his brow as these considerations passed through his mind. It was possible, of course, that the bullet mark recorded merely some accident; Ardvore had fought in the war and no doubt had an army pistol. He might have been showing it to his wife and forgotten that it was loaded. But against that idea was this extraordinary ghost machine, with its suggestion of some sinister purpose. One thing seemed to be certain at any rate; the shot had missed its mark. Had anyone been wounded there must have been a great outcry.

He bent down and rolled the carpet further back so as to expose the switch more completely. Then his eye detected a dark stain on one of the varnished boards. He knelt to look at it and once more experienced a thrill of astonishment.

The stain was almost certainly blood.

He moistened the corner of his handkerchief and rubbed it on the surface. A rusty discoloration rewarded his efforts.

So it was possible that the man who had fired the shot in the direction of the door had himself been fired at!

He swung round to examine the wainscoting behind him and a moment later found what he sought—a bullet mark similar to that on the opposite side of the room. In this case, however, the direction of the shot was upwards from the floor, as though the pistol had been discharged by someone actually lying thereon.

An expression of bewilderment came into his eyes. It almost seemed as though the same individual must have fired both shots, the first while yet he stood facing the door, the second after he had fallen to the ground wounded. That would mean that he was dealing with two assailants, unless indeed—

Doctor Hailey started as the new idea flashed into his mind. Suppose that after opening fire he had slipped and fallen, or been borne down by his intended victim, and suppose that in his fall his pistol had been discharged a second time. In that case the bullet might have passed through his body before it became lodged in the wall behind him.

The doctor took a pinch of snuff in the manner habitual to him when excited; but a moment later the eagerness faded out of his eyes. Satisfying as this explanation appeared to be, it took no account of the fact that, had anyone been wounded in that serious fashion, some report of the matter must have become public. The servants would certainly have heard about it.

He sat down again and took more snuff. How could a man wounded so badly as to lose that quantity of blood be restored without arousing the suspicion of the most suspicious folk in the world? How, too, had the reports of the pistol escaped the ears of the servants—for it seemed reasonable to think that the shooting must have taken place during the day when Mrs. McCallien was not in the room?

Suddenly he caught his breath. There had been one period—one night—in which Mrs. McCallien had been in the room and yet been far removed from all anxiety about the events occurring there, the night of her death. On that night the superstitious Highland servants would keep away as far as possible from this apartment, would, indeed, shut themselves up in their own remote quarters. *It was on that night that the laird of Ardvore had disappeared leaving only his hat at the bottom of the cliff as an indication of the fate which, as it was assumed, he had courted!*

He tried to picture the scene: the coffin, supported on its trestles at the foot of the bed. Ardvore, distracted with grief, becoming aware suddenly that he was not alone with his dead wife…snatching up his pistol to defend himself…the frantic rush of the mysterious stranger to avert his doom… the final shot as the two struggled together on the floor…

The stranger's shouldering of the body to bear it to the cliff…
His furtive departure through the eerie night…

Who was this stranger? And what had brought him to Ardvore at the time when the mistress of the castle was lying in her coffin? Why, too, should the husband of the dead woman have received him thus murderously?

Doctor Hailey paced the floor with ever quickening steps as these questions sprang to his mind. In his pursuit of this mystery he seemed to forget everything—Tarbet and Tarbet's illness, the storm now sobbing itself out over the ocean, even his own comfort. His huge face wore an expression of intense concentration which, however, did not entirely mask its native geniality.

Suddenly he stood still. If it was assumed that Ardvore had suspected the stranger of a guilty relationship with his wife, his subsequent conduct would be explicable. He started. In that case the ghost machine might be a device employed to recall to a conscience-stricken woman an event, the recollection of which she was trying to blot from her memory; it might even represent a deliberate attempt to test her innocence.

An exclamation escaped him. Mrs. McCallien of Ardvore had died suddenly, as a nervous woman, haunted by some spectre of the past, might die who heard, in the dead of night, these dreadful, accusing footsteps.

But it was almost necessary, if that idea were to be accepted, to assume that the man, whose steps were being reproduced, was himself dead at the moment when the reproduction took place. And such an assumption robbed the attack on the stranger of all its meaning unless indeed it could be further assumed that this individual appeared at that precise and tragic hour to falsify a previously received report of his death.

Doctor Hailey's instinct as an amateur investigator of crime, was opposed to any such elaboration of coincidence, though his experience furnished examples of the dovetailing of events which no writer of fiction would have dared to offer to his readers. He came back to the fireplace and opened his snuff-box with a deliberation which indicated cessation of mental effort. It was his habit, when a problem became too complicated, to go to bed and sleep over it. Before he could do that, however, he must satisfy himself that Tarbet was fully recovered.

He left the room and walked slowly along the corridor leading to the staircase. He ascended the stair and came to Lord Tarbet's bedroom door.

It stood open. The room was in darkness.

He spoke his host's name and then, when he received no reply, felt for the switch and turned up the light. There was nobody in the room. He glanced at the bed and saw that it had not been disturbed.

Evidently Tarbet had not come here at all when he left the smoking room. The doctor experienced a thrill of uneasiness which intensified with the movements. Where could the man have gone at this hour of the night and in this weather? He went to his own room but that also was untenanted. Then he tried the other bedrooms, in series. There was no sign of his host in any of them.

He returned to the staircase and descended it again. His wits were fully awakened now and the sense of weariness which had assailed him a few minutes earlier had completely passed away. He strode quickly back to the smoking room, glanced in there again and then proceeded to a systematic search of the other public apartments.

But that search was as fruitless as had been the examination of the bedrooms. The truth, that Tarbet was not in the castle, stared him in the face. It was confirmed when he reached the front door and found that it stood ajar.

Doctor Hailey was counted a brave man, but at that moment he felt his nerves a trifle unsteady. He pushed the heavy door before him and came out, almost timidly, into the threatening darkness of the night. The storm had passed but the thunder growled still among the mountains, fitfully like some giant beast wounded almost to death. The air seemed heavy and charged with fresh catastrophe. He groped his way across the gravel patch in front of the house and came to the lawn. The ground, as he knew, sloped steeply from this point towards the cliffs. He stood gazing into the sullen face of the night, seeking in these inscrutable features some hint of the fate which had overtaken his friend.

The night refused him so much as a gleam of enlightenment. He turned back to the house and possessed himself of his electric lamp, an accessory which long experience had taught him never to omit from his personal equipment. By the help of the generous beam he found the footpath leading to the bottom of the lawn and thence out from the grounds across the bare promontory on which Ardvore Castle stood.

He had chosen this way rather than any other because it was while he stood at the window overlooking the sea that his host had apparently been taken ill. The memory of Tarbet's ashen face, of his ghastly expression as he staggered back across the room, rose up clearly in the doctor's mind, bringing with it a great new anxiety. What had the man seen on this dismal heath which had so stricken his spirit? With what further spectacle of dread had the old castle furnished its latest tenant?

Doctor Hailey could not answer these questions. A vast complication of mystery, like an entangling web, seemed to bind his wits. He stumbled on, groping in the darkness, and scarcely daring to envisage the possibilities which the situation afforded.

He stood still. Far away, as it seemed, a tiny gleam of light shone to warn him that he was not alone on these wild headlands. The light came from a point on his left, removed some distance, as he judged, from the pathway which he was now following. He extinguished his own lamp and remained watching intently.

Then he switched on the current again and struck out across the turf towards the beckoning flame. As he approached it, he saw that it came from the window or doorway of a hut—that, probably, of which he had noticed the roof while the storm was raging. He paused again and once more extinguished his lamp. Then he advanced carefully step by step, keeping his eyes the while fixed on the enlarging square of light.

And suddenly a gasp of astonishment escaped his lips. Instinctively he crouched down.

The rays which had served as his beacon in the darkness were proceeding from the interior of a tomb!

There could be no doubt about this because he was able to distinguish the pattern of the wrought iron gate of the sepulchre. He was able to see, too, the gleam of white marble within the building itself. Breathlessly he crept forward over the rough ground.

The tomb was set on the edge of the cliff as though the

lairds of Ardvore desired that the voices of the sea should hold unending communion with their spirits. Sighings of an ebb tide rose wistfully on the air. He came to a point from which a clear view of the interior could be secured. As he looked he exclaimed in new bewilderment.

Within the sepulchre, facing the gateway, but bending down so that his face was partially hidden, was a man whose age seemed to be about forty years, a tall, dark-visaged man dressed in highland costume. He held a long screwdriver in his hands with which by the light of a storm lamp he was engaged in re-affixing its lid to one of the several coffins which lay, side by side, on the slabs with which the place was furnished.

So intent was the fellow on this ghoulish task that never once did he raise his eyes from it. Doctor Hailey studied him closely while his own mind groped anew among the confusion of ideas that the night had thrust on him. So far as he could see the coffin which had just been violated was the latest addition to the number of the Ardvore dead. At any rate it lay nearest to the entrance to the tomb. That would mean that it must contain the body of the woman the circumstances of whose death he had just been investigating.

He started at the thought. It was apparent that his misgivings about that event were more securely founded than he had known, since this man shared them to the point, seemingly, of doubting the identity of the dead.

The fellow finished his task and stood erect. His face was revealed, long and lean, sallow, with a furtive, cunning expression which betrayed his nature. His eyes, or so it seemed, shone maliciously, as though he had achieved more even by this sacrilege than he had expected or hoped to achieve. He took a silver case from his pocket and extracted a cigarette. He proceeded to light it.

Doctor Hailey heard a faint sound, rather like the chirp of a grasshopper.

He turned his head, and his eyes caught a dull gleam cast by the light from the tomb, on some shining object protruding from a near-by tuft of grass. With a gasp of horror he recognised the barrel of a pistol. In a sudden flash of revelation the mystery of Tarbet's disappearance from the castle was made plain to him.

He sprang to his feet, throwing away all caution in this moment of supreme danger and anxiety. He rushed to the gate of the tomb and flung his huge weight against the iron work. The gate was not secured and it fell back with a loud and discordant clatter, precipitating him almost into the arms of the man whom he had been watching.

Pale, haggard with fear, the man shrank back among the coffins.

Doctor Hailey managed to regain his feet. He turned on the fellow with a shout of indignation which carried, as he meant that it should carry, out to the darkness beyond.

"What are you doing here?" he cried furiously.

There was no reply. The man drew back farther to the limits of the sepulchre. The doctor raised his voice so that its tones rang under the vaulted roof.

"I will tell you what you are doing," he cried. "That coffin you have just opened contains not the body of the woman whose name is inscribed on its lid, but that of a man, her husband. You came to verify the fact because you supposed that knowledge of it would enable you to exact more, and yet more, hush money from those whom you suppose to be guilty of a crime. Ha! You are a fool! a dolt!"

He threw back his immense head and laughed loudly. And the sound of his laughter seemed to strike the man, whom he addressed, with new fear.

"Don't you know that this crime has been investigated down to its minutest detail, and proved to be no crime at all, but the just vengeance of Heaven on a ruffian? Ardvore was not murdered, he died by his own hand and by his own folly, as the walls of his castle bear witness at this present hour."

The doctor leaned forward, as he spoke, across the newly violated coffin. His voice fell suddenly to a conversational tone.

"You must have been mad," he said, "to suppose that such a man as Lord Tarbet would neglect to establish the facts in the proper quarter."

He paused, watching his antagonist as one duellist watches another. To his surprise the fellow drew a sharp sigh of relief. His sinister face was thrust forward.

"So," he sneered, "that is the game, is it? As Tarbet's friend you follow me here and attempt to carry the thing off in this fashion. Unfortunately for that little stratagem I happened to know the facts."

He pointed a lean finger at the coffin.

"People who have nothing to fear," he added, "do not bury a man in his wife's coffin and then pay blackmail in order to keep him there undisturbed."

The insolence of the words made the doctor choke. No wonder that Tarbet aimed that pistol! But he mastered his feelings and set his eyeglass in his eye.

"You do not know, perhaps," he remarked, "who I am or why I am here. My name is Hailey and it happens that I enjoy the confidence of both the Scottish and the English police. I am completely satisfied, as the result of personal investigation that the present Lady Tarbet, who was formerly the wife of the laird of Ardvore, is innocent of the death of her husband." His voice assumed a grim accent. "I am further satisfied that you are a blackmailing scoundrel and I mean here and now, to effect your arrest."

He swung round and called "Tarbet!" in loud tones. Lord Tarbet appeared at the door of the sepulchre, pistol in hand. But the man whose freedom was thus threatened acted with amazing promptitude and daring. He sprang at the storm lamp and struck it to the ground. There was a clatter of breaking glass on the stone floor of the sepulchre and then darkness.

"Guard the door," Doctor Hailey cried.

The warning came too late. The hunted man had sprung at Lord Tarbet and borne him down heavily. The sound of their breathing as they struggled together in the darkness came to the doctor's ears. He flashed his torch. He was just in time to see the stranger leap to his feet and spring out into the wide darkness of the night.

Lord Tarbet closed his eyes as Doctor Hailey finished his account of the investigations he had made. He was pale and looked as though the struggle in which he had engaged at the entrance to the tomb had exhausted all that remained of his nervous energy. Then he raised himself on his elbow and regarded the doctor with deep thankfulness.

"How wonderful you are!" he said in low tones.

He rose from the sofa and threw himself down in an armchair. He pointed to the bullet hole in the wall of the room.

"It happened," he said, "exactly as you have conjectured. I stood there, by the door, facing him." Again he closed his eyes. When he reopened them Doctor Hailey saw that they were glowing.

"Let me begin at the beginning. Mrs. McCallien was my kinswoman; we had been friends from childhood. I did not know it but her husband was desperately jealous of that fact, jealous in the dark implacable way of the Highlanders. Had I known, I would not have come here as I did while on leave from France, and stayed in the castle alone with her."

He broke off and caught his breath. "My God, what humiliation and suffering that visit was to inflict on her! Ardvore returned himself a week after my visit, shell-shocked, a sick man, newly discharged from the Army, gloomy and suspicious. He accused her of infidelity and tortured her with his inquisitions so that her reason began to shake. Denials, entreaties, the most solemn assurances—all were useless against his insane jealousy. Then, when his accusations failed to elicit a confession, he had recourse to falsehood."

Lord Tarbet's voice fell to a whisper. "He informed her that I had been reported killed."

He leaned forward towards the doctor.

"That news," he said, "came as a terrible shock and brought on a fainting attack. I think a kind of catalepsy. The poor girl lay inanimate for several hours. But when she recovered new and far more terrible sufferings were inflicted on her. Those dreadful footsteps of which you have discovered the secret began to visit her bedroom. Even then she did not suspect her husband of an ingenuity in devising torture of so devilish a kind. One night while the footsteps were approaching the cataleptic state reasserted itself."

"A doctor was summoned and pronounced her life extinct."

He jumped up. His face was now transformed with lively horror, as though memory had opened to him its darkest recesses. He cried in awe-struck tones:

"She was placed in her coffin. And on that night, as God willed it, I returned to Ardvore. I had a fortnight's leave and was spending it motoring in Scotland. I had planned to spend a couple of days in the castle and meant my arrival to be a pleasant surprise. Ardvore himself met me when I arrived."

Again he broke off. He drew his hand across his brow.

"He brought me here and showed me the open coffin. When I cried out in horror, he laughed, shrilly, horribly, so that I realised that I was in the presence of a madman. Next moment I was looking down the barrel of an Army pistol. Then he began to talk and I learned a little of what the poor girl, his wife, had suffered on my account. I protested as she had protested. I swore as she had sworn, but that availed me nothing at all. Only his terrible eyes grew wilder and fiercer, like the eyes of a tiger before it springs. He shouted my name and the sentence of death he had passed on me so that the walls re-echoed his voice. Then he thrust his hand forward to shoot."

Lord Tarbet's eyes became gentle suddenly and a look of awe dawned on his face. He whispered:

"And then God's miracle was wrought in my favour. The trance in which his wife lay was broken suddenly. *She sat up in her coffin.* At that sight his aim was distorted. He fired and missed. And then I sprang at him and we fell together on the floor. There was a second pistol shot. Afterwards, when we realised that no one had heard anything of this fearful encounter, it seemed better to put his body in the coffin and close it down there and then."

Tarbet sank back again into the chair. He covered his face with his hands. Doctor Hailey adjusted his eyeglass.

"That was your great mistake," he said. "You should have foreseen that, sooner or later, somewhere, somebody would discover your secret. The bullet marks would have established your innocence."

Lord Tarbet raised his head and faced his companion. "I was so desperately afraid," he said, "that her mind would give way if there were inquiries and investigations. I took the dead man's hat and threw it over the cliffs then and there. We left in my car for Glasgow the same night. I had arrived after dark, as it happened, and nobody seems to have known of my arrival, for Ardvore, as I told you, met me at the door. The servants were hidden in their own wing of the castle. Mrs. McCallien lived in Cornwall after that till the armistice and then went to South America to her sister. I followed her there last year and we were married. In the ship coming home was that scoundrel, Ardvore's cousin, whom you saw tonight. He recognised my wife."

He closed his eyes again and lay back. He added:

"She managed to hide it all from me for a time in order to spare my feelings. But I found out after we reached London. By this time the ruffian had obtained from her a substantial sum. I learned too that he was coming up here to make personal investigation. That was why I took the castle."

Again he sprang to his feet.

"Tonight," he cried, "when the lightning showed me his face passing the window and when, later, I saw him at work, I was mad, crazy. The resolutions I had formed to do no violence in any case, were blotted from my mind. But for your marvellous gifts and intuition, but for the fact that you reached the tomb before me and contrived that I should hear what you said—"

His voice failed. He stood looking at the doctor with shining eyes. Doctor Hailey took a pinch of snuff.

"There is a limit," he said, "to all human endurance. When that limit is passed each of us becomes a madman." He was silent a moment and then added:

"Tomorrow with your consent I will put all the facts before the Procurator Fiscal of Argyll. After that, if he thinks fit, action can be taken against that abominable scoundrel."

The White Line

John Ferguson

John Ferguson (1871–1952) was born in Callander in Perthshire. He worked in his hometown as a railway clerk before a dramatic change of direction saw him become ordained as a clergyman and pursuing his ministry in places as far away as Guernsey in the Channel Islands. At one point he lived in Dunimarle Castle in Fife, by tradition the scene of Macbeth's murder of Lady Macduff. He also spent time as school chaplain in Kent. Although his travels were extensive, much of his writing has a flavour of Scotland. He achieved success as a playwright in 1921 with a one-act play called *Campbell of Kilmhor*; set in 1745 at the time of the Jacobite uprising, it opened in the Royal Theatre, Glasgow, and was televised by the BBC in 1939.

He first tried his hand at crime fiction in 1918, with *Stealthy Terror*, which earned high praise in H. Douglas Thomson's early history of the genre, *Masters of Mystery*

(1931). Thomson said that Ferguson's work inclined towards the sensational, but that he was "one of the most delightful stylists in the genre." His series detective was the criminologist Francis McNab, London-based but of Scottish origin. McNab's cases included *Night in Glengyle* (1933), of which Dorothy L. Sayers said in the *Sunday Times*: "The action takes place in Scotland and goes with a whizz—so much so that in the excitement of the chase your reviewer quite forgot to be cunning and was properly taken aback by the surprise-packet at the end." *The Grouse Moor Mystery* (1934) was a venture into the locked room mystery, again set in Scotland. "The White Line" appeared in a 1929 anthology, *The World's 100 Best Detective Stories* and was probably published in an unknown magazine at an earlier date.

———

BEFORE MCNAB HAD NEGOTIATED THE PIVOTED CHAIR at the dinner-table in the *Magnificent*—it was her first night out from Sandy Hook—he was greeted by a feminine welcome.

"So we meet again, Mr. McNab."

Mrs. Westmacott looked up at him with a smile on her clever face. She was a chance acquaintance made on the journey from Washington. McNab expressed his pleasure.

"You are in luck," said she with a nod.

"So I see," he returned with a ceremonious bow.

"Poof! It's not because they place you next *me*. You didn't think I meant *that*?"

McNab looked around as he picked up his spoon.

"Well, it's the luckiest thing I perceive at the moment. Quite enough to content me," he added.

"Why, man, they've given you a front seat for the comedy, and you don't know it. What a waste! There are people on board who'd give a thousand dollars, cash down, to change places with you."

"I wouldn't accept," said McNab, "unless you changed also."

"Ah! And in the train you denied you were Irish!"

To this McNab's only response was an enigmatic smile. People at the tables *were* a little hushed, subdued. But that was the usual state of affairs on the first night out. Later, when they got to know each other, the laughter and the chatter would flow. But the scene that met his eye was gay enough with the women's multi-coloured frocks and the shimmer of their jewels.

"Do you never ask questions, Mr. McNab?"

As he turned to her Mrs. Westmacott made a moue at him, evidently anxious to impart the information his roving glance had failed to discover. He laughed—internally—at the notion that he was an incurious person. His head ached yet with investigations which had kept his mind keyed up for weeks.

"I was looking for the comedy you spoke of," he said.

Mrs. Westmacott turned to him, the morsel of fish poised on the end of her fork.

"And found it?"

He shook his head.

She leant towards him confidentially.

"To the right—opposite—the girl in black—between the two young men. You must recognise her."

"I am not up in types of American beauty—not feminine ones anyhow," he amended. "Still, I seem to—"

"I should think so, indeed. Her picture is in every paper. That is Sally Silver."

"Really? Sally Silver? Now where have I heard that name before?"

Mrs. Westmacott laughed.

"How perfectly delicious you are. Oh, how I wish she could hear you!"

"I can be wonderfully dense," McNab admitted. "The times I've missed things under my very nose—you'd never believe. Tell me about her."

"She's Henry Silver's only child—and you won't say you haven't heard of *him*! She's just twenty, and the biggest catch that ever came out of a Chicago pig-pen. But no man's caught her yet."

McNab was regarding the girl with interest. He had wondered already why her presence there had drawn all eyes in her direction. The girl was undeniably pretty, but scarcely beautiful. There was not enough repose in her face for real beauty. The headlong pursuit of pleasure, the eager search for new sensations, were visibly marked on her restless and uneasy face. Her face, McNab thought, would miss the beauty designed for it, and become in a year or two the ruins of what it had *never* been! He felt a certain pity for her.

"The most envied girl we have just now," Mrs. Westmacott remarked. "Her diamonds alone make the women hate her."

"She is wearing none."

"No. That is her pose for the moment. The little puss knows very well all the women on board are dying to see the famous Vernese necklace her doting father has just bought for her. That is why she has left it in her cabin."

"And they hate her still more for that?"

"Naturally."

McNab resumed his dinner.

"The men don't seem to miss the diamonds," he observed.

"No. She has a fine neck, and her shoulders are—well, brave."

McNab again looked over at the two men and the girl. With both elbows resting on the table, and with her chin on her clasped hands, she was still listening to the young man on her right, while the youth on her left, who had been getting her shoulder all through, sat crumbling his bread gloomily.

"The two favourites in the race," Mrs. Westmacott explained *sotto voce.*

"Not much doubt which is making the running."

Mrs. Westmacott looked at him almost in contempt.

"You men!" she said. "You think because at the moment she's showing a preference for Jefferson Melhuish she has turned down young Hilary Harben for good."

"Well, by the look on his face, young Hilary Harben seems to share my view."

"Very likely he does, being a man. But any woman could tell him it doesn't follow. The minx knows the betting has lately been on Harben."

McNab was startled.

"What!" he cried. "You don't mean to say people are betting on it. I call that almost indecent."

"Indecent? I like that! You English who flog horses to make

them run races for you to bet on—you call this indecent! Why, Sally Silver is proud to know America is betting on this, and both men must know it. Notoriety, Mr. McNab, may not be so fine a thing as fame, but it is better than obscurity. As for Hilary's chances, I'm not sorry my money is on him."

"*You* have a bet on this?"

"I have. I stand to win what will pay my six months' trip to Europe twice over. You are surprised? You think I should have backed Melhuish, who is good-looking and wealthy, while Harben is almost poor, and still has the limp he got in the war?" She tapped McNab lightly on the arm and breathed into his ear: "That lameness is no handicap in a woman's eyes. You put something on him, too. You'll get long odds. No? Well, you'll see, in two days there won't be a soul on board from the ambassador to the stewardess who hasn't made a bet on it."

And Mrs. Westmacott proved to be right. The daily sweep-stake on the ship's progress was thin and tame compared with the zest and excitement aroused by the betting on Melhuish and Harben. McNab marvelled over it. They were all like children, he thought. There was nothing to show—so far as he could see—that Miss Silver must necessarily choose either of her suitors, much less choose one of them before they reached port. It was just a chance. He pointed out the absurdity of the thing one night in the smoking-room, and half a dozen voices promptly offered to bet him on that very chance. McNab went away puzzled. They could not really know. Of course, on board a liner the pace and rhythm of life quickened enormously. Minutes were as hours on land, and hours held as much in them as days. So many things happened quickly, things that would scarcely happen at all, to the same people anyway, ashore. That must be why they were all so confident something was bound to happen in the matter of Sally Silver.

Now, McNab was a keen student of human nature. Professionally his concern was with the darker side, but his connection with New Scotland Yard had not made him a narrow specialist; he remained interested in humanity, in all its infinite variety, which fact is probably the secret of his great professional success. Therefore, McNab turned an eye on Miss Silver, on her two suitors, and on the betting over their chances with all the interest he was wont to give to the study of innocent human foibles in his moments of leisure. The men, he found, all betted on Melhuish, who appeared to be well aware of the fact. He had a way of twirling up his moustache, a way of smiling till you caught just a glimpse of his gold-filled teeth that seemed to irritate the women. But the men backed him as confidently. And the women without exception backed Harben.

For three long days the good-looking, immaculate Melhuish basked in Miss Silver's honeyed smiles, while young Harben limped along the deck to his solitary chair, followed by the sympathetic glances of the ladies.

Then on the fourth day a change came. It came just at the moment when Melhuish's triumph seemed complete, when the men, convinced their bets were safe, were ceasing to chuckle among themselves, and the women almost began to doubt. That is to say, just when interest threatened to die down, Miss Sally Silver took it into her wayward head to readjust matters. Very early on the fourth morning one of Melhuish's backers, coming on deck, found her and Harben, their deck chairs side by side, holding each other's hands! The news circulated with mysterious quickness. At breakfast the men exchanged uneasy glances with each other. By lunchtime they were whispering together about it in odd corners. And all through the long afternoon there was a *hush* on the ship that reminded McNab of a Sunday afternoon he once had to pass in Tunbridge Wells. For all that afternoon Miss Silver and young Harben sat together, and Melhuish paced the deck alone, gnawing the end of his moustache. To the men who covertly watched the pair on the hurricane deck the afternoon seemed an eternity. What it seemed to Melhuish none but Melhuish knew, and he did not tell.

At tea Mrs. Westmacott crossed to the corner in which McNab sat with Colonel Baylis.

"Well?" she said brightly.

The colonel almost scowled.

"It won't last!" he snapped.

The lady thrilled with triumph.

"I hear some of you men are already trying to hedge. Now *we* never did that!"

"Our man's not done yet."

She turned to McNab.

"Is that your view?"

"Well, I don't know. He's of the type that takes what he wants."

"It won't last, you'll see," the colonel repeated as Mrs. Westmacott returned with the sugar basin. "That monkey is only taking Harben up to give the women a bigger drop. She knows that the cats don't love her much."

He stirred his tea angrily. Mrs. Westmacott held out the sugar basin to him.

"An extra lump today?" she suggested sweetly.

But after dinner that night the affair took a new turn, one which brought McNab into the business in real earnest in his professional capacity.

It was a fine, still night, with the moon approaching the full, and McNab had gone up to the long hurricane deck to finish his cigar while taking a little gentle exercise. It was still early, but most of the men were down below in the smoking-rooms, while the ladies were in the music saloon. McNab therefore had the deck almost to himself as he paced up and down, first up one side and then down the other, with the long row of state rooms occupying the centre. So quiet was it that above the throb-throbbing of the vessel, as she cut her way across the smooth sea, McNab could distinguish the distant tinkling of a piano. But the deck, with its row of white, untenanted cabins, was like a deserted village, dominated by four great red incongruous chimney stacks. He was watching the silent rolling columns of black smoke from the funnels, following the smoke till it thinned out and the moonlight came through it, when his ear caught a sharp sound behind him. It was like the opening of a door which had been recently varnished when some of the varnish has adhered close to the hinges—a crack, short and abrupt. The unexpectedness of the sound on that quiet, deserted deck, the contrast it made to the continuous throbbing of the screw caught his attention. But after the little start it gave him, interrupting his thoughts, he resumed his silent promenade without giving any more heed to the occurrence. When he reached the aft termination of the deck, however, he found something that amused him—Miss Sally Silver was sitting there *alone*.

Several times that evening in the course of his promenade he had come close enough to see Harben seated by her side and hear the murmur of their voices. Not ten minutes earlier Harben had been there; but now his chair was vacant, a rug lying on the deck looked as if it had been tossed aside. The girl, her elbow on the arm of the chair, and her hand beneath her chin—a characteristic attitude—seemed to be gazing dejectedly into vacancy. If there had been a quarrel, and all the symptoms pointed to it, McNab smiled to think how, once known, it would stir the ship from end to end. Who would have dreamed that the affair would end, not with Sally Silver leaving Harben, but with Harben leaving Sally Silver!

Now, McNab was by instinct and occupation an observer, not a talker. So he simply turned on his heel and continued his promenade. Turned on his heel, he distinctly remembered that afterwards. That is to say, instead of crossing over the deck and continuing down the other side as he had been doing for the best part of an hour, he for the first time went back the way he had come.

He had gone half the length of the deck when he saw a man step out of a state room a little way ahead, close the door gently, and come quickly towards him. Then the man pulled up suddenly, as if at sight of McNab, hesitated an instant, and came on again. McNab, though the figure passed him with down-bent head and in the shadow of the deck houses, recognised him from his limp as young Harben. He was probably on his way to make it up with the girl, McNab thought with a smile, observing as he passed that the cabin bore the number 13. Looking back, he saw Harben now in the full moonlight awkwardly, painfully limping aft. McNab, tossing the butt of his cigar overboard, took out his watch. It was thirteen minutes to nine: his exercise was over. So he went to the lower deck.

He had been in the crowded smoking-room for nearly an hour, indolently watching a group playing poker for rather high stakes, when a man entered so hurriedly and noisily as to attract immediate attention.

"Heard the latest?" he asked almost breathlessly.

There was so much significance in his tremulous tones that even those who had not cast a glance at his entrance looked up from their game. Indeed, everyone present looked up hopefully. Men reading put their magazines on their knees, even the man dealing out the cards arrested his arm in mid-air to regard the speaker. For it was obvious there was something new in the Silver-Melhuish-Harben affair—or, at least, they hoped so. McNab thought he knew what it was, and that he could have told them as much when he had entered an hour ago. He was slightly amused by this man's snatching at a piece of news which gave him a temporary importance.

"No!" came a chorus of impatient voices as the fellow hung on, enjoying the interest he had aroused.

"Sally's necklace has gone!"

"Gone?"

"Stolen from her cabin tonight."

"Is that all? Serve her jolly well right!" someone grunted in disgust. There came a chorus of approval.

The dealer continued with his cards and the old gentlemen lifted their magazines again.

"What else could she expect—canoodling up there with *that* fellow?"

The chorus of agreement seemed to McNab unfair. Had the thing happened when Melhuish was the girl's favourite the judgment would have been otherwise, and Melhuish would not have been "*that* fellow."

"She'll never get it back. The crooks on liners are smart."

"But on a ship—after all—they can't run away."

"You'll see. Depend on it they had a hiding place ready for the swag before it was lifted."

"This comes of her choosing cabin 13 out of pure bounce."

"I remember once—"

McNab heard no more. He left the saloon. He wanted to think.

Cabin 13! He was quite sure that was the one out of which he had seen Harben come. Harben, of course, might have been sent there for some purpose by Miss Silver herself. There was against that theory—it could easily be settled by Miss Silver—his hesitation on catching sight of someone approaching, and the furtive manner in which he had slunk past, in the shadow, close to the deck houses. But, again, Harben must have known that his limp would betray him. If he had no guilt, why had he been furtive?

Harben was no professional crook, of course, for the expert would not have been taken by surprise, and besides, he was, like his rival Melhuish, an old friend of the Silver family. But why had Harben been surprised to see him? It was to this question McNab recurred most. Harben must have been aware that he had been walking the deck all the time. Then whence came the surprise? He had hesitated and stopped a moment at sight of him. Why?

Suddenly the detective smote his fist on the taffrail as an explanation burst upon him. Of course!

"I'd been walking round and round the deck houses until I saw the girl and the empty chair," he muttered. "Just like a policeman on his beat. But that last time I *turned back*. And when he came out of the cabin he calculated that I'd be on the other side. But what a fool the man was not to put the thing back once he *knew* he had been seen."

McNab lighted another cigar reflectively. Perhaps, he mused, Harben had no chance to go back. Perhaps, as was not uncommon, he supposed his lameness less noticeable than it actually was, and believed he had avoided detection. The furtive slinking along in the shadows suggested he had that belief.

The detective, in his dark corner, grinned to himself. Harben would probably stick to the diamonds; he did not know with whom he had been playing that little game of "Here we go round the mulberry bush" up there in the moonlight! There was little danger of such an amateur in crime as Harben getting frightened and dropping the things overboard. He must need them badly indeed. Had he come away without sufficient funds for the trip? He could not take money from Miss Silver, and he would salve any qualms by telling himself it was for her sake, her ultimate happiness. Later he would tell her all, perhaps; own up, and she would cry out: "You poor boy! Why didn't you ask me for the money?" So the young fool would picture the happy ending!

McNab had no desire to thrust his professional services on those concerned—indeed, he did not suppose his services would be required—but being well aware of a witness's duties in such matters he went to see Miss Silver. Miss Silver, however, had retired, prostrated by her loss, so the maid informed him. Well, his knowledge of Harben's movements would keep till morning. McNab himself sought his berth.

Next morning he was much later at breakfast than usual. He had slept badly. He had not, somehow, been able to dismiss this case from his mind so easily. He had lain awake, thinking it out. He had traversed all the facts repeatedly, and some features of the thing left him doubtful. He was, however, scarcely seated before he sensed that something new had happened. People stood about in little groups with their heads together. There were noddings and whisperings. Mrs. Westmacott, observing him, came across and took a place beside him.

"Well," she said, "you've heard what they're saying?"

"No. What is it?"

"They say the thief is a man with a limp. He was seen coming out of her state room."

McNab almost bounded out of his chair.

"What?" he cried. "What's that you say?"

"Ah, you know what that means. There aren't many lame men aboard, are there?"

"I've seen only one."

"Well, that seems to fasten the thing on him all right. Do *you* think he did it?"

McNab regained his self-control. He looked at her fixedly.

"I did," he said, "till you told me others are saying he did it."

"What on earth do you mean by that?"

"It sounds odd, but the explanation is simple: *I* was the only person who saw him come out of her state room."

Her woman's wit took her at a bound to the vital point.

"And you have not mentioned it to anyone?"

McNab looked at her in admiration.

"Not unless I've been talking in my sleep."

"And do you?" she asked anxiously.

"No," he replied with a grin. "That is one of the things forbidden us at Scotland Yard."

Her face changed from anxiety to amazement.

"Scotland Yard! Are you—"

"Hush! Just tell me who you think did it?"

"Melhuish," she rejoined promptly. "He is your man."

McNab shook his head.

"It doesn't follow. The first question to ask in the presence of a crime is, *cui bono—who benefits*?"

"Well, *he* does. Sally will certainly—"

He put a hand on her arm restrainingly.

"Yes, but this Vernese necklace in itself supplies a sufficient motive to a few hundreds of us, perhaps. Melhuish had *one* motive which no one else but Harben shared, that is Sally Silver herself. But the motive of Sally Silver's diamonds would be equally strong for a far larger number."

"Still, I feel *sure* it was Melhuish. Something tells me."

"Yes, your dislike of him. And if I were to put the case before any of these men, they would, for the same reason be equally sure it was Harben."

"And you?" she asked.

"I suspect everyone but you. That is why I ask your help."

"Me!" she flushed with excitement. "Women are said to talk."

"They do. So do men. Look at them."

As he reached for the marmalade he nodded towards a group of men in eager converse.

"You mean to take up this case?"

"Yes. You see this infernal thief has brought me into it. He *used* me. That's what it amounts to. For it was someone who imitated Harben's limp and affected hesitation at the sight of me, he expects me to say I had seen Harben coming out of the cabin. He used *me*: that stings, you know. If it was Harben himself—"

McNab broke off pensively.

"You need my help because the thief knows you know and will be on the watch?" Mrs. Westmacott asked.

"Especially when he finds I shall say nothing. You see," he went on, "we have not merely to detect the thief but to keep him, if he is startled, from dropping the necklace over the side."

Mrs. Westmacott sighed with a half wry smile.

"To think I should find myself trying to save *her* necklace. I shouldn't *dream* of doing it if I wasn't *sure* Hilary Harben is innocent. You can't be sure that someone else wasn't hiding up there, watching both you and him."

"I don't deny it. Anything is possible. And if Harben is cleared, so much the better for your bet. Can I count on you?"

"What do you wish me to do?"

"Very little—and that little easy. I am not going to report what I saw to Miss Silver or to the captain. I am not going to make any enquiry. I am going to sit out on the promenade deck entirely absorbed in a book. All I want you to do is to stroll over, and give me news of what happens from hour to hour."

"It sounds just a man's idea of a woman's job. But what if nothing happens?"

"Then come and tell me."

At eleven she came to him with her first report. Harben had tried to see Miss Silver, but had been refused admission. A notice had been posted asking anyone who had been on the hurricane deck between the hours of eight and ten to see the purser in his office.

At half-past eleven she reported having seen Miss Silver and Melhuish together on the upper deck.

At noon she returned with the news that Harben's cabin was then being searched. There was a crowd outside the door. McNab sent her off to join the crowd, while he sat on apparently engrossed in his book.

She was back in half an hour. Nothing had been found, of course. She laughed:

"The amusing thing is that Harben finds that he himself has been robbed. Oh, it's nothing of consequence—just a leather collar-box missing."

"Ah!"

There was so much significance in the ejaculation that she was startled.

"Did Harben mention it?"

"No, the steward who does his cabin did."

"A leather collar-box? It would just do to hold the necklace, I suppose."

McNab lay back again in his chair and shut his eyes, while Mrs. Westmacott waited.

She waited a long time, or so it seemed to her. She began to think McNab must have fallen asleep, so still was he. Then he startled her again.

"What is the colour of Harben's door, red or green?" he asked.

"Neither; it is white," she replied, wondering if he were mad.

"Good! Do you think you could get me a ball of wool?"

"A ball of wool?" she cried. "What for?"

"To snare the thief. If any lady friend can provide a ball of wool, we have him."

"Heaven above us!" she murmured, aghast.

"Let me see," he went on, "there is to be some sort of entertainment tonight, isn't there?"

She welcomed what seemed a return to sanity.

"Yes—a concert. The Orpheus String Quartette have kindly—"

"Well," he cut in, "for the sake of variety we'll provide a conjuring trick also—if you can find me that ball of wool."

Mrs. Westmacott was very nervous at the concert— thoroughly disquieted about McNab. Of course, the recent events had upset everyone; but the soothing effect of classical music is well known, and perhaps that is why practically every passenger in the ship was present. Even Miss Silver came in before the interval, looking very pale and tired, leaning on the arm of Melhuish. Melhuish, after finding her a seat, left the saloon, returning with a wrap for her just before the interval. McNab, Mrs. Westmacott saw, was very fidgety. He kept looking at his watch, glancing keenly about him. When the interval came, most of the men seemed ready for a stimulant. She saw Colonel Baylis approach McNab with an invitation on his face; and she did not miss the curt refusal he received. The men began to filter towards the door. Captain York, who was acting as chairman, rose and tapped the table.

"Gentlemen," he said, addressing those who were moving towards the door, "I regret very much that for the moment it will be impossible for anyone to leave this saloon. You are aware that a necklace, a very valuable necklace, has disappeared from the cabin of one of our lady passengers. A general search for it, which I am sure no honourable or innocent person here will resent, is now in progress. There are, unfortunately, black sheep in most ships of—"

Mrs. Westmacott saw McNab rise to his feet.

"Excuse me," he said in calm, determined tones. "There is no need to detain these gentlemen, nor to disarrange their baggage. The necklace is in a leather collar-box in Mr. Hilary Harben's cabin."

A tense hush fell on the saloon—a moment's breathless silence, and then Harben, pushing aside the men in his way, came towards the platform with blanched face and clenched fists.

"That is a lie!" he called out. "I'll make you eat those words. How do you know what is, or what is not, in my cabin? Who are you?"

"I am the person who saw the man with the limp come out of Miss Silver's cabin last night."

An "Ah!" of astonishment ran round the saloon like a wave, and Mrs. Westmacott sparing a glance for Miss Silver, saw the girl sink in her chair with both hands covering her face. Melhuish, standing beside the captain, was, like most, eagerly intent on McNab.

"I was not that man, I swear it!" Harben cried out

helplessly, as if he did not expect them to believe him. And certainly nobody seemed to. Mrs. Westmacott saw the gleam of gold as Melhuish smiled. In the tense, painful silence which ensued, the ship's purser entered and handed up to Captain York the little leather collar-case. As he opened the thing and took out the necklace, the man whispered something to him, and it was evident to all from the way in which he stared at McNab, who was still on his feet that it had been found where McNab had said.

"I swear I had no hand in this—I never took it!" Harben cried passionately again.

"I know you didn't," said McNab.

Melhuish, who had gone forward to receive the necklace from the captain, turned sharply.

"Since you know so much," said the captain, "perhaps you know who did?"

"I do," the reply came quietly, electrifying the whole saloon. "You see, at first I did think the thing had been done by this young gentleman. The man who passed me outside cabin thirteen I took for Mr. Harben. But in the morning, when I heard that a man with a limp was seen coming out of the cabin, I knew it was someone else. I knew it must be someone else because I was alone on that deck, and had not spoken *to anyone* of what I saw. Anyone might have imitated his walk. Later in the day, when I heard of the missing collar-box, it was clear that the guilty person, through fear of discovery or some other reason, meant to fix the guilt on Mr. Harben. That little box which was missing in the forenoon would be found when the general search was made. The inference would be that it had been hidden till the earlier search was over, and when it was discovered later in his cabin with the necklace inside the conclusion would be irresistible."

McNab paused while everyone hung on his words.

"All that was easy. The real difficulty lay in detecting the guilty man. It was, of course, useless to watch Mr. Harben's cabin all day. The real thief would not venture to go in so long as anyone was in sight. Well, the road was left open, and he did his trick exactly as I thought it would be done, about half an hour ago, and not a soul saw him do it."

Mrs. Westmacott sighed miserably as she saw Melhuish's face brighten on hearing McNab's last words. Captain York himself voiced her fear:

"Then you cannot prove who this black sheep is? I suppose we must be content with—"

McNab held up his hand. "Pardon me, but that is exactly the task I set myself. I have *marked* the black sheep."

"How?"

Half a dozen cried out the question, and did not know they had spoken.

"The door of Mr. Harben's cabin is white. I fastened a length of wool from one side to the other five feet five inches high, chalking it so that it was invisible against the door. The two broken ends will be found hanging there now, and the man who entered the cabin ought to have a chalk line across the lapels of his coat exactly five feet five inches from the floor."

Instinctively Melhuish had looked down. He saw what all saw, a thin white line across the collar of his faultless dress coat.

Pitiably the man wilted. The tense silence was broken suddenly by a girl's voice.

"Hilary, oh Hilary, I am so glad! *So glad!*"

The words in themselves might have committed her to nothing, but there was that in her tones which led every man who heard them to settle his bet without a murmur.

The Body of Sir Henry

Augustus Muir

Augustus Muir was the principal writing name of Charles Augustus Carlow Muir (1892–1989), born in Ontario, Canada, to Scottish parents. He was a versatile and prolific author, and Scotland often featured in both his factual work and his fiction. His publications included *Heather-Track and High Road: A Book of Scottish Journeys*. The endpapers of *Scotland's Road of Romance* feature a map of Scotland, showing the route from Arisaig to Edinburgh taken by Prince Charlie Edward Stuart ("Bonnie Prince Charlie") in 1745. His novel *The Blue Bonnet* was promoted as "a rousing tale of Scottish life" and concerned a boy who escapes from an orphanage. He also edited a volume on the subject of *How to Choose and Enjoy Wine*.

Muir's career as a writer of novel-length thrillers began in 1924 with publication of *The Third Warning* and lasted almost thirty years, encompassing a couple of novels in the early thirties written under the name Austin Moore. His short fiction earned a considerable reputation, and according to the IMDb website, he "used to read his own short stories on radio, as well as doing radio security sensor work for the Home and Overseas news." He was a regular contributor of feature articles as well as fiction to the *Strand Magazine*, and the anthologist Jack Adrian speculated that he may at one time have been on the staff of the magazine. This story, set in the Scottish border country, first appeared in *Detective Fiction Weekly* on 13 April 1929.

I

I HAD BEEN SO ENGROSSED IN MacIVER'S TALK THAT my cigarette had burned right down to my fingers and, cursing it heartily, I hurled the wretched thing into the fire.

MacIver laughed.

"That reminds me of a queer thing that happened to me once," he said, lying back in his chair and smiling at me out of his keen grey eyes—the shrewdest eyes I think I have ever looked into. On MacIver's face are clearly written the qualities that have helped him to rise from the ranks of the police force to be one of the really big swells at Scotland Yard. I count it worth losing five hours' sleep any night to hear the man tell of some of the strange people he has run up against.

"That reminds me," he repeated, "of a mighty queer thing that happened to me in the Border country soon after I joined the force." MacIver pronounces the word "force" as though he were speaking of the most marvellous affair in all Christendom; it is his only vanity.

"The case," he continued, "has to do with the most beautiful woman I've ever seen. I'm mebbe no great judge. I certainly never saw the woman yet that made me feel like—like, well, what's called falling in love. But if ever a woman made me melt with the sheer witchery of her, it was Lucille Vallandri. Aye, and she was a devil, yon young woman. A beautiful devil. She should have hung; I'm not joking. She missed it by the skin of her teeth. I'll tell you all about her—and the burning cigarette that cost the life of the man whose mistress she was at the time—no; the facts never came out. He cheated the gallows before they even got him the length of trial; he kept poison ready in his wrist-watch."

As far as I was concerned (went on MacIver) it began one night when I was on duty at Battlekirk. I had only been in the district about a couple of months, and I used to wonder how many years it would be before anything happened to break the awful monotony in yon out-of-the-way corner of the Borders. I can mind how the rain was pelting down that night, and the wind from the Cheviots lashed round you like a whip. It seemed that everybody else in Teviotdale was in bed except myself, and just because I had been fool enough, as I thought, to join the force, in preference to trudging behind a plough on my father's small holding in the Merse, I had to be out there on duty—aye, and shivering under a doorway with the rain trickling down my neck, and wishing to God somebody would break into the Clydesdale Bank or commit a murder, just to stir things up a bit.

I nearly gave three cheers when I saw a white smudge of light show up in the distance. It was a motor car coming down from the North. So I wasn't the only body in Scotland out in the storm that night! It cheered me up to watch the light getting nearer, and soon a big car went rushing past the cross-roads. Then I heard the brakes go on and the tyres grinding and grinding on the rough surface till the car stopped.

It started to reverse. It was a big yellow limousine, I could see from the shelter of my doorway, and a man was leaning out of the driving seat. He turned the car in to the side, so that his headlights shone on the signpost. At this, I stepped out of the doorway and hurried over to him.

"Can I help you?" I asked. I noticed that he wasn't dressed like a chauffeur, but had a cloth cap pulled down over his face.

"Are we near Battlekirk?" he inquired, and I told him he was already in Battlekirk.

"Is it far to Milne Easter?" he said.

"Three miles, sir," I replied. "And Milne Wester is five miles down this other road," I added, for it struck me that Milne Wester, a decent-sized village with a lot of gentlefolk living in it, was the place he really wanted to get to. Milne Easter being only a few poor cottages with no houses of any size near it at all.

But it seemed to be Milne Easter he wanted right enough. He thanked me, and began to turn back to the south road again. As if he'd had an afterthought, he leaned out and said:

"How many miles is Newcastle?"

I told him, but I had a queer feeling, by the way he spoke, that he didn't care a rap how far Newcastle was. And then I saw something that took my breath away, and left me standing on that road as stiff as the white signpost beside me.

In turning the nose of the car, the headlamps had blazed into the shop window five or six yards away. The light was reflected back, just as if it had shone against a mirror. The driver was half-blinded. He swore good-naturedly, and swung the wheel quickly round. But not before I had seen into the back of the car.

A woman sat there, with dark furs round her face, and I'll never forget her expression. It was one of unspeakable horror. Beside her, a man lay huddled stiffly back on the cushions. Right up to his chin he was covered with a travelling rug. He was elderly and had thick grey hair. His skin was chalk white, and his eyes were wide open and staring straight upward. The light didn't seem to dazzle them. It would have dazzled mine if I hadn't had my back to it. But one quick glimpse at him was enough to tell me the important thing. The man was dead.

In a flash the woman's hand came out from her furs and pulled the travelling rug up over his face, from which it had apparently slipped down. The car swerved away from the shop window, and the reflected light snapped out.

The limousine gathered speed and was gone. I stood there with my head buzzing round as I watched its shape getting less and less against the glow of its lights ahead of it. And then the little red tail-light moved around the bend and disappeared.

II

I tell you I could have kicked myself right over the crossroads and back again. I hadn't even had the gumption to cast an eye on its number-plate. A fine fool I'd look when I reported this to the sergeant, as I'd have to do—and I was to meet him in a little less than half an hour's time.

But Sergeant Gailes just laughed at me.

"A dead man?" he said. "You young fellows read ower much o' that sensational trash nowadays. Drunk mebbe, but not dead. Na, na, MacIver. I'm thinking ye were ower dazzled by the lights yoursel' to see very clear. Na."

"I'm sure the man's mention of Newcastle was just a pure blind," I declared.

Sergeant Gailes grunted, and shook some of the rain from the top of his flat-peaked cap. "Ye'd better keep your tongue between your teeth about it," he advised. "That kind o' thing is no' likely to do ye any good wi' the inspector at Teviothead. Ye'll be reporting that ye've seen a ghost next, laddie. Na, na."

But I wasn't satisfied. As I cycled back toward Battlekirk, I kept chewing the matter over. It was just before I got to the main road that an idea struck me, and instead of going home to bed I turned south toward Milne Easter. I had suddenly remembered that about a mile from the village was a big house called Black Weir—in fact, the only house of any size round about. If that car was really making for Milne Easter, Black Weir was probably the actual destination. Then I remembered something else. The house was shut up. It belonged to an old bachelor, Sir Henry Ellison-Stewart. I didn't know him by sight, but in the couple of months I'd been stationed at Battlekirk I had heard plenty about him. He lectured to antiquarian societies, and was supposed to have a wonderful collection of antique Scottish and French jewels. He was wealthy, of course, and they called him half-daft—seemingly he thought nothing of sending all his servants home on holiday for three months, and going away on his travels, with Black Weir House shut up. Aye, and it was shut now. When I remembered this, the only thing that kept me going on was sheer dourness. The chances were that I was on a wild-goose chase.

I got off my cycle, and went forward to the big iron gates. They were padlocked. So that finished it.

My spirits were away down in my boots—along with a lot of rain-water—and, turning back, I started to mount. But I nearly sprawled across my machine in surprise. Curving in from the main road to the avenue were the fresh marks of motor car tyres.

It took me about two minutes to wheel my cycle along the road, hide it in a ditch, and climb over the high stone dyke beyond the lodge. The lodge, I knew, was unoccupied—and had been since the head gardener left—so there was no good trying to seek information there.

The night was desperately black. Rather than risk losing my way by taking the short cut through the woods, I preferred to trudge the quarter of a mile of twisting avenue. And a long quarter of a mile it was.

Black Weir House, when I got to it, was the most dismal-looking thing you ever saw—a great rambling place with turrets and crow-step gables, and not a chink of light showing anywhere. And then, beside the doorway, I made out the shape of a motor car. I had been right about the tyre-marks, but it remained to be seen whether I had been right in jumping to the conclusion that I was on the track of trouble—trouble, I mean, for other folk.

I walked round the car, and went up the steps to the front

door. I was about to switch on my lantern when my eye caught a slit of light in a window on my left. The curtains had been pulled close, but not close enough. By craning out over the stone balustrade, I was able to see into the room.

A lamp stood on a table, and beside it was a leather suitcase with the lid lying back. There were also two bunches of keys, one of them on a long chain.

And then I saw a detail that gave me a jar.

I had run into the real thing at last! I had been wishing that something would happen to break the monotony of life. Well, it looked like being broken into half a hundred bits now! For a door stood open in the opposite wall of the room with another small but very thick door of steel behind it. I could see enough to tell me that I was looking into an open safe.

I thought of Sergeant Gailes, and how long I would take to get hold of him. Hours, probably. That was no good. If I was going to do anything, I had to do it myself—and at once. I wasn't afraid of rough work—I was a match for most of the brawny lads of the Borders—but I was helpless against firearms. However, I'd have to risk that.

Then I got a brain-wave. Whatever action I took, they would try to get away in the motor car—it was their quickest means of escape. I went back down the steps and opened up the bonnet. I knew a little about motor cars, and I shone my lantern in till I got the top off the float-chamber, and saw the petrol running out. I watched it till the last drop had gone; then I closed the bonnet, satisfied that I had scored the first point.

As I straightened up, I thought I heard a low thudding noise. It wasn't the bough of a tree in the wind; it was too near at hand for that. Then I noticed another sparkle of light. This time it was in a grating in the wall, close down to the ground. Somebody, I knew, must be busy in the cellar. A queer occupation for anybody after midnight. Flashing my lantern up, I clanged the bell.

The thudding stopped. I looked over the balustrade. The light down at the grating moved, and went out. Then silence. I could still see the light at the window of the room on my left, but only a glimmer, for the narrow slit in the curtain had been closed.

I waited for a matter of three or four minutes, then rang the bell again.

The front door was at once thrown open, as if somebody had been waiting behind it in case I rang again. Half a dozen candles had been lit in the big hall, and standing in the doorway was the man who had been driving the motor car.

"Good Lord," he said, "I wondered who the deuce it could be at this time of night. Come in, constable. It's too damned stormy to be out of doors."

III

I was glad he had spoken first, for I was a bit flustered, and not very sure of what line to take. I decided to go very cautiously, and bide my time.

"And what can I do for you, constable?" he said, lighting a brier pipe. I could see he was a man of about fifty-five. He was dark, and thin, but he looked wiry, and he had a frank and extremely pleasant smile. "Nothing wrong, eh?"

"Nothing, I hope sir," I said. "I'm doing what I thought

was my duty. I knew Sir Henry had been away for about a month, and hadn't come back, so, seeing the marks of a car at the gates, I thought I'd have a look around."

"Quite right," said the man at once. "Glad the police are so wide awake. Didn't we pass you at the crossroads, eh?"

"That's correct, sir."

"Thought so." He nodded. "Hadn't you better have a drink? It's a foul night, and I've just been down in the cellar opening a case of Sir Henry's brandy."

Which explained the thudding I had heard, but I couldn't think why his hands looked as if they had been scraping among brown earth.

"My name's Norgate," he went on. "Colonel Norgate. We're on our way to Newcastle. We should have been here quite early in the evening, but Sir Henry wanted to collect some goods and chattels—and some odd things from his safe. I told him he shouldn't leave valuables here, with the house empty. It's asking for trouble—don't you think so? He hadn't even warned the police to keep an eye—Hullo!" He broke off and stared at me in amazement. He must have read some of my suspicions in my face, for he burst into loud laughter. "You don't mean to say you've been thinking that—Come in and have a drink, constable—that's worth a drink any day!"

He led me into a large room on the left—the one I had seen through the chink in the curtains. It was lined with books, and had some big carved furniture. The safe was closed, I noticed, and the door in the wall looked like any ordinary door. The suitcase still lay on the table near the lamp, but it was shut. The bunches of keys had gone. Away at the other end of the room a fire was crackling and spluttering in a grate as if it had only recently had a match put to it.

On the hearthrug, with her back to the fire, was the woman I had seen in the car. Her fur coat was open, her hat was off, and in the lamplight she looked wonderful. She was laughing and chatting with a man who sat in an armchair.

And then I saw that Providence had prevented me from making a grand fool of myself. I couldn't see the man's face, for his back was to me, but I recognised his thick grey hair at a glance. He was the man I had spotted beside her in the motor car. A half finished tumbler of spirits was on a little table at his elbow, and a long spiral of smoke curled up from the cigarette in his fingers.

"My wife and Sir Henry Ellison-Stewart," said Colonel Norgate, nodding in their direction. "It was only the local police constable," he called out to them. "I've brought him in for a drink."

The woman looked up, gave me a smile that set my raw young heart astir, wished me good evening, and went on chatting.

Colonel Norgate had stepped to the sideboard near the door and was pouring me out a drink.

"Sir Henry turned very groggy on the way here," he said in a lowered voice. "I thought we'd have to stop the night at some wayside pub and call in a doctor. However, a good stiff dose of brandy has pulled him together. I don't think it's anything very serious—Yes, my dear?"

The woman crossed the library with an empty glass. "Another drink for Sir Henry, Jim—he says he's feeling all right again." She turned to me. "Oh, constable, by the way, would you do Sir Henry a favour? It'll save him writing."

"Certainly, ma'am," I said readily.

"You see, Sir Henry is coming abroad with us," she explained. "We'll be yachting, and he won't be back for three months, and perhaps longer. He wonders if you'd mind telling this to the police sergeant, or to whoever should be told, so that the house will be looked after. Will that be all right? Thanks most awfully for all your trouble."

Charm is a queer thing. That young woman stood talking to me by the sideboard for less than five minutes, but by the time she had finished I think I would have done anything in the world for her. Because she had merely taken notice of me I felt a good two inches taller. And then I remembered what I had done to their motor car, and I wondered how in heaven's name I was going to blurt out what a fool I had been! I wondered if I should clear out and say nothing, hoping that they'd have some spare petrol on the car. It was a devilish awkward situation, I can tell you. I was on the point of broaching the subject when she turned away with a bright laugh and a friendly nod.

"Give the constable another drink, Jim," she said. "It'll keep out the cold and wet."

While the colonel was refilling my glass, I followed her in admiration with my eyes. She sauntered back to the hearth, carrying herself superbly with that easy swing of hers. And then my eyes fastened on one detail, and for a long second I felt as though I'd had a sudden icy douche. Everything became plain to me—everything. The colonel handed me my glass.

"I wonder, sir," I said, in a steady voice, "if you'd mind signing my book? It'll keep me right with the sergeant tomorrow."

"Certainly," he declared, taking the pencil and notebook I held out to him. And when his hands were together, I clicked the handcuffs on his wrists.

With one leap I was at the door and had locked it, and slipped the key in my pocket.

"What the hell are you getting at?" The man's face was twisted and white as I pulled a little automatic pistol from his hip pocket.

"The murder of Sir Henry Ellison-Stewart," I said, "and the attempted robbery of his safe—with the keys you took from his body. It was a good idea to bury him in the last place they'd look for him—his own cellar."

The man was crouching like an animal, but he knew I had him beat. Everything I said was going home on him like successive blows.

"You had to pull the wool over me somehow," I said, watching him closely. "You had to convince me he was still alive. When you saw me there at the front door just now, you knew I'd seen too much back at these crossroads. I've no doubt you stopped the car on that lonely bit of road on Soutra and killed him in cold blood. Aye. Well, I compliment ye both, and especially the lady. You're clever devils, the two of you. But for one thing, aye, one thing only, I'd have left this house without a single suspicion in my mind—which is what ye've been playing for!"

I pointed toward the hearth.

With a cry, the woman had run forward. But the grey-haired man, who sat with his back to us, had not stirred.

His white hand rested on the arm of his chair. The lighted cigarette burned right down until it had charred the flesh of the dead fingers.

Madame Ville d'Aubier

Josephine Tey

Elizabeth MacKintosh (1896–1952) enjoyed literary success, under two different pseudonyms, as a playwright and a detective novelist. She was born in Inverness and attended Inverness Royal Academy prior to starting to publish fiction under the name Gordon Daviot (Daviot is a Highland village five miles south east of Inverness). Her first detective novel, *The Man in the Queue* (1929) introduced Inspector Alan Grant, who appeared in most of her mystery novels. The book was at first attributed to Daviot, but thereafter was published under the name by which she is best remembered today—Josephine Tey. The novel won two awards and, as Tey's biographer Jennifer Morag Henderson points out, one of its attractions is the action: "the sections where Grant careers off to the Highlands makes the book like a more sedate Buchan… and one of its strengths is that Daviot knows all the places she describes." There is also a strong and memorable

Scottish flavour to Grant's final case, the posthumously published *The Singing Sands* (1952).

Jennifer Morag Henderson's *Josephine Tey: A Life* (updated in 2021) gives a detailed account of Tey's early short stories, written under the Daviot name. I am grateful to her for drawing this story to my attention. As far as I know, it has never appeared in print since publication in the *English Review* in February 1930.

———

I PUT DOWN THE NEWSPAPER FEELING EMPTY AND rather sick, as though someone had hit me in the wind. Outside, the white dead moors stared blankly back at me as the train trailed its slow length across the Grampians. The hills stood withdrawn and cold and magnificent. Even the winter sunlight that lit them to beauty could not make them less aloof, less symbolic of eternity. And suddenly the chugging train with its load of little mortals, each busy with his own futilities, was somehow heart-breakingly pathetic. If we were to count so little, it was surely unfair that we should suffer so much.

I was conscious that the man opposite murmured a polite request and took the paper from my knee, but I did not answer. I was remembering that summer morning and smelling the lilac and the hot *croissants*. Late spring, it was, hardly summer, and we had spent a whole morning wandering in the woods near Paris; those dear stage-scenery woods, so naïve in their first green, so conventionally wild. Michael, whose latest picture was not "marching," had been upset by the sight of the chestnut tree that dreamed in the sun below the studio window. He had hurled his palette into a corner, stuck his hat on the back of his head, and asked me if we had enough money to take us out of this damned sewer (Paris) so that we could see more trees and forget that we had ever scraped a palette or shoved a pen. Long before we had passed the fortifications, of course, he had regained his good humour and his zest for life, and we dawdled along the forest paths in a content that was nearly ecstatic, making for nowhere in particular and finding all that came good. We met no one— only the birds were alive there, it seemed—but now and then we would come suddenly upon small villages in clearings. So sudden were they and so still in the morning sunlight that they had the quality of an apparition. An enchantment was upon the woods this morning. Over the high, white secretive walls of the villas the lilac hung motionless, and the air was sweet with its flowering. Laburnum dripped in pale showers behind wrought-iron gates that might have guarded a fairy-tale. It was as if a wanton word or a careless movement might break a spell, and the vision vanish into the limbo of things that are too good to be true.

At noon we walked into Ville d'Aubier, drunk with satisfaction and very hungry. Here, too, the lilac and the laburnum drooped over the walls, but we were satiated with beauty and wanted food. The street was deserted except for two dogs, and with a clairvoyance born of famine I saw that Ville d'Aubier shorn of its blossom would be a commonplace and deadly dull little village. A search for an eating-place revealed nothing better than a solitary baker's shop, and even that had nothing at all in the window.

"They'll have bread, anyhow," said Mike, and we went in.

The shop had a counter and one marble-topped table, but there was no sign of food anywhere. As we sat down, a woman came through the door at the back and crossed the little room slowly towards us. She was middle-aged and heavily-built and pale, and she wore the habitual black of the French working woman. Her sullen face was quite expressionless, but there was something oddly hostile, almost intimidating, in her immobility.

"Yes, messieurs?" she said.

We asked what we could have to eat.

There was nothing, she said. They did not bake today.

But, Michael explained, if we did not have something quickly, we should die on her doorstep, and she would not like to have that happen.

She did not smile. If we liked to wait, she said, her son was making *croissants,* and we could have some of them.

"Good!" said Mike. "We will have *croissants* and coffee."

She could not supply coffee, she said. She did not cater except in the summer. We could have lemonade, if we wished.

Even Michael was daunted by her antagonism. He consented to the lemonade. And as she turned to go, I saw that a man was standing in the doorway at the back, watching. He was youngish, and dressed in floury grey overalls. But it was not at us that he was looking, as one would have expected; it was at the woman. He watched her in silence as she came up to him, and passed beyond him into the dark passage. As soon as she had passed, he turned quickly on his heel and followed. And as they went out of sight, he said something in a rapid undertone. The sentence was too low and too rapid for us to catch the words, but the tone was unmistakeable; it was either a reproof or a threat.

Mike had turned to watch her go, and now sat with his head screwed round, gazing at the black doorway. He, too, had been arrested by something strange in the atmosphere.

"The Gorgon is not very accommodating," was all the comment he made, however.

Presently she came back with the hot *croissants* and the lemonade—a sufficiently vile mixture, but we were in no state to care whether our bacon had beans or not. I made a conventional remark about the glorious weather, hoping to dissolve her, if not into talk, at least into some semblance of amiability. She agreed, without looking at me and without altering the dead tones of her voice, that it was very fine. Suddenly Michael, whose French is better than mine, said in English:

"You are not French."

"No," she replied. "I am a Londoner."

She had not raised her eyes from the *croissants*, but the bitterness—I had almost said, the venom—in her voice staggered us as much as if she had lifted her thick white hand and hit us. She turned away without looking at us and without waiting for Michael's rejoinder, and I noticed that the man had come to the door again.

And all at once I wanted to get out of the place. Something I did not understand was happening here. The air was thick with it, bulged with it as air does before an explosion. We were being crushed and pressed down by the potency of someone's misery, and it was as if at any moment that pressure of misery might burst the thing that held it. I wanted to get away before something happened. I had the unreasoning uneasiness that I always have when I am close to a dynamo.

We ate quickly and without remark. Even Mike, I thought, was anxious to be gone. In answer to our summons the man came, and we paid him. He gave us a fleeting unpleasant smile and retired into the back regions without bidding us good-day or waiting to see us go.

Out in the sunlight and walking down the white road among the blossoming trees the horror faded and the thing seemed merely strange. We marvelled mildly at our reception.

"The lady is not a good daughter of France, that is evident," Michael said.

I thought of Ville d'Aubier in the winter time: the black dripping days in that narrow street buried in the woods, when no one came from the outside world and few stirred in the village. Did she miss even yet the comfort of traffic and lights and companionship?

"But she has a son," I said aloud.

"You saw him," Mike remarked. "He didn't look much of a widow's comfort."

"Do you think she hated us because we were English? Or does she hate all the world?"

Mike said she probably hated folk coming in when she was busy with the washing. And with that there was born a tacit agreement to be flippant about the affair; though we both knew that Mike's remark was nonsense. It was not a mood that had darkened the woman's face, nor a brewing squall that had poisoned the laden atmosphere.

In the months that followed, Madame Ville d'Aubier, as Mike called her, passed into legend for us. We would say "as cheerful as Madame Ville d'Aubier," or "as hospitable as Madame Ville d'Aubier." And gradually the reality faded into the legend. When her name was mentioned, a faint discomfort crossed the surface of my mind, but it was as impalpable and as fleeting as a gull's shadow on the sea.

And now—

"A cold country, even in summer," said my companion, indicating the white moors that I was still staring at. "As cold and self-contained as the people."

"They have the reputation of being less so than ourselves," I reminded him.

"I don't think there's much to pick and choose. We are both thoroughly insular, I suppose. 'Insulated' is a better word." He chuckled happily. "I don't wonder the continental people find us cold fish. You never catch us running amok. Like this, for instance."

He held up the paper and flipped it with careless fingertips, and I caught sight of the headlines again. "Triple Murder at Ville d'Aubier. Woman Kills Husband and Two Sons."

"Only a Frenchwoman goes in for wholesale murder like that. We have too good a sense of proportion."

What was the use? Why spoil his insulated comfort?

"I expect we have," I said.

The door crashed open. "Taking luncheon, sir?" said the attendant.

And we went to luncheon, watched by the staring indifferent hills.

The Man on Ben Na Garve

H. H. Bashford

Sir Henry Howarth Bashford (1880–1961) was, like Arthur Conan Doyle, a doctor who wrote prolifically but was knighted for reasons other than his fiction. Bashford trained in medicine in London and was chief medical officer to the Post Office, receiving a knighthood in 1938. He served as honorary physician to King George VI from 1941–44 and for a time he was chief medical officer to the Treasury. In later life he settled in Easton Royal, on the edge of the Salisbury Plain. He became a local benefactor and historian. A blue plaque was placed on his residence by English heritage to commemorate his generosity towards the rural community.

Bashford was a fluent writer who turned his pen to many subjects, including specialist articles on industrial medicine and a series of sketches of medical life which were gathered in *The Corner of Harley Street*. A keen angler, he wrote a book about fishing and in addition to producing occasional novels he also found time to write a variety of short stories. "The Man on Ben Na Garve," with an account of an incident in a remote part of the Scottish Highlands, strikes me as a first-rate example of Golden Age crime fiction by an author seldom associated with the mystery genre. It was first published in the *Strand Magazine* in February 1933.

———

IT WAS THE LAST WEEK IN NOVEMBER. WE WERE SIT-ting, the six of us, round Joe Torrance's dinner-table in Wimpole Street, and I had supposed it was Chiltern—I am not quite so sure now—who was responsible for the argument that had grown up between us. Like all Joe's parties, it had been purely fortuitous, the result of chance meetings during the day. But Lady Torrance, who was the only woman present, had accepted and provided for us with her usual kindness.

Being an assistant physician on the staff of St. Julian's, where old Joe was the senior surgeon, I was, of course, as familiar with his apple-cheeked face as with the street in which he lived; and only the week before I had enjoyed the dubious privilege of being cross-examined by Chiltern for nearly an hour. I don't think he had seriously shaken my evidence—I had been one of the medical witnesses for the defence—but it was certainly pleasanter, I reflected, to be sitting opposite to him at dinner than measuring swords with him at the Old Bailey. In the mellow light, indeed, and unframed by a K.C.'s wig, his sardonic countenance was almost urbane; and it was difficult to believe that he was the same man who had so acidly tried to discredit me before the jury.

Of the other two guests I knew nothing except what I had learned during the evening. Wentworth, who was sitting next me, and had apologised for not changing, was a second cousin, it appeared, of Lady Torrance. He was a hard-bitten, middle-aged man, who looked more like a sailor than an engineer, but was actually in charge of a railway in Bolivia that was being built by the Gordon, Barran firm of Sheffield. Altogether, he had been out there, he had told us, for seven years, and was returning that night via Southampton, having taken the day off, he said, to get washed and brushed while his party and plant wallowed round from Tilbury. He was also interested in birds, and, according to old Joe, a well-known authority and collector.

As for Darenth, who was sitting next Chiltern, he was a dark-eyed young man with an olive complexion and the puckered scar of a gunshot wound seaming his left cheek just below the bone. He was something ornamental—again according to Joe—at the embassy at Paris, and a son of the man from whom Joe and Chiltern rented a mile of the Test. Joe had produced a box of cigars, the gift, he explained, of a grateful patient.

"Well, you can't wonder," he was saying. "Every Englishman's brought up to regard tale-bearing as a low-down trick."

"And yet, I suppose," said Darenth, "that fewer people get away with crime in England than in most places you could name."

"Possibly that's true," said Chiltern. "But then, by and large, we're a law-abiding nation."

"Cuts both ways, too," said Wentworth, "this difficulty

in getting witnesses to come forward. Teaches the fellows on the job how to do it. And, after all, it is their job; not other people's."

"Well, I know this," said Joe. "I'd rather live in a country where the bias was against coming forward than for it."

Chiltern grinned.

"That's because you're essentially lazy."

"Tolerant," said Joe.

"Won't be bothered," said Chiltern.

"In fact, English," said Lady Torrance. "Well, I'll leave you to your coffee."

She glanced at Wentworth.

"I've ordered the car for ten o'clock, but, of course, I'll be seeing you before you go."

She patted the sparse grey hairs on her husband's head, and closed the door behind her.

Chiltern helped himself to a cigar, and looked across at me.

"Take that case, for instance," he said, "we were in last week. Your people won. But they wouldn't have had an earthly if that grocer round the corner hadn't kept his mouth shut."

"So I heard tell," I said.

"And it means that a murderer has got off."

"But you can't be certain of that," said Joe, "surely."

"Not absolutely, of course. But it illustrates my point."

He lit his cigar.

"And you have to remember," he added, "that for every case that comes into court there are probably a dozen that the police daren't bring there—to say nothing of the other dozen that they haven't a chance to look into because somebody or other has lain low."

"Then you consider," said Wentworth, "that if anybody happens to see something that may possibly have a—well, a criminal significance, it's his duty to tell the police?"

"His civic duty," said Chiltern, "certainly. Of course, it depends. Everything depends."

Wentworth lit his own cigar.

"You mean," he said slowly, "on the degree of the possibility? Well, if you'd be so kind, I should like to give you an instance. It was something that happened to me last year in Scotland."

He glanced at his watch.

"I was in much the same position," he said, "as I am at this moment. It was the last day of my leave, or, rather, the last day but two, and I was at Invercorrig, in Ross-shire. I dare say you know it. It's on the edge of the Struan Forest. But if you don't, it's not much more than a fishing inn. Six beds, and three miles of the Corrig—not a bad place if you don't want a Ritz."

He finished his coffee, and helped himself to another half-inch of Joe's ninety-year-old brandy.

"Well, I had had a bit of fishing," he said, "not much good—weather too bright, and the water too low—and on this particular day, the sixth of June, it was, I decided to go out and have a look at the birds. It was a good day, with an early mist and the sort of mountain smell that you only get in Scotland; and I suppose I had done about ten miles of heather and bog before I came to anchor under Ben Na Garve. I had seen from the map that this divided me from Glen Carra—with Meallan Dearg on the other side of it; and being pretty fit, I decided to keep my sandwiches till I'd got to the top of the mountain. That meant another thousand feet of fairly hard going, and when I got there I might have been the only man in the world; and I'm not going to tell you that it was the finest view in Scotland, because I change my mind about that every time I go there. Anyway, it was good enough, with the Carra below me—one of the little rivers that run into Loch Bhuin—and the shoulder of Meallan Dearg across the way, and half a dozen other mountains beyond it. Altogether, I was feeling pretty pleased with myself, especially as I had come upon a pair of red-throated divers nesting on the edge of a small tarn; and after eating my sandwiches, I curled myself up under a warm bit of granite and went to sleep.

"I must have slept for a couple of hours, for when I woke up it was four o'clock—three o'clock by Nature's time—and the glen was so still that I might have been staring at a picture. I hadn't seen a soul, of course, since I left Invercorrig, but now there wasn't a sign of a movement anywhere, not a cloud or a breath of wind, and I was far too high up to see the movement of the river.

"Well, I lit a pipe, and was pondering turning back on my tracks, when I saw a speck of darkness detach itself from the horizon; and getting my glasses on to it, I followed it across the face of Meallan Dearg and across the glen to somewhere below me. Then I saw another coming up the glen, high above the river from the direction of the loch, and—well, to cut it short, they were a pair of golden eagles; and that was quite enough to make me change my plans. I didn't know the country. But I had any amount of daylight—I had been fishing the night before till after eleven—and if there was an eyrie about, as I hoped and suspected, I meant to have a look at it, if it was at all possible."

Wentworth paused, and I saw his eye meet Chiltern's.

"Perhaps you're not a bird-lover," he smiled. "But there was something rather thrilling to be there alone with a couple of golden eagles on a June afternoon in the heart of the Struan Forest; and I sat there for about half an hour considering my tactics and waiting for them to cruise again and give me a lead. Just below me, for a couple of hundred feet or so, there was a steep, but not very difficult piece of rock, and below that a broad ledge of bog, with a fringe of heather and granite boulders. To the right this seemed to pan out upon the shoulder of the mountain, but to the left it looked as if it were sloping towards the glen; and just as I had made up my mind to get down to it, the eagles appeared again over its farther edge.

"I marked the spot, and waited while they hovered over the glen, and then cruised westwards out of sight; and a quarter of an hour later I was down on the ledge with the crest of Ben Na Garve behind me. I now saw that I could get back towards Invercorrig without going the way I had come; and, in fact, there seemed to be traces of a sort of sheep-track or path following the ledge, and crossing the shoulder of the mountain. It can't have been very frequented—the presence of the eagles showed that—and looking down over the brink of the ledge I saw that this was the roof of an immense corrie, dropping another three hundred feet to a slope of heather. It was a savage bit of rock, even in the June sunshine, with a tilt to the right towards the head of the glen; and as it was quite unclimbable, I decided to work towards the left, where the path bore away from it towards a belt of pines.

"These were the first trees that I had seen all day—they were still a goodish way below me—and for the first time, as I left the ledge above me, I picked up the sound of the river below. I followed the path for about fifty yards down and then left it, working back towards the corrie, and at last found a crevice on the left side of the precipice from which I could command the whole of the corrie. It was just what I wanted. I judged I was pretty well out of sight, and having settled down between a couple of boulders, I got out my glasses, and at last, to my great satisfaction, located the eyrie. It was upon the farther side of the corrie and partly hidden from me by a projecting bit of rock, but I could just see the heads of two young birds, and I felt that my trouble hadn't been wasted. I was also commanding, I found, about a mile of the glen, though the loch at the foot of it was out of sight; and this is what I am coming to—I saw a man fishing what seemed to be the highest salmon pool of the river.

"It was at the bottom of a little fall, of which I couldn't see the top. But I watched him casting for a few minutes; and then—somewhere about six o'clock, it was—I saw a fellow with a rucksack coming down the shoulder of Meallan Dearg. At first I could only see him through my glasses. He was waist-deep in heather, and the side of the mountain was in shadow; and it took me two or three minutes to find him, again after I had had another look at the eyrie. But he was evidently coming down into the glen.

"He had probably climbed over, I imagined, from the road along the north of Loch Bhuin; and ten minutes later I saw him waving to the man at the salmon pool. The other man stared at him for a moment and then waved back, and I saw him pointing up the river. He was fishing on my bank, and appeared to be signalling to his friend where he could get across the stream. Then I forgot them both as one of the parent eagles came over the skyline beyond the corrie; and for the next few minutes I was watching him dropping down to the eyrie with a mountain leveret for the larder.

"To be exact, that was at half-past six. I generally keep notes of that sort of thing for my bird diaries; and when I looked at the river again I saw the man with the rucksack just coming down to the near edge of the pool. I saw the fisherman greet him. If I had to guess, I should say that he was a little surprised to see him; but they obviously knew one another—or so it seemed to me—and then they disappeared towards the tail of the pool. This was hidden from me, and I never saw the fisherman again. But ten minutes afterwards I saw the man with the rucksack; and after hesitating for a moment, I saw him leave the river, apparently with the intention of climbing Ben Na Garve.

"By then the first eagle was away again. But the second had returned, and was hovering over the eyrie; and the fellow was within twenty yards of me, on the path I had left, before I thought about him again. I didn't want to be disturbed. So I didn't hail him, and he went by without seeing me; and it was another half-hour before I tore myself away and started back to Invercorrig. But he had spent the night there, for I saw him the next morning, starting out just as I had begun to shave; and I saw from the visitors' book, when I came down, that he was a Mr. Smith of Leeds."

Wentworth paused again and removed his cigar-ash.

"I'm sorry to be so long," he said, "in coming to the point.

But, as I told you, this was the end of my leave, and a week later I was on the high seas. Meanwhile, however, I had left behind me at Invercorrig a couple of bird books that I valued; and when I discovered it, I wrote to Mrs. McKenzie, the innkeeper's wife, and asked her to forward them to me. The parcel arrived in due course. But it was three months before I opened it; and I was then fifty miles beyond railhead up the Ignacio in the heart of Bolivia. The books had been sent out to me wrapped in brown paper, but underneath this they had been packed in a local newspaper; and my eye was caught by the account of a public inquiry on a Mr. Croome, who had been found drowned in a pool on the Carra.

"I read it carefully—I was pretty short of reading matter up there—and saw that the date of his death was June the 6th; and the pool in which he had been found was at the head of the glen at the foot of Meallan Dearg and just under Ben Na Garve. He had been staying, it appeared, at a lodge on Loch Bhuin, the guest of a General Henderson; and it was General Henderson himself and a ghillie who had found him there about half-past eight.

"The inquiry was very brief. Mr. Croome had gone up the glen salmon-fishing. Nobody had seen him since ten o'clock in the morning; and it seemed quite clear that he had somehow slipped, and owing to his heavy waders been drowned in the pool. What interested me, however, was the fact that he must have been the man I was looking at; and that I had therefore been the last person to see him alive—or rather the last but one.

"But what about the last person? That struck me as a little odd, though very possibly there was nothing in it. But it had evidently been a friend of his; and it was difficult to believe that he hadn't heard of the accident and death. I read the account again. Being a local paper, it was important news, and the inquiry had been fully reported. But there it was. Nobody had seen him since ten o'clock; and the friend, who had been with him at half-past six, hadn't, as you would have said, come forward."

Wentworth sipped his brandy and looked again at Chiltern.

"That was in October," he said, "and I was several thousand miles from England. Do you think it was my duty as a citizen to have taken any steps?"

"Then you didn't?" said Chiltern.

"No, I didn't. After all, I thought, there wasn't much to make a song about, except that, after the two of them had passed out of my sight, I hadn't seen the fisherman again. In fact, I shouldn't have bothered you with the story at all, if another rather odd thing hadn't happened. I've discovered quite lately—in fact, only today—that Mr. Smith, of Leeds, wasn't the friend's real name."

He glanced at his watch.

"And I'm leaving in half an hour. Given this new circumstance, what would be your advice?"

"I think," said Chiltern, "that you ought to tell the police, or at any rate write to them fully about all you know."

Wentworth glanced at me.

"And you?"

"I agree," I said, "with Chiltern."

He looked at old Joe.

"Well," said Joe, "as you're just off, I suppose that's the right thing to do. But if you'd had time, I think I'd have suggested asking the fellow for an explanation."

Wentworth smoked for a moment and then looked soberly at Darenth.

"Well, Mr. Darenth," he said, "what *is* the explanation?"

There was a little sound as Chiltern turned sharply in his chair. Old Joe leaned forward an inch and dropped back. Darenth's dark eyes were fixed upon Wentworth.

"You must have been pretty well hidden," he said.

"I was."

Darenth lit a cigarette.

"Did you know that Croome was at the Foreign Office?"

Wentworth nodded.

"So the newspaper said."

"Well, he'd been selling confidential papers for nearly a year. It was definitely established on June the 4th. They knew he was a friend of mine. In fact, he was engaged to my sister. So they let me tell him. I left him standing beside the pool."

Before Insulin

J. J. Connington

Alfred Walter Stewart (1880–1947) was born in Glasgow. His father had been Professor of Divinity at Glasgow University, and Stewart duly studied there himself. His subject was chemistry, and he became an expert in spectroscopy. He pursued an academic career in Marburg and London before moving to Belfast, and combined lecturing with author-ship, beginning with scientific textbooks. His first novel, *Nordenholt's Million* (1923), was a dystopian story which features a survivalist colony in a part of his homeland that he knew well: the Clyde Valley. He published his fiction under the name J. J. Connington, an alias inspired by the name of the translator of Horace, John Conington.

Taking his lead from Richard Austin Freeman's success in blending scientific inquiry and detective work, he turned to crime fiction. *Death at Swaythling Court* involves the inven-tion of a lethal ray, and elements of science fiction (although these prove to be bogus). Soon he was demonstrating a strong commitment to "fair play" plotting in his novels, which benefited from his scientific and technical know-how and earned the admiration of T. S. Eliot among others. *The Eye in the Museum*, first published in 1929, contains a very early example of a "cluefinder," with footnote references appended to the explanation of the crime to point out the pages where information relevant to the solution was provided. Connington's novels are mostly set in England, but the eponymous isle in *Tom Tiddler's Island* (1933) is off the Scottish coast. His short stories are few and far between; this one first appeared in the *London Evening Standard* on 1 September 1936.

———

"I'D MORE THAN THE FISHING IN MY MIND WHEN I ASKED you over for the weekend," Wendover confessed. "Fact is, Clinton, something's turned up and I'd like your advice."

Sir Clinton Driffield, Chief Constable of the county, glanced quizzically at his old friend.

"If you've murdered anyone, Squire, my advice is: keep it dark and leave the country. If it's merely breach of promise, or anything of that sort, I'm at your disposal."

"It's not breach of promise," Wendover assured him with the complacency of a hardened bachelor. "It's a matter of an estate for which I happen to be sole trustee, worse luck. The other two have died since the will was made. I'll tell you about it."

Wendover prided himself on his power of lucid exposition. He settled himself in his chair and began.

"You've heard me speak of old John Ashby, the ironmaster? He died fifteen years back, worth £53,000; and he made his son, his daughter-in-law, and myself executors of his will. The son, James Ashby, was to have the life-rent of the estate; and on his death the capital was to be handed over to his offspring when the youngest of them came of age. As it happened, there was only one child, young Robin Ashby. James Ashby and his wife were killed in a railway accident some years ago; so the whole £53,000, less two estate duties, was secured to young Robin if he lived to come of age."

"And if he didn't?" queried Sir Clinton.

"Then the money went to a lot of charities," Wendover explained. "That's just the trouble, as you'll see. Three years ago, young Robin took diabetes, a bad case, poor fellow. We did what we could for him, naturally. All the specialists had a turn, without improvement. Then we sent him over to Neuenahr, to some institute run by a German who specialised in diabetes. No good. I went over to see the poor boy, and he was worn to a shadow, simply skin and bone and hardly able to walk with weakness. Obviously it was a mere matter of time."

"Hard lines on the youngster," Sir Clinton commented soberly.

"Very hard," said Wendover with a gesture of pity. "Now as it happened, at Neuenahr he scraped acquaintance with a French doctor. I saw him when I was there: about thirty, black torpedo beard, very brisk and well-got-up, with any amount of belief in himself. He spoke English fluently, which gave him a pull with Robin, out there among foreigners; and he persuaded the boy that he could cure him if he would put himself in his charge. Well, by that time, it seemed that any chance was worth taking, so I agreed. After all, the boy was dying by inches. So off he went to the south of France, where this man—Prevost, his name was—had a nursing home of his own. I saw the place: well-kept affair though small. And he had an English nurse, which was lucky for Robin. Pretty girl she was: chestnut hair, creamy skin, supple figure, neat hands and feet. A lady, too."

"Oh, any pretty girl can get round you," interjected Sir Clinton. "Get on with the tale."

"Well, it was all no good," Wendover went on, hastily. "The poor boy went down hill in spite of all the Frenchman's talk; and, to cut a long story short, he died a fortnight ago, on the very day when he came of age."

"Oh, so he lived long enough to inherit?"

"By the skin of his teeth," Wendover agreed. "That's where the trouble begins. Before that day, of course, he could make no valid will. But now a claimant, a man Sydney Eastcote, turns up with the claim that Robin made a will the morning of the day he died and by this will this Eastcote fellow scoops the whole estate. All I know of it is from a letter this Eastcote man wrote to me giving the facts. I referred him to the lawyer for the estate and told the lawyer—Harringay's his name—to bring the claimant here this afternoon. They're due now. I'd like you to look him over, Clinton. I'm not quite satisfied about this will."

The Chief Constable pondered for a moment or two.

"Very well," he agreed. "But you'd better not introduce me as Sir Clinton Driffield, Chief Constable, etc. I'd better be Mr. Clinton, I think it sounds better for a private confabulation."

"Very well," Wendover conceded. "There's a car on the drive. It must be they, I suppose."

In a few moments the door opened and the visitors were ushered in. Surprised himself, the Chief Constable was still able to enjoy the astonishment of his friend; for instead of the expected man, a pretty chestnut-haired girl, dressed in mourning, was shown into the room along with the solicitor, and it was plain enough that Wendover recognised her.

"You seem surprised, Mr. Wendover," the girl began, evidently somewhat taken aback by Wendover's expression. Then she smiled as though an explanation occurred to her. "Of course, it's my name again. People always forget that Sydney's a girl's name as well as a man's. But you remember me, don't you? I met you when you visited poor Robin."

"Of course I remember you, Nurse," Wendover declared, recovering from his surprise. "But I never heard you called anything but 'Nurse' and didn't even hear your surname; so naturally I didn't associate you with the letter I got about poor Robin's will."

"Oh, I see," answered the girl. "That accounts for it."

She looked inquiringly towards the Chief Constable, and Wendover recovered his presence of mind.

"This is a friend of mine, Mr. Clinton," he explained. "Miss Eastcote. Mr. Harringay. Won't you sit down? I must admit your letter took me completely by surprise, Miss Eastcote."

Wendover was getting over his initial astonishment at the identity of the claimant, and when they had all seated themselves, he took the lead.

"I've seen a copy of Robin's death certificate," he began slowly. "He died in the afternoon of September 21st, the day he came of age, so he was quite competent to make a will. I suppose he was mentally fit to make one?"

"Dr. Prevost will certify that if necessary," the nurse affirmed quietly.

"I noticed that he didn't die in Dr. Prevost's Institute," Wendover continued. "At some local hotel, wasn't it?"

"Yes," Nurse Eastcote confirmed. "A patient died in the Institute about that time and poor Robin hated the place on that account. It depressed him, and he insisted on moving to the hotel for a time."

"He must have been at death's door then, poor fellow," Wendover commented.

"Yes," the nurse admitted, sadly. "He was very far through. He had lapses of consciousness, the usual diabetic coma. But while he was awake he was perfectly sound mentally if that's what you mean."

Wendover nodded as though this satisfied him completely.

"Tell me about this will," he asked. "It's come as something of a surprise to me, not unnaturally."

Nurse Eastcote hesitated for a moment. Her lip quivered and her eyes filled with tears as she drew from her bag an envelope of thin foreign paper. From this she extracted a sheet of foreign note-paper which she passed across to Wendover.

"I can't grumble if you're surprised at his leaving me this money," she said, at last. "I didn't expect anything of the kind myself. But the fact is… he fell in love with me, poor boy, while he was under my charge. You see, except for Dr. Prevost I was the only one who could speak English with him, and that meant much to him at that time when he was so lonely. Of course he was much younger that I am; I'm twenty-seven.

I suppose I ought to have checked him when I saw how things were. But I hadn't the heart to do it. It was something that gave him just the necessary spur to keep him going, and of course I knew that marriage would never come into it. It did no harm to let him fall in love; and I really did my very best to make him happy, in these last weeks. I was so sorry for him, you know."

This put the matter in a fresh light for Wendover, and he grew more sympathetic in his manner.

"I can understand," he said gently. "You didn't care for him, of course…"

"Not in that way. But I was very, very sorry for him, and I'd have done anything to make him feel happier. It was so dreadful to see him going out into the dark before he'd really started in life."

Wendover cleared his throat, evidently conscious that the talk was hardly on the business-like lines which he had planned. He unfolded the thin sheet of note-paper and glanced over the writing.

"This seems explicit enough. 'I leave all that I have to Nurse Sydney Eastcote, residing at Dr. Prevost's medical Institute.' I recognise the handwriting as Robin's, and the date is in the same writing. Who are the witnesses, by the way?"

"Two of the waiters at the hotel, I believe," Nurse Eastcote explained.

Wendover turned to the flimsy foreign envelope and examined the address.

"Addressed by himself to you at the institute, I see. And the postmark is 21st September. That's quite good confirmatory evidence, if anything of the sort were needed."

He passed the two papers to Sir Clinton. The Chief Constable seemed to find the light insufficient where he was sitting, for he rose and walked over to a window to examine the documents. This brought him slightly behind Nurse Eastcote. Wendover noted idly that Sir Clinton stood sideways to the light while he inspected the papers in his hand.

"Now just one point," Wendover continued. "I'd like to know something about Robin's mental condition towards the end. Did he read to pass the time, newspapers and things like that?"

Nurse Eastcote shook her head.

"No, he read nothing. He was too exhausted, poor boy. I used to sit by him and try to interest him in talk. But if you have any doubt about his mind at that time—I mean whether he was fit to make a will—I'm sure Dr. Prevost will give a certificate that he was in full possession of his faculties and knew what he was doing."

Sir Clinton came forward with the papers in his hand.

"These are very important documents," he pointed out, addressing the nurse. "It's not safe for you to be carrying them about in your bag as you've been doing. Leave them with us. Mr. Wendover will give you a receipt and take good care of them. And to make sure there's no mistake, I think you'd better write your name in the corner of each of them so as to identify them. Mr. Harringay will agree with me that we mustn't leave any loophole for doubt in a case like this."

The lawyer nodded. He was a taciturn man by nature, and his pride had been slightly ruffled by the way in which he had been ignored in the conference. Nurse Eastcote, with Wendover's fountain pen, wrote her signature on a free space of each paper. Wendover offered his guests tea before they departed, but he turned the talk into general channels and avoided any further reference to business topics.

When the lawyer and the girl had left the house, Wendover turned to Sir Clinton.

"It seems straight enough to me," he said, "but I could see from the look you gave me behind her back when you were at the window that you aren't satisfied. What's wrong?"

"If you want my opinion," the Chief Constable answered, "it's a fake from start to finish. Certainly you can't risk handing over a penny on that evidence. If you want it proved up to the hilt, I can do it for you, but it'll cost something for inquiries and expert assistance. That ought to come out of the estate, and it'll be cheaper than an action at law. Besides," he added with a smile, "I don't suppose you want to put that girl in gaol. She's probably only a tool in the hands of a cleverer person."

Wendover was staggered by the Chief Constable's tone of certainty. The girl, of course, had made no pretence that she was in love with Robin Ashby; but her story had been told as though she herself believed it.

"Make your inquiries, certainly," he consented. "Still, on the face of it the thing sounds likely enough."

"I'll give you definite proof in a fortnight or so. Better make a further appointment with that girl in, say, three weeks. But don't drag the lawyer into it this time. It may savour too much of compounding a felony for his taste. I'll need these papers."

———

"Here's the concrete evidence," said the Chief Constable three weeks later. "I may as well show it to you before she arrives, and you can amuse yourself with turning it over in the meanwhile."

He produced the will, the envelope, and two photographs from his pocket-book as he spoke and laid them on the table, opening out the will as he put it down.

"Now first of all, notice that the will and envelope are of very thin paper, the foreign correspondence stuff. Second, observe that the envelope is of the exact size to hold that sheet of paper if it's folded in four—I mean folded in half and then doubled over. The sheet's about quarto size, ten inches by eight. Now look here. There's an extra fold in the paper. It's been folded in four and then it's been folded across once more. That struck me as soon as I had it in my hand. Why the extra fold, since it would fit into the envelope without that?"

Wendover inspected the sheet carefully and looked rather perplexed.

"You're quite right," he said, "but you can't upset a will on the strength of a fold in it. She may have doubled it up herself, after she got it."

"Not when it was in the envelope that fitted it," Sir Clinton pointed out. "There's no corresponding doubling of the envelope. However, let's go on. Here's a photograph of the envelope, taken with the light falling sideways. You see the postal erasing stamp has made an impression?"

"Yes, I can read it, and the date's 21st September right enough." He paused for a moment and then added in surprise, "But where's the postage stamp? It hasn't come out in the photo."

"No, because that's a photo of the impression on the back half of the envelope. The stamp came down hard and not only cancelled the stamp but impressed the second side of the envelope as well. The impression comes out quite clearly when it's illuminated from the side. That's worth thinking over. And, finally, here's another print. It was made before the envelope was slit to get at the stamp impression. All we did was to put the envelope into a printing-frame with a bit of photographic printing paper behind it and expose it to light for a while. Now you'll notice that the gummed portions of the envelope show up in white, like a sort of St. Andrew's Cross. But if you look carefully, you'll see a couple of darker patches on the part of the white strip which corresponds to the flap of the envelope that one sticks down. Just think out what they imply, Squire. There are the facts for you, and it's not too difficult to put an interpretation on them if you think for a minute or two. And I'll add just one further bit of information. The two waiters who acted as witnesses to that will were given tickets for South America, and a certain sum of money each to keep them from feeling homesick… But here's your visitor."

Rather to Wendover's surprise, Sir Clinton took the lead in the conversation as soon as the girl arrived.

"Before we turn to business, Miss Eastcote," he said, "I'd like to tell you a little anecdote. It may be of use to you. May I?"

Nurse Eastcote nodded politely and Wendover, looking her over, noticed a ring on her engagement finger which he had not seen on her last visit.

"This is a case which came to my knowledge lately," Sir Clinton went on, "and it resembles your own so closely that

I'm sure it will suggest something. A young man of twenty, in an almost dying state, was induced to enter a nursing home by the doctor in charge. If he lived to come of age, he could make a will and leave a very large fortune to anyone he choose; but it was the merest gamble whether he would live to come of age."

Nurse Eastcote's figure stiffened and her eyes widened at this beginning, but she merely nodded as though asking Sir Clinton to continue.

"The boy fell in love with one of the nurses, who happened to be under the influence of the doctor," Sir Clinton went on. "If he lived to make a will, there was little doubt that he would leave the fortune to the nurse. A considerable temptation for any girl, I think you'll agree.

"The boy's birthday was very near, only a few days off; but it looked as though he would not live to see it. He was very far gone. He had no interest in the newspapers and he had long lapses of unconsciousness, so that he had no idea of what the actual date was. It was easy enough to tell him, on a given day, that he had come of age, though actually two days were still to run. Misled by the doctor, he imagined that he could make a valid will, being now twenty-one; and he wrote with his own hand a short document leaving everything to the nurse."

Miss Eastcote cleared her throat with an effort.

"Yes?" she said.

"This fraudulent will," Sir Clinton continued, "was witnessed by two waiters of the hotel to which the boy had been removed; and soon after, these waiters were packed off abroad and provided with some cash in addition to their fares. Then it occurred to the doctor that an extra bit of confirmatory evidence might be supplied. The boy had put the will into an envelope which he had addressed to the nurse. While the gum was still wet, the doctor opened the flap and took out the 'will,' which he then folded smaller in order to get the paper into an ordinary business-size envelope. He then addressed this to the nurse and posted the will to her in it. The original large envelope, addressed by the boy, he retained. But in pulling it open, the doctor had slightly torn the inner side of the flap where the gum lies; and that little defect shows up when one exposes the envelope over a sheet of photographic paper. Here's an example of what I mean."

He passed over to Nurse Eastcote the print which he had shown Wendover and drew her attention to the spots on the St. Andrew's Cross.

"As it chanced, the boy died next morning, a day before he came of age. The doctor concealed the death for a day, which was easy enough in the circumstances. Then, on the afternoon of the crucial date—did I mention that it was September 21st?—he closed the empty envelope, stamped it, and put it into the post, thus securing a postmark of the proper date. Unfortunately for this plan, the defacement stamp of the post office came down hard enough to impress its image on *both* the sheets of the thin paper envelope, so that by opening up the envelope and photographing it by a sideways illumination the embossing of the stamp showed up—like this."

He handed the girl the second photograph.

"Now if the 'will' had been in that envelope, the 'will' itself would have borne that stamp. But it did not; and that proves that the 'will' was not in the envelope when it passed through the post. A clever woman like yourself, Miss Eastcote, will see the point at once."

"And what happened after that?" asked the girl huskily.

"It's difficult to tell you," Sir Clinton pursued. "If it had come before me officially—I'm Chief Constable of the county, you know—I should probably have had to prosecute that unfortunate nurse for attempted fraud; and I've not the slightest doubt that we'd have proved the case up to the hilt. It would have meant a year or two in gaol, I expect.

"I forgot to mention that the nurse was secretly engaged to the doctor all this while. And, by the way, that's a very pretty ring you're wearing, Miss Eastcote. That, of course, accounted for the way in which the doctor managed to get her to play her part in the little scheme. I think, if I were you, Miss Eastcote, I'd go back to France as soon as possible and tell Dr. Prevost that... Well, it hasn't come off."

The Case of the Frugal Cake

Margot Bennett

Margot Bennett was born in Lenzie in Dunbartonshire in 1912. Her family subsequently emigrated to Australia, and she also spent time in New Zealand before returning to Britain when she was twenty-three. She worked in advertising and met and married a journalist, Richard Bennett. Her first crime novel, *Time to Change Hats*, appeared in 1945, and in the years that followed she published crime fiction infrequently but nevertheless became one of the outstanding British mystery novelists of the Fifties. *The Widow of Bath* (1952) and *The Man Who Didn't Fly* (1955) have both been published as British Library Crime Classics to considerable acclaim.

In 1959, Margot Bennett was elected to membership of the Detection Club and also published *Someone from the Past*, which won the Crime Writers' Association award for the best crime novel of the year. Astonishingly, after this achievement she never wrote another crime novel, although she did write for television (for series such as *Maigret*) until 1968; she died in 1980. In the early part of her career, she wrote a number of short stories for magazines and newspapers. "The Case of the Frugal Cake" was published in the *Evening News* on 18 August 1955.

———

AUNT ELLEN WAS RICH; AUNT ELLEN WAS A MISER. SHE kept her money in a trunk in the bedroom, and counted it by candlelight. So they said. She was too mean to buy cow's milk and kept a goat in the garden.

The goat and Cousin Hilda were Aunt Ellen's only extravagances. Cousin Hilda had lived in the cottage with Aunt Ellen for twelve years. Cousin Hilda milked the goat, fetched the water from the well, sifted the cinders, and didn't eat enough to stretch a mouse-skin. They said she'd get it all back one day. She was only forty-two. The money would come to Hilda in the end. She was the only relation, so they said in the village until Jeremy turned up.

Jeremy was a flabby little man in his forties; some kind of nephew. He had come from distant parts; he was asked in; he stayed the night; then he stayed on. They said Aunt Ellen was nervous about burglars, and she had worked out he would be cheaper than a dog to feed.

Everything about the cottage pleased him. He lounged in the brutally hard chairs; basked by the tiny fire that burned dubiously in the grate; participated eagerly in the ceremony of tea.

Aunt Ellen always made the tea with her own careful hands. At this meal there was only plenty of bread, and a little cube of margarine on each plate.

On Sunday there was cake for tea. Aunt Ellen made this too, for who else could be trusted with the sugar? She was skilled at omitting the usual ingredients. A little fat and sugar, a cupful of goat's milk, a great deal of flour and baking powder and sometimes a few caraway seeds—this was Aunt Ellen's cake.

She always took a little walk before tea, shuffling, secret and cunning as far as the woods, her head sunk in her greasy coat, purple streaks of leg bulging from her wrecked stockings, shoes flapping from her feet. Little Jeremy trotted round her, his face sharp with cold, and lean Cousin Hilda marched behind. They returned to the cottage shaken with hunger, then Aunt Ellen ate her own cake greedily. Jeremy said the cake was delicious. Cousin Hilda, suddenly, outrageously, spat it on to the plate.

There was a row, one of those rows women have that are never forgiven, then she rushed out of the house.

She went as housemaid to the doctor. It was a comfortable job, but thirty years ago she had worn silk dresses and gone to dancing classes. She had something to think about as she polished the consulting-room floor.

It was Cousin Hilda who answered the door when the news came at last one Monday morning. It had to be admitted she gave the message at once, but when the doctor called, Aunt Ellen was already dead, and Jeremy was being sick.

The doctor sent for the police. The village constable came first, then an inspector and his team. Ugly words about arsenic were exchanged, and the constable provided the local gossip.

Jeremy, pale and emptied but no longer sick, was able to give frightened answers. They hadn't eaten anything queer, only tea, and he hadn't eaten much of that owing to loss of appetite, he said, with an outburst of the coughing that had taken him more than once to the doctor's surgery.

The tea-table didn't show much. There was a thin slice of half-eaten cake on Jeremy's plate. There were only crumbs on Aunt Ellen's plate.

Cousin Hilda was sent for. Jeremy was already cringing. He was the only heir. If he hadn't been alive they'd never have suspected him. He raised his weak, hopeful eyes to Hilda, begging for her help.

The police also wanted her help. They would like to hear her account of Aunt Ellen's Sunday routine.

She spoke slowly, in a puzzled voice, as though she was trying to fit Jeremy into a picture that she seemed to see on the tea-table. She bent forward and peered at the cake more than once. Then she turned on Jeremy.

"Aunt Ellen didn't make that cake," she said in a flat, stiff voice.

"But she always did. You know she did," Jeremy said weakly.

Everyone waited for what this suddenly terrible, this at last triumphant, woman was going to prove.

She waved her hand and they stared obediently at the cake. It was an ordinary sort of yellow cake. A piece had been cut from it for analysis.

"That cake's a good cake," Cousin Hilda shouted. "You can see it. You ask anyone. That cake's got eggs in it. She never put an egg in a cake. Did you make it, Jeremy?"

"Aunt Ellen made it."

"To poison herself?" Hilda demanded. "That's likely."

"I never made a cake in my life," Jeremy said, cowering.

"You used a cookery book. That would say eggs, wouldn't it? What else did you put in?"

It was the village constable who stopped her apologetically at the door.

"It's true enough, sir," he said hesitantly to the inspector, "that Aunt—that she would never put an egg in a cake. But she was meaner than that. They say she had never bought an egg in her life. If the cake was cooked in this house, sir, where did the eggs come from? Anyway, we haven't found any eggshells, have we?"

That was when Cousin Hilda screamed and tried to run from the house. There was nowhere to run, but she died before the case came up, poor thing.

It was a clear enough case. She always baked for the doctor on Sundays. She had borrowed some white powder from the dispensary for the last cake, the cake she had changed for Aunt Ellen's when the old lady was out walking.

There was only one egg in it, anyway. It wasn't, they said, a very good cake.

Thursday's Child

Cyril Hare

The author known to detective fans as Cyril Hare was born Alfred Alexander Gordon Clark, at Mickleham in Surrey, in 1900. He died regrettably young, at the age of fifty-eight, after a period of indifferent health. A busy practising barrister who also served as a judge, he found time to publish nine detective novels and about forty short stories. Although his professional commitments meant he was far from prolific, he earned an enviable reputation in the genre which owes something to his sharp prose and crafty plotting but also reflects his willingness to try to do something a little different in his mysteries. His most famous mystery, *Tragedy at Law* (1942) is notable not only for its authentic portrayal of legal life but also for an unusual plot and an appealing, unorthodox protagonist in the barrister Francis Pettigrew. Pettigrew is a reluctant detective, but his appeal was so great that Hare brought him back on a number of occasions and married him to a young woman whom he first encounters in *With a Bare Bodkin* (1946).

As far as I know, Hare's connections with Scotland were limited, but he was a keen angler, and I expect that he used to go north of the border for the fishing. This little story is one of a group of six that Michael Gilbert included in the posthumous collection *Best Detective Stories of Cyril Hare* (1959).

———

"Thursday's child has far to go"

"IS THAT THE ISLAND?" MR. WILKINSON ASKED.

"Aye. That's Cara right enough."

"Cara!" Mr. Wilkinson stood on the jetty looking out at the long, low shadow of the island, dark against the setting sun. Beyond it, he knew, the nearest land was North America. He was at the ultimate edge of the Western Isles. It was a supremely romantic spot, and he looked supremely ridiculous there, in his dark city suit, with his neat city brief-case under his arm.

"Cara!" he repeated. "A beautiful place, and a beautiful name."

"It's the Gaelic word for a corpse."

Mr. Wilkinson looked again. Seen against the light, the island did resemble a human body, laid out upon its back. He could distinguish the shrouded outline of a head, a waisted trunk, a pair of stiff, upturned feet... He shivered. It was getting distinctly chilly down by the shore.

"I shall see you tomorrow, then?" he said to the boatman.

"Aye. The tide will be right about ten. If it's fine we shall be in Cara within the hour."

"And if it's rough?"

"If it's rough we shall no' be going." There was a flat finality about Dugald Macdougal's pronouncement that precluded argument. "The sound is no place for a small boat when the wind's blowing up from the sou'-west. There was a man tried it last spring. He hired Rory Maconner's boat and went alone. Rory was lucky. He got his boat back. She came ashore three days later, bottom up. The other fellow wasn't so lucky."

———

The next day was bright and warm, with hardly a breath of wind. The trip to Cara was like a pleasure cruise. Mr. Wilkinson watched the island slowly grow larger. He could distinguish a few goats on the grassy slopes, but no other sign of life.

"Where does Mr. James Filby live?" he asked.

"On the other side of the headland."

"All alone?"

"All alone. He likes it that way. Maybe he won't want to see you."

"I wrote to tell him I was coming."

"There's no postal delivery on Cara. Your letter's still at the post office waiting for him to collect it. He's not been on the mainland for six months."

Dugald steered the boat into a tiny harbour and tied up to the crumbling stone jetty.

"I'll wait for you here," he said. "If you go up yon path, maybe you'll find him."

Wilkinson found him very quickly. He was waiting for him round the first bend in the path, a tall, bearded figure, not sun-tanned as might have been expected, but pale-faced, with bright, sunken eyes.

"This island is private," he announced, and advanced on the intruder. Wilkinson became aware that Filby was holding a very purposeful-looking cudgel in his right hand. He began to talk extremely fast.

"I know that I am on private property," he said, "and I apologise most sincerely for my intrusion. But I have come all the way from London to see you, Mr. Filby, on a matter of very important business, and I do beg you to give me a few minutes of your time."

Filby stared at him in silence for a full half-minute. Then he said abruptly, "Ye'd best come into the house," turned on his heel and walked away.

Wilkinson followed him to the ramshackle cabin that was the only house on the island. Filby motioned him into the one chair and stood opposite him. Between them was a rough table that had evidently served recently as a chopping-block for meat. It was foul with grease and dried blood. Looking at his menacing figure, Wilkinson felt glad of even that protection.

"So you're on business from London?" said Filby. "You'll have known my brother Fergus in London, no doubt."

"I'm afraid not, Mr. Filby. It's a large place, you know."

"Did you not? He called himself Farnby in London, I'm told."

"Fergus Farnby! Yes, as a matter of fact I have—er—heard of him."

"And where is my brother now, do you know?"

"Mr. Filby," said Wilkinson, "I have not come all this way to talk about your brother. My being here is nothing to do with him. I have an important proposition—"

"Fergus came to no good, I have no doubt."

"He went to prison for fraud, if you must know. I don't know what has happened to him since."

"I see. That is very much what I would have expected. And now your proposition, Mr. Wilkinson?"

"I should like to buy Cara."

"It is not for sale."

"Alternatively," went on Mr. Wilkinson as if he had not spoken, "to acquire the mineral rights for a term of years. The group I represent would pay very handsomely for the privilege."

"Mineral rights? Are you crazy?"

"Not at all. A month ago a friend of mine and a party from a yacht came on shore at a sandy bay on the west of the island for a picnic."

"I did not see them, or I'd have turned them off quick enough."

"My friend is a geologist. He found in the dunes above the bay a deposit of silicate sand."

"And what is that?"

"It is the type of sand used in glass manufacture—common in some parts of the world, very rare in Britain, consequently very valuable."

Filby's eyes were glittering.

"Where is this deposit exactly?"

Wilkinson took from his case a large-scale map of the island and spread it out upon the table. He pointed to the pencil marks which indicated the boundaries of the deposit, and Filby spanned the distance with finger and thumb. He chuckled softly.

"Fergus had to go to London to seek his fortune," he said. "And it was waiting on Cara all the time. That is what you might call ironical, is it not, sir?"

When Wilkinson's plane touched down at Glasgow airport it was met by two specially selected police officers. Quietly and unobtrusively they took Wilkinson in tow, and escorted him to a car. At headquarters his brief-case was taken from him and its contents examined by experts. While this was going on, two very senior officers—one Scottish and one from Scotland Yard—were questioning him closely.

Presently a plain-clothes man joined them. He had with him Wilkinson's map of Cara.

"This has Fergus Farnby's prints on it all right," he said. "I'm much obliged, sir. It's a good clear set."

"It ought to be," Wilkinson observed. "That table was greasy enough in all conscience."

"So he did get to Cara in Rory's boat after all," said the man from Scotland Yard. "He was one jump ahead of us all the way. What happened then, do you think?"

"There wasn't room on the island for two of them," said his Glasgow colleague. "Jamie Filby tried to turn his brother away,

I have no doubt. The brother stayed and Jamie—disappeared. It's a grim thought."

"I had a quick look over the island before I left," said Wilkinson, "and there is a patch of soft ground near the house that might repay attention. Or possibly something will turn up when we start exploiting the silicate sand."

"You mean to go on with that, if you can?"

"Bless you, yes! We've been after the Cara concession for years. Filby would never so much as talk to anyone we sent to discuss the matter. This man was interested as soon as I started to talk business. I didn't need fingerprints to tell me he was your man."

The Alibi Man

Bill Knox

Bill Knox—as William Knox (1928–99) was always known—
was a Glaswegian who became a familiar face on Scottish
television as a result of presenting the long-running series
Crimedesk. He followed his father, who was sports editor on
the *Sunday Post*, into journalism, joining the *Glasgow Evening
News*. His specialities were crime and motoring. When he
interviewed the bestselling thriller writer Alastair MacLean,
he was encouraged to try his own hand at crime fiction. Once
his career as a novelist was launched, he proved prolific, and
his series about the cop duo Thane and Moss was especially
popular. As well as writing under his own name, he used the
pseudonyms Webb Carrick, Robert MacLeod, Noah Webster,
and Michael Kirk. His books were widely translated, and in
1986 he was given the Police Review award by the Crime
Writers' Association.

I never met Bill Knox, but I feel an affinity with him

as a result of having been commissioned to finish his final book in the Thane and Moss series, *The Lazarus Widow*, which begins with a body being retrieved from the River Clyde. That strange yet interesting experience enhanced my enthusiasm for his crisp, unfussy style of storytelling. This story first appeared in *Edgar Wallace Mystery Magazine* in February 1965.

———

MANNY DAVIS WINCED AND GAVE A GROAN AS THE white light of the torch beam lanced into his eyes. Daybreak or dusk, time was meaningless inside his prison, a half-existence measured only by the sparse meals which the torch beam heralded.

Booted feet grated on the stone floor of the cellar, and he shrank back against the damp brick of the wall, waiting. He heard a mild curse in the voice he'd come to anticipate—the only voice he'd heard since he'd first been brought to the place, the only human sound he'd heard since the last meal.

He had almost stopped caring. The cellar's perpetual chill had numbed his mind and frozen his senses. But why was it happening to him—why, in this way?

"Don't move." The gruff voice rapped its usual order and he obeyed. A rough hand clamped briefly to his forehead for a moment. "Got to make sure you stay healthy. Right—" the hand was withdrawn and he looked up, then away again as the white light seared his eyes.

"Now eat." He heard a tin mug laid down beside him, fumbled for it, felt the shock of the warm, friendly heat within, and swallowed down the thick, scalding soup. "And these—" a thick packet of sandwiches was thrust into his lap. The shape behind the light moved back.

The heavy footsteps retreated, the cellar door-hinge creaked, and there was a clatter as it was closed and locked. The last glow of the torch had gone. He was alone again. He undid the package carefully and took out the first sandwich. He tasted it delicately—food was important, food was life and interest rolled into one.

The sandwich was ham, heavily flavoured with mustard. The taste helped him forget the darkness for a moment then just as suddenly emphasised it. He began to quiver but no longer wept. That time had passed.

The two men who left the old grey-stone house closed and locked the door behind them, and strolled off together along the darkened street. A jukebox blared from a brightly lit basement coffee bar; a group of schoolgirls went chattering past them, going home to bed after a first house visit to the local cinema.

The shorter of the two men chuckled as the youngsters turned a corner and disappeared. "Like magpies, eh? Kids— their tongues are never still."

His companion, slim, serious-faced in the glow as they neared another street lamp, gave a curt nod. Children reminded him too much of the past—and the past was not pleasant.

They walked on, and a car approached, travelling slowly. It pulled into the kerb and one of its two occupants reached back and opened the nearside rear door. They climbed in, closed the door, and the car drew away again.

"How is he?" The driver glanced back for an instant.

"All right." The slim man answered for them both. "That cellar wasn't built for comfort."

"Can't have him complaining, Andrew." The driver gave a grim chuckle. "Anyway, another twenty-four hours and it'll be over. At least you don't have to go back to that flea-pit hotel tonight." He turned the car into the next street, driving aimlessly. There were few safer places to hold a meeting than in a moving car—it was strange the tricks you learned when you needed them.

The man in the front passenger seat cleared his throat and spoke for the first time. "There are some last details to be taken care of—shall we begin?"

The others nodded. Andrew Gunn took out a cigarette and lit it. Only twenty-four hours now and it would be finished...

"Andrew—"

He jerked his mind to the present and made an apologetic grunt.

The man in front sighed. "Look, how much of what I've said have you been hearing?"

"Sorry." He made a grimace. "What was that last point?"

"I asked if you had everything you needed."

He nodded. "Everything. Don't worry about me."

In the outside world it was an hour before dawn. In the solid darkness of the cellar, Manny Davis stirred uneasily in his shallow sleep. The door lock clicked and hinges creaked.

The torch beam had found and pinned him before he rewoke to the usual regular sequence of nightmare reality. The vague figure approached him. By the wet feel of the sleeve which brushed against his face and the cold touch of the hand on his forehead, he guessed it must be raining outside. There was warm milk in the cup this time. He drank it greedily. As the sandwiches were dropped in his lap, he screwed his eyes in one more bid to beat the torchlight, to see even the rough outline of the face so close to his.

"Only a few more hours," said the same gruff voice.

The shape receded. He looked up at the beam, ignoring the watering pain it brought to his eyes. The vague mixture of contempt and something close to pity there had been in the words started his lips moving and he began a trembling, incoherent cursing.

The hinges creaked, the lock clicked and the darkness returned. He gave up, and felt for the sandwiches. They'd slipped from his lap, and it took a few moments of fumbling panic before he found them on the stone floor.

If he was right, he'd been in that cellar for ten days... though that was guesswork, backed up only by the patchy beard which had sprouted on his chin and the number of visits which his gaoler had made.

Only a few more hours. He took a deep breath of hope.

It had been a Friday when it had begun—and he could remember every detail of it. He'd had a few drinks that evening, then had started back to his bachelor flat. He'd put his key in the lock, he'd stepped inside, and then there'd been that blow on the head.

They must have drugged him after that. They—because

he knew there were at least two of them. When he came round, he'd been in the dark cellar. His clothes had been changed. Instead of the neat fawn lightweight suit he'd been wearing, he was now dressed in an old wool sweater and thick, coarse trousers. No ropes, no gag restrained him. He'd explored the cellar by touch and found it was just four brick walls, a stone floor, and a stone ceiling—swept absolutely bare except for two blankets as his bed.

When they came the first time, behind that torch beam, he'd tried to rush them. They'd simply knocked him down and gone away, leaving the food beside him.

He'd tried shouting, but the noise only beat back against his ears. At last the torch beam had come, shining on his face for a moment then clicking out. He'd been left alone for a long time after that.

No violence, no threats—just the simple, unspoken lesson that to shout and rage meant no food or water. When at last the food did come, the man with the torch had seemed vaguely amused at his acceptance.

Now he felt tired again, very tired. His eyes were closing against his will, his limbs felt heavy, heavier… He thought of the milk and realised he'd been drugged. By then he was halfway to oblivion and nothing more than a twinge of anger managed to register before he slumped down.

A lorry drove down the street with a rattle of cased milk-bottles as Andrew Gunn left the house and closed the door behind him. He walked briskly through the faint drizzle of rain. A distant church clock chimed six a.m.

The car, a sturdy but perfectly commonplace black saloon, was standing where they'd arranged. He unlocked the door, got in, and decided it was still dark enough to need sidelights. He switched them on, started the engine, then drove off, handling the car deftly and carefully.

Two and a half hours later the black saloon purred into the morning rush-hour traffic of the city. It had covered nearly eighty miles to get there.

A point-duty policeman stopped the traffic ahead; Gunn used the wait to glance up at the sky. Though the rain had stopped, the clouds were still thick—not that the weather entered into calculations. As the traffic moved again, he flicked the trafficator lever and joined the filter lane of cars drawing off to the left.

A few minutes more and he reached his goal, the dark bulk of an old office block. Across the street a sergeant and two police constables strode past, talking busily. The sight brought a quick, dry smile to his lips. He slowed the car and stopped it at the pavement's edge.

He left the vehicle and strolled into the office block, nodding casually to the liftman but using the stairs. He went up two flights, stopped outside a frosted glass office door. He tried it, found it was locked, and knocked quietly. There was no reply. Satisfied, he took a small, flat package from his pocket and pushed it through the letterbox. It fitted easily— that detail had been carefully attended to, like all the others.

He left the building as unostentatiously as he'd entered, walked back to the car, and drove off. A little later he was having breakfast at a cafe half a mile away, eating with the leisurely enjoyment of a man with time to spare. He waited an hour then drove back, parked the car a few streets away from the office block, and walked the rest of the distance.

Outside the building a chattering, curiosity-drawn crowd was gathered round an ambulance and two police cars. He looked up, and saw the broken raw-edged glass which was all that remained of a blast-smashed window two floors above. The crowd parted as two ambulance men came out of the block, carrying a stretcher with a blanket-covered burden. They loaded it into their vehicle and a grim-faced constable climbed aboard before the doors were closed.

Andrew Gunn turned and walked away. At ten-forty he entered a call-box and dialled a local number. He let it ring for a moment then pressed the receiver rest and broke the connection. He released the rest, dialled the same number again, let it ring once more, then hung up.

Five minutes later he was driving out of the city. It had never been his home and he didn't expect to be back.

When Manny Davis came round he knew he was lying on the metal floor of a moving vehicle. There was a faint scent of exhaust fumes in his nostrils and the low, throbbing vibration of the engine pulsed against his body. There was something tight tied against his eyes. He groaned, pulled himself into a sitting position, and groped to remove the bandage.

"Take it off," invited a voice. "But when you do, stay right where you are."

He did, his eyes gradually focussing in the dull gloom of

the vehicle's interior. It seemed a medium-sized van and the partition to the driver's cab was closed. But, sitting cross-legged on the floor opposite him, were two men. Each had a nylon stocking mask over his face. One held an automatic, pointed casually in his direction.

"What's going on?" Davis licked his lips. There was no reply. Gradually, he became aware of other things. He was back in his fawn lightweight suit. He was wearing a clean shirt—one of his own shirts. Even his shoes had been polished. He felt clean again. He put a hand up to his face and found the stubble of beard had gone.

"Just as you were seven days ago." There was grim amusement in the voice of the man with the gun.

"Seven—?"

"You thought it was longer, eh?" The man gave a grunt. "It wasn't long enough by half."

"Who are you?" demanded Davis, with a sudden spurt of courage. "Look, once I get out of this I'm going straight to the cops. You'll find out you can't kidnap someone like this—you'll find out all right."

"The police?" The second masked man shook his head. "As of now, they're your worry, not ours." A harsher note came into his voice. "Manny Davis, I've been given the task of telling you why you're here, and what faces you."

"And I've had just enough—" Davis began scrabbling to his feet in the lurching van, then subsided as the automatic swung to point steadily at him.

"Stay still and be quiet," said the man behind it.

"Just listen, Davis," advised his companion. "A little over a year ago a man named Henry Prinner was arrested by the police on a charge of murder. He set fire to a bookmaker's office. The fire spread, and five perfectly innocent people in a rented flat above died in their sleep. Five people, Davis—a man, his wife, and their three children."

Davis stared at the masked man in a sudden terror of understanding. "I wasn't involved in it—and anyway, Prinner wasn't the man. They took him in, but…but they let him go again."

"They let him go," growled the man with the gun. "They let him go because they had a weak case and he produced an alibi out of the blue. You were the alibi man, Davis."

"I only told the truth," protested Davis vigorously. "Prinner was with me—we played poker together that night until two o'clock."

"That's what you claimed," agreed the second man. "That was part of the bargain—that you'd give Prinner an alibi if he needed one. Because you employed him to start that fire, to get even with a bookie who wouldn't pay out on a bet." He pointed a sudden forefinger. "You supplied the alibi. And a green young lawyer who believed you did some smart manoeuvring which made them set Prinner free."

"You're crazy." Davis beat the floor of the van with one fist. "I didn't do anything. Look, if there had been this bet, wouldn't the bookie have talked? Wouldn't the police have traced it back?"

"Men who put a heavy bet on a fixed race don't use their own name on the ledger. We know what happened, Davis— even though it took time to find out, even though we couldn't prove it the way a court would require, even though you cleared out of the city, and tried to disappear."

He stared at them, puzzling. Who were these men? Relatives? No, that was out. The family had left no kin.

He steadied his voice. "I didn't do anything."

The man opposite shrugged. "Well, hear the rest. You've been out of circulation for a week—and some strange things have happened in this city in those seven days. Each time there's been a man who looks pretty like you around, a man using your name and clothes. There's been a hotel room occupied by you. The police will find a tumbler with your fingerprints, some of your clothing, other things lying around it. They'll check—because nobody slept in that room last night and there's an unpaid bill and a false address.

"They're already looking for you, Davis. Because somebody put a parcel bomb through Prinner's letterbox this morning—somebody who knew enough about his habits to know he worked in a one-room office all alone, and never got there before ten o'clock. There's a liftman who'll remember someone dressed like you.

"The police have already had an anonymous tip that you'd quarrelled with Prinner. If there are any paper fragments left from that bomb's wrapper, they'll find your prints on them. And the police will wonder why you wanted to kill the man you once saved. They'll wonder if the reason could be that he was blackmailing you in some way. They'll trace where you've been living, and be interested in the scraps of cut tin and electric wiring they find lying around. They'll put two and two together."

"You mean...you've framed me!" Davis swallowed hard, then forced a laugh. "Suppose I go straight to the cops, and tell them how you had me in that cellar?"

"Will they believe you?" he was asked. "Would you believe that kind of a story? Could you take them to the cellar? It's a very long way from here, Davis." The stranger rose and knocked lightly on the driver's partition. The van's engine-note changed and gradually slowed.

"We're going to drop you off here," said the masked man, quietly. "Take my advice. If you see a policeman, start running. Not that you'll get far—but this time you're going to need something more than a too-clever lawyer."

The van stopped, the rear door opened, and Davis found himself pushed forward by the gun muzzle.

"Who the hell are you?" he asked bitterly.

"Just people—people who liked that family," said one of the men.

A sudden shove sent Davis toppling out. He fell on the roadway, heard the van door slam shut. Even as he dragged himself up, the vehicle was drawing away.

He cursed and stared after it through the late dusk. It was a plain dark van, like thousands of others. The registration plates were dull, muddy, and unreadable.

Manny Davis looked around him. He was in a street near the docks, with tall, gaunt buildings on either side. There was no one in sight. He patted his jacket, made sure he still had his wallet, and gnawed his lip for a moment.

First of all he needed a drink. There would be somewhere near; there always was, down by the docks. Then he'd contact that young lawyer who'd swallowed the last story and got Prinner off the hook. Maybe he'd swallow this one too. That lawyer—he frowned, trying to remember his name. It had been common enough... it was almost on the tip of his tongue.

A drink might help him remember. He started walking, still trying to recall the lawyer's identity. Then, suddenly, he stopped. There was a car coming towards him, a car with a blue light flashing on its roof. He saw the peaked caps of the occupants and panic began to grow.

The car stopped and its police crew climbed out. Manny Davis screamed once at them—and began running.

They were overhauling him fast when he remembered. Gunn…that had been the lawyer's name. Andrew Gunn.

The Fishermen

Michael Innes

John Innes Mackintosh Stewart (1906–94), who published detective fiction under the name Michael Innes, was born in Edinburgh, where his father was for several years Director of Education. In his memoir *Myself and Michael Innes* (1987), he said that: "My mother, who was nothing if not romantic, would have been happy to believe me descended from that Simon Fraser, Lord Lovat, who was the last man to be beheaded on Tower Hill for high treason. I possess to this day, as a consequence of the characteristic Scottish concern with 'connections,' whether real or imagined, a formidable volume…which records verbatim the entire proceedings at the impeachment of Simon Fraser in Westminster Hall." He was educated at Edinburgh Academy and later at Oxford, where he would establish a distinct reputation as an academic.

Having enjoyed success with cerebral whodunits featuring the Scotland Yard man John Appleby, Innes made what he called a "detour into thrillers." He acknowledged the influence of his countrymen Robert Louis Stevenson and John Buchan: "I have been told that *Lament for a Maker* smells strongly of *The Master of Ballantrae*." As for *The Secret Vanguard* (1940): "the actual hunting of the girl, Sheila Grant, over the Scottish moor, is…far and away, I judge, the most emphatic writing I have anywhere achieved." In *The Man from the Sea* (1955): "The young man upon whom the story opens, as he lies naked upon a Scottish beach at night…is prone to brooding darkly on the difference between disgrace and dishonour." This story was first published as "Death of a Fisherman" in *Argosy* in March 1970, then as "Comedy of Discomfiture" in its outing for *Ellery Queen Mystery Magazine* in 1971 before appearing in the collection *The Appleby File* (1975) under the title reprinted here.

———

IN SCOTLAND TROUT-FISHING, ALMOST AS MUCH AS deer-stalking and grouse-shooting, is an amusement for wealthy men. Appleby was not particularly wealthy. From a modest station he had risen to be London's Commissioner of Metropolitan Police—a mouthful which his children, accurately enough, had turned into better and briefer English as Top Cop.

Top Cop's job turning out, predictably, to be more purely administrative than was at all enlivening, Appleby had retired from it earlier than need be, and now lived as an unassuming country gentleman on a small estate in the south of England which was the property of his wife. This, very happily, had proved not incompatible with getting into odd situations from time to time. Sir John Appleby liked odd situations. As a country gentleman he also, of course, liked fishing.

So he had accepted Vivarini's invitation to bring a rod to Dunwinnie, although he didn't really know the celebrated playwright particularly well. Now here he was, cheek by jowl with four other piscatory enthusiasts in what had once been a crofter's cottage. Crofters, and all such humbly independent tillers of the soil, had almost vanished from this part of the Scottish Highlands. Whether in small patches or in large, the region had been turned into holiday terrain for those rich men.

Appleby didn't brood on this. At least the hunting-boxes and shooting-lodges were (like everything else) thin on the ground. From the cottage one saw only the river—a brawling flood interspersed with still-seeming pools, brown from the peat and with trout enough—with an abandoned lambing-hut on its farther bank and then the moorland that stretched away to the remote line of the Grampians. Dr. Johnson, Appleby remembered, had once surveyed this scene and disliked it. *A wide extent of hopeless sterility,* he had written down. *Quickened only with one sullen power of useless vegetation.* That had been the heather.

There was a brushing sound in the heather now. Appleby looked up from his task of gutting fish for supper, and saw that his host was returning. Vivarini had been the last to leave the water. He seemed to be a keen angler. In his stained waders, Balmoral bonnet festooned with dry-flies, and with his respectably battered old creel, he certainly looked the part. But perhaps the playwright had enough of the actor in him for that. Snobbery and expensive rural diversions are inextricably tied up together in Britain, and in pursuit of some elusive social status men will go fox-hunting who in their hearts are terrified at the sight of a horse. Perhaps Vivarini with his costly stretch of trout-stream was a little like that.

Very rightly, Appleby felt mean at harbouring this thought, particularly as Vivarini looked so far from well. Even in the twilight now falling like an elfin gossamer over these haunted lands one could distinguish that about the man. Perhaps it was simply that he was under some sort of nervous strain. Appleby knew nothing about his London way of life, but there could well be things he wanted to get away from. A set-up like this at Dunwinnie—a small all-male society gathered for a secluded holiday on a bachelor basis—might well have been planned as wholesome relief by a man rather too much involved in something altogether different.

"Cloud coming up," Vivarini said, "and that breeze from the west stiffening. Makes casting tricky. I decided to stay with Black Gnat, by the way." He indicated the fly still on the end of his line. "A mistake, probably. Not sultry enough, eh?"

Clifford Childrey, ensconced with a three-day-old copy of the *Scotsman* on a bench beside the cottage door, glanced up—not at Vivarini but at Appleby—and then resumed his reading. He was Vivarini's publisher. A large and ruddy out-door man, he had no need whatever to look a part.

"You deserve a drink, Vivarini," Appleby said.

"Not so much as you do, sweating away as cook. I'll see to it. Sherry, I suppose? And you, Cliff?"

"Sherry." Childrey momentarily lowered his newspaper.

"Don't know about the other two. They've gone downstream to bathe."

"Right. I do like this American make." Vivarini had leant his rod against the cottage's low thatched roof. "No more than five ounces to the six feet. Flog the water all day with it."

"Umph." This response came from behind the *Scotsman*, which had been raised again. But it was tossed to the ground when Vivarini had entered the cottage. "No need to be supercilious," Childrey said.

"I've been nothing of the kind." Appleby was amused at the charge. "And if 'umph' isn't supercilious, I don't know what is."

"Well, well—Freddie Vivarini and I have been chums for a long time." Childrey chuckled comfortably. "A damned queer lot writers are, Appleby. I've spent my life trying to do business with them. Novelists are the worst, of course, but dramatists run them close. Always getting things up and trying out roles. What they call *personas*, I suppose. Thingamies, really. Chimeras."

"You mean chameleons."

"That's right. No reliable personal identity. Shelley said something about it. Right up his own street."

"Keats. You think our host is playing at being a sportsman?"

"Oh, at that and lots of other things. What he's run on all his life has been folding up on him. Unsuccessful literary man."

"Unsuccessful?"

"Of course he's made a fortune. But that's what he's taken to calling himself. You're meant to regard it ironically. Uneasy joke, all the same." Childrey checked himself and got to his feet, perhaps aware of talking too casually about his host. "I'll start that grill for you," he said. "I see you'll need it soon."

As if in one of Vivarini's own neat plays, Childrey's exit-line brought the subject of his late remarks promptly on-stage again. Vivarini was bearing glasses and a bottle which, even in the gloaming, could be seen as lightly frosted. The cottage was not wholly comfortless. Warmth was laid on for chilly evenings, and there was hot water and a refrigerator and a compendious affair for cooking any way you liked, all served by a few cylinders of butane trundled across the moor on a vehicle like a young tank. Not that their actual culinary regime wasn't simple enough. Elderly Englishmen of the sort gathered at Dunwinnie rather enjoy pretending to be public-schoolboys still, toasting crumpets or bloaters before a study fire. Of course there are limits, and when it is a matter of a glass of dry sherry or opening a bottle of hock, they don't expect the stuff to reach their palate other than at the temperature it should. Nor do they care to couch in straw. Appleby was just reflecting that the cottage's bunks had certainly come from an expensive shop when he became aware that his host, uncorked bottle in hand, was laughing cheerfully.

"I heard the old ruffian," Vivarini said. "Trying out roles, indeed! Well, what if I am?"

"What, indeed. I myself shall remain grateful to you. This is a delightful spot."

"My dear Appleby, how nice of you to say so. But I do enjoy fishing, as a matter of fact. And—do you know?—as far as renting the cottage and this stretch of river goes, it was actually one of these chaps who egged me on. Positively ran me into it! But I won't say which." Vivarini was laughing again—although with the effect, Appleby thought, of a man not wholly at ease. "No names, no pack-drill. Ah, here come Mervyn and Ralph."

Appleby couldn't afterwards remember—not even with a dead body to prompt him—who at the supper table had introduced the topic of crime. Perhaps it had been Ralph Halberd, since Halberd was one of that not inconsiderable number of millionaires to have suffered the theft of some enormously valuable pictures. This might have given Halberd an interest at least in burglars, although his line (outside owning shipping lines and luxury hotels) was a large if capricious patronage of artists expressing themselves in mediums more harmless than thermal lances and gelignite. Perhaps it had been Mervyn Gryde. Gryde wrote theatrical notices for newspapers (being dignified with the style of dramatic critic as a result), and the kind of plays he seemed chiefly to favour were, to Appleby's mind, so full of violence and depravity that crime must be supposed his natural element. Or it might have been Vivarini himself. Certainly it had been he who, exercising a host's authority, had insisted upon Appleby's recounting his own part in certain criminal *causes célèbres*. But it had been left to Childrey, towards the end of the evening, to insist with a certain flamboyance on toasting the retired Metropolitan Commissioner as the finest detective intelligence in Britain. The hock, Appleby thought, was a great deal too good for the toast; it had in fact been Halberd's contribution to the housekeeping and was quite superb. But he acknowledged the compliment in due form, and not long afterwards the company decided to go to bed.

Rather to his surprise, Appleby found himself obscurely relieved that the day was over. Everyone had been amiable enough. But had something been stirring beneath the talk, the relaxed gestures, the small companionable-seeming silences? As he dropped to sleep he found himself thinking of the deep still pools into which the Dunwinnie tumbled here and there on its hurrying and sparkling scramble towards the sea. Beneath those calm surfaces, whose only movement seemed to be the lovely concentric ripples from a rising trout, a strong current flowed.

He had a nightmare, a thing unusual with him. Perhaps it was occasioned by one of the yarns he had been inveigled into telling at the supper table of his early and sometimes perilous days in the C.I.D. In his dream he had been pursuing gunmen down dark narrow corridors—and suddenly it had been the gunmen who were pursuing him. They caught him and tied him up. And then the chief gunman had advanced upon him with a long whip and cracked it within an inch of his face. This was so unpleasant that Appleby, in his nightmare, told himself that here was a nightmare from which he had better wake up. So he woke up—not much perturbed, but taking thought, as one does, to remain awake until the same disagreeable situation was unlikely to be waiting for him.

The wind had risen and its murmur had joined the river's murmur, but inside the cottage there wasn't a sound. The single-storey building had been remodelled for its present purpose, and now consisted, like an ill-proportioned sandwich, of a large living-room in the middle, with a very small bedroom at each end. The bedrooms contained little more than two bunks set one above the other. Childrey and Halberd shared one of these cabin-like places, and Appleby and Vivarini had the other. Gryde slept on a camp-bed in the living-room. These dispositions had been arrived at, whimsically, by drawing lots.

Appleby turned over cautiously, so as not to disturb Vivarini underneath him. Vivarini didn't stir. And Appleby suddenly knew he wasn't there. It was a simple matter of highly developed auditory alertness. Nobody was breathing, however lightly, in the bunk below.

The discovery ought not to have been worth a thought. A wakeful Vivarini might have elected for a breath of moorland air. Or he might have been prompted to repair to the modest structure, some twenty yards from the cottage, known as the jakes. Despite these reflections, Appleby slipped quietly down from his bunk.

It was dark, then suddenly not dark, then dark again. But nobody had flashed a light. Outside, the sky must be a huddle of moving cloud, with a moon near the full sometimes breaking through. Vivarini's bunk was indeed unoccupied. Appleby picked up a torch and went into the living-room. Gryde seemed sound asleep—a little dark man, Appleby passingly told himself, coiled up like a snake. The door of the farther bedroom was closed, but the door giving direct on the moor was open. Appleby stepped outside, switching off the torch as he did so. He now knew why he was behaving in this way—like an alarmed nursemaid, he thought. It was because of what had happened in his dream.

He glanced up at the clouds, and in the same moment

the moon again came serenely through. The Dunwinnie rose into visibility before him, like a sudden outpouring of hoarded silver on dark cloth. On the other bank the lambing-hut with its squat square chimney suggested some small humped creature with head warily erect. And something was moving there. Momentarily Appleby saw this as a human figure slipping out of the door. Then he saw that it was only the door itself, swinging gently on its primitive wooden pivot. But no sound came from across the softly chattering flood; no sound that could have transformed itself into another sound in Appleby's dream.

There were stepping-stones here, practicable enough for an active man. But they faded into darkness as Appleby looked; the moon had disappeared again. He had to switch on the torch or risk a ducking. He risked the ducking, although he could scarcely have told himself why he disliked the idea of being seen. When he reached the hut he reconnoitred the ground before it with a brief flicker close to the earth. He felt for the door and pushed it fully open; it had been firmly shut, he remembered, and with an old thirl-pin through the latch, the evening before. Now he was looking into deep darkness indeed. The hut was no more than a square stone box with a slate roof; it had a fireplace more for the needs of the ewes and lambs than their shepherd; and in one wall—he couldn't rec-ollect which—there was a window which had been boarded up. Treading softly, he moved through the door and listened.

No sound. No glimmer of light. Nothing to alert a single sense—unless it was a faint smell of old straw, the ghost of a faint smell of carbolic, of tar. Then suddenly, and straight in front of him at floor level, there was an illusive suggestion of light. All but imperceptibly, the small glow grew; it was as if a stage electrician were operating a rheostat with infinite care. It grew to an oblong, with darkness as its frame. And now within the frame there was a picture, there was a portrait. It was the portrait of Vivarini—but something had happened to his forehead. It was Vivarini himself.

Appleby was on his knees, his ear to the man's chest, his fingers exploring through a sports-coat, a pyjama-jacket. His face close to the still face, he flashed his torch into unclosing eyes, saw uncontracting pupils. He turned his head, gazed upwards, and was looking at a square of dimly luminous cloud. Nothing more than the moon's reflected light filtering down the chimney had produced that moment of hideous melodrama. Vivarini himself at his typewriter, or pacing his study while dictating to his secretary, couldn't have done better. It was backwards into the rude fireplace that he had crashed, a bullet in his brain. And hence the crack of that ugly whip in the other dimension of dream.

Twenty minutes passed before Appleby re-entered the cottage. Arrived there, he didn't waste time. He gave Gryde a rough shake and rapped smartly on the closed bedroom door. Within seconds his three fellow-guests were around him, huddled in dressing-gowns, dazed and blinking.

"Vivarini is dead," he said quietly. "In the lambing-hut. Shot through the head."

"My God—so he meant it!" This exclamation was Ralph Halberd's, and it was followed by a small silence.

"One of us," Appleby went on, apparently unheeding,

"must get down to Balloch, and telephone for a doctor and the police. But something a shade awkward comes first."

"Awkward?" It was Mervyn Gryde who repeated the word, and his voice had turned sharp.

"Well yes. Let me explain. Or, rather, let me take up what Halberd has just said." Appleby turned to the millionaire. "'*My God—so he meant it!*' Just what made you say that?"

"Because he told me. He confided in me. It was a fearful shock." In the cold light of a hissing gas-lamp, Halberd, who normally carried around with him an air as of imposing boardrooms, looked uncertain and perplexed. "On Tuesday—the day we arrived. It was because I happened to see him unpack this thing, and shove it under his shirts in that drawer over there. A pistol. It looked almost like a toy."

"Vivarini said he was going to kill himself with it?"

"Not that, exactly. Only that he had thoughts of it, and couldn't bring himself not to carry the weapon round with him."

"Did he give any reason?"

"No. It seemed to be implied that he was feeling discouraged. His plays—all those Comedies of Discomfiture, as he called them—are a bit outmoded, wouldn't you say?"

"Perhaps so. But, Halberd, did you take any steps? Even mention this to any of the rest of us?"

"I wish to God I had. But I thought he was putting on a turn." The patron's indulgent scorn for the artist sounded for a moment in Halberd's tones. "That sort of fellow is always dramatising himself. And people don't often kill themselves just because they're feeling discouraged."

"That's certainly true. There are psychologists who

maintain that suicide never happens except on top of a clin-
ically recognisable depressive state. An exaggeration, perhaps,
but no more than that. But here's my point. Whatever Vivarini
said to you, Halberd, he can't have made away with himself.
I found no weapon in that hut."

There was a long silence in the cottage.

"That's just according to one witness—yourself—who
was the first man on the scene." Gryde's voice was sharper
still. And with a curiously reptilian effect, his tongue flickered
out over dry lips.

"Exactly. You take my point." Appleby smiled grimly.
"Anybody can tell lies. But let's see if there's a revolver under
those shirts now."

Watched by the others, Appleby made a brief rummage.
No weapon was revealed.

"I may have killed him," Halberd said slowly. "And made
up a stupid story about suicide, which the facts disprove."

"Certainly you may." Appleby might have been discussing
a hand at bridge. "But you're not going to be the only suspect."

"Obviously not." Childrey spoke for the first time. The
least agitated of Appleby's companions, he might have been
a rosy infant doubly-flushed from sleep. "Nor are we—the
four of us here—characters in a sealed-room mystery. Why
the lambing-hut? Why did Vivarini go over there secretly
in the night? To meet somebody unknown to us, one may
suppose—and somebody who turned out not to care for him."

"It might still have been one of ourselves," Appleby said.
"But may I come back to the business of going for help? I'm
thinking of the weapon. If one of us killed Vivarini, he may
then have had enough time to get quite a distance across the

moor and back for the purpose of hiding the gun where no search will ever find it. On the other hand, one of us may have it on his person, or in a suitcase, at this moment. Whichever of us goes for help must certainly be searched first. Or perhaps all of us. Do you agree? Good. I'll search each of you in turn—over there in that bedroom—and then one of you can search me."

"I'll come first," Childrey said easily. "But behind that closed door. Less shaming, eh?"

Appleby's was a very rapid frisking. "By the way," he asked at the end of it, "have you any notion how this fishing-party originated? You didn't by any chance suggest it to Vivarini, or in any way put him up to it?"

"Lord, no! Came as a complete surprise to me. We'd been on bad terms, as a matter of fact."

"I'm sorry to hear it. Send in Halberd."

Five minutes later, they were all in the living-room again. In another ten, the whole place had been searched.

"No gun," Appleby said. "But another lie—or the appearance of it. Vivarini told me one of you had egged him on to organise this little fishing-party. But each of you denies it."

"All according to you," Gryde said.

"Yes, indeed. I'm grateful to you for so steadily keeping me in mind. And now, who goes to telephone? It's at least five miles. I suggest we draw lots."

"No. I'm going to go." It was Childrey who spoke. "Trekking over the moors in darkness is my sort of thing. I'll just get into a jacket and trousers."

"The cunning criminal makes good his escape," Gryde said. "But it's all one to me." He turned to Appleby. "While

Cliff is louping over the heather—I believe that's the correct Scots word—I suggest we open a bottle of whisky and have a nice friendly chat."

It didn't prove all that friendly. Childrey's, it struck Appleby, had been the genuinely genial presence in the fishing-party; now, when he had gone off with long strides through a darkness with which the moon had ceased to struggle, the atmosphere in the cottage deteriorated sharply.

"Odd that Vivarini should have made *you* that confidence, Ralph." Gryde said this after the whisky bottle had clinked for a second time against his glass. "And odd that he asked you here. Wanted to make it up with you, I suppose. Tycoons make ugly enemies."

"What the devil do you mean?" Halberd had sat bolt upright.

"And it's going to be awkward for that girl. He'd miscalculated, hadn't he? Thought she was just one of your notorious harem, no doubt, and that you wouldn't give a damn. Actually, you were ludicrously in love with her. Not unusual, once a man has reached the age of senile infatuation. Everybody was talking about it, you know. And I'm surprised you came."

"One might be surprised that cheerful idiot Childrey came." Halberd had controlled himself with an effort in face of Gryde's sudden and astonishing assault. "He told me that *he* had been on poor terms with Freddie. And, for that matter, what about yourself, Mervyn? I believe—"

"I don't filch other men's trollops."

"You certainly don't. What you'd filch—"

"One moment." Appleby had set down his glass—and he plainly didn't mean to take it up again. "If we're to have this sort of thing—and experience tells me it may be inevitable—it had better be with *some* scrap of decency. No venom."

"Venom is Mervyn Gryde's middle name." Halberd reached for the bottle, but glanced at Appleby and thought better of it. "Read the stuff he writes about any play in which the *dramatis personae* aren't a bunch of sewer rats. Read some of the things he's recently said about Freddie. He had his knife in Freddie. You'd suppose some hideous private grudge." Halberd turned directly to the dramatic critic. "How you can have had the forehead to accept an invitation from the poor devil beats me, Snaky Merv. That's what they called him at Cambridge long ago, you know." This had the character of an aside to Appleby. "Snaky Mervyn Gryde."

"I'm afraid," Appleby said drily, "that I can't contribute much to these amiable exchanges. I don't know a great deal about our late host. But of course—as you, Gryde, will be quick to point out—you have only my word for it. What I do see is that this party is revealing itself as having been organised by way of sinking differences and making friends again. And it hasn't had much luck. One result has been that, in your two selves, it brought here a couple of men with an undefined degree of animus against Vivarini. Perhaps Childrey has been a third. Can either of you explain what Childrey meant by telling me he'd been on bad terms with Vivarini?"

"I can, because Freddie told me. Not that you'll believe me." Gryde, having apparently seen danger in too much whisky, was chain-smoking nervously, so that he was like some small dark devil risen from a nether world amid mephitic vapours. "Childrey had refused to do a collected edition of Freddie's plays. And Freddie had found out it was because he was planning something of the sort for a rival playwright. Freddie was furious."

"I can certainly believe that. But it's scarcely a reason why Childrey should murder Vivarini. Rather the other way about."

"True enough." Gryde laughed shrilly. "But Freddie believed he was on the verge of exposing Childrey in some disreputable sharp practice about it all. He said he could wreck his good name as a publisher, and that he meant to do it."

"And had meantime invited him to this friendly party? It's an uncommonly odd tale."

"I said you wouldn't believe me."

"On the contrary." Appleby's smile was bleak. "I'm inclined to believe that the dead man told you just what you say he did."

"Thank you very much." It wasn't without looking disconcerted that Gryde said this. "And where the deuce do we go from here?"

"Exactly!" Halberd had got up and was restlessly pacing the room to the sound of a flip-flap of bedroom slippers. "Where the deuce—and all the damned to boot."

"We wait for the local police," Appleby said. "No doubt they will clear the matter up quickly enough."

"Stuff and nonsense!" There was sudden violence in Halberd's voice. "And I don't see this as an occasion for superior Scotland Yard irony, Appleby. The rotten business is up to you."

"Well, yes. And I'm sorry about the irony. As a matter of fact, I rather agree with you. And I can't complain. You have both been most communicative—about yourselves, and about each other, and about Childrey. Childrey, too, has made his little spontaneous contribution. I really confront an *embarrass de richesses*, so far as significant information goes. You have laboured as one man, I might say, to give it to me."

"And just what do you mean by that?" Gryde asked sharply.

"Perhaps very little." Appleby yawned unashamedly. "One tends to talk at random in the small hours, wouldn't you say?" He stood up, and walked to the open door of the cottage. "Lights in the lambing-hut," he said. "Childrey has made uncommonly good time. And here he is."

"And here you are." Clifford Childrey echoed Appleby's words as he stood in the doorway. "I was beginning to think I'd dreamed up the whole lot of you. Too fantastic—this affair."

"Is that," Halberd asked, "what the doctor and the local copper are saying?"

"I don't know about the copper. He's an experienced sergeant, settling in to a thorough search, and not saying much meanwhile. As for the sawbones, he's the nice old family-doctor type. Agrees, of course, that the poor devil has been stone dead for at least a couple of hours. Seems to be wondering whether he was dead first, and dragged into the hut second. Suspects something rigged, you might say. Position of the body, and so forth. Appleby, what do you say to that?"

"I certainly felt an element of the theatrical to be present. But other things were present, too."

"Clues, do you mean?"

"Clues? Oh, yes—several. Enough, in fact, to admit of only one explanation of the mystery."

Sir John Appleby glanced from one to another of three dumbfounded faces, as if surprised that his announcement had occasioned any effect at all.

"As it happens," he said, "there is rather a good reason why the local sergeant won't find them—the clues, that's to say. But, as he is going to spend some time in the hunt, I propose to while away a quarter of an hour by telling you about them. Do you agree?"

"You'll have your say, I think, whether we agree or not." Halberd had sat down heavily. "So go on."

"Thank you. But, first, I'd like to ask you something. Does it strike you as at all odd that the three of you—each, apparently, with a rather large dislike of Vivarini—should have accepted his invitation to come here in this particular week?"

"He took a lot of trouble to arrange it," Gryde said. Gryde's voice had gone from high-pitched to husky. "Dates, and so forth."

"And there was this let-bygones-be-bygones slant to it." Perhaps because his night tramp had been exhausting, Childrey might have been described as almost pale.

"Just that," Halberd said. "Wouldn't have been decent to refuse. Rum sort of coincidence, all the same—the lot of us like this."

"Coincidence?" Appleby said. "The word is certainly worth holding on to. Vivarini, incidentally, was holding on to something. Literally so, I mean. I removed that something from his left hand, and have it in my pocket now. I don't intend to be mysterious about it. It was the cord of the silk dressing-gown that Gryde is wearing at this moment."

"That's another of your filthy lies!" Before uttering this, Gryde had clutched grotesquely at his middle. Even as he did so, Appleby had produced the missing object and placed it quietly on the table.

"Making a bit free with the evidence, aren't you?" Childrey asked. He might have spoken out of a benevolent wish to give Gryde a moment in which to recover himself.

"Dear me! Perhaps I am." Appleby offered this piece of innocence with perfect gravity. "As a matter of fact, I've done rather the same thing with what appears to be property—or the remains of property—of your own, my dear Childrey. If photostatic copies of papers with your firm's letter-head are to be regarded as your property, that's to say. You remember the little place we made to boil a kettle, down by the river, the other afternoon? I discovered that a small file of such papers had been burnt there. And no time ago at all; I could still blow a spark out of them. Might they conceivably have been awkward—even compromising—documents that Vivarini had managed to get copies of—fatally for him, as it has turned out?"

"It's true about that collected edition," Childrey said abruptly. "I declined to do it, simply because there wouldn't be anything like an adequate market for it. It is untrue that I behaved improperly. And the notion of my killing Vivarini in order to recover and destroy—"

"But there's something more." Appleby had raised a hand in a civil request for silence. "Just to the side of the door of the lambing-hut there happens to be a patch of caked mud. The first thing I found was a footprint in it. Not of a shoe, but of a bedroom-slipper—with a soft rubber sole which carries a diamond-shaped maker's device on the instep. Yes, Halberd, you are quite right. You are wearing that slipper now."

"Well," Gryde said maliciously, "that's something the sergeant *will* find."

"Actually, I'm afraid not." Appleby looked properly conscience-stricken. "I was rather clumsy, I'm afraid. I trod all over the thing."

"Can we have some explanation of all this madness—including your own totally irresponsible conduct?" It had been after a moment of general stupefaction that Gryde had put this to Appleby.

"Why, certainly. You all had a bit of a motive for killing Vivarini—or at least you can severally think up motives with which to confront one another. And in the case of each of you we now have a clue—a real, damning, mystery-story clue. There is a fairly simple explanation, is there not? One of you killed Vivarini, and deliberately planted two clues leading to the other two of you severally. If just one of these clues was noticed, there would be one suspect; if two, there would be an indication that two of you had been in collusion. But in addition to planting those two clues *deliberately*, the murderer also dropped one, pointing to himself, *inadvertently*. Would you agree"—and Appleby glanced from one to another of his companions—"that we now have an explanation of the observed facts?"

"A singularly rubbishing one," Childrey said robustly.

"Very well, let me try again." Appleby paused—and when he resumed speaking it was almost as if a current of icy air had begun to blow through the cottage. "There *was* collusion, and between all three of you. And so incompetent have you been in your evil courses that you have all three made first-class errors. Childrey failed completely to destroy the papers he had managed to recover, and Gryde and Halberd both left physical traces of their presence in the lambing-hut. Will that do?"

"My dear Appleby, I fear you have a poor opinion of us." Sweat was pouring down Gryde's face, but he managed to utter this with an air of mild mockery. "Should we be *quite* so inept? And there's something you just haven't accounted for: you own damnably odd conduct."

"Do you know, I'd call that right in the target area? Although I'd say it was not so much a matter of my conduct as of my mere presence." With an air of conscious relaxation, Appleby began to fill his pipe. "We were talking about coincidence. Well, the really implausible coincidence was my being here at all. Don't you see? I was *meant* to be here. Vivarini wanted me here—and that although he and I were no more than casual acquaintances. That was the first thing in my head when I found him dead. And it led me straight to the truth."

"The truth!" There was a dark flush on Halberd's face. "You mean to say you know the *truth*, and you've been entertaining us to a lot of damned rubbish notwithstanding?"

"I certainly know the truth."

"May we be favoured"—Gryde hissed this—"with some notion of when you arrived at it?"

"Oh, almost at once. Before I came in to tell you that

Vivarini had been shot. First I *thought* for a few minutes, you know. It's always the advisable thing to do. And then I went to have a look at the gas cylinders. That settled it."

"Vivarini," Appleby said, "didn't like any of you. You'd refused to publish him as a classic, you'd reviewed him waspishly, you'd been in a mess-up with him about a girl. But what he really resented was being treated as outmoded. His so-called Comedy of Discomfiture you all regarded as old hat. Well, he decided to treat you to a whiff of that Comedy all on your own." Appleby paused. "After all," he said—blandly and with apparent inconsequence—"I was his guest, you know. I owed him something. It would have been a shame to knock that comedy too rapidly on the head."

"The man was a devil," Gryde said. "And you're a devil too."

"No, no—Vivarini wasn't really an evil man. He had me down so that there would be a sporting chance of giving you all no more than a bad half-hour."

"Three hours." Childrey had glanced at his watch.

"Very well. And I've no doubt that he'd taken other measures. A letter on its way to Australia, by surface mail, perhaps, and then due to come back the same way. At the worst you'd have had no more than a few months in quod."

"Go on," Halberd said grimly.

"There's very little to tell! He spread a few useful lies: that one of you had egged him on to arrange this fishing-party; that he was nurturing something between thoughts and intentions of suicide (although that was *not* a lie); that he had evidence of some discreditable sharp practice on

Childrey's part. Then, similarly, he prepared his few useful
clues: making that footprint, filching the cord from Gryde's
dressing-gown, making his little imperfectly burnt heap of
old business letters. After that, he had just one more thing
to prepare."

"You mean to tell us," Halberd said, "that he killed himself
just for the fun of playing us a rotten trick?"

"Certainly. It was to be his last masterpiece in the
Comedy of—"

"Yes, yes. But surely—"

"My dear Halberd, didn't you notice he was a sick man?
It's my guess that he was very sick indeed—with no more
than months, or perhaps weeks, before him."

"My God—the poor devil! Ending his days with a revolt-
ing piece of malice." Halberd frowned. "What was that you
said about gas cylinders?"

"There are three stored at the back of the cottage. Two
contain butane, all right, but the third contains hydrogen.
And all he needed apart from that was a fair-sized child's
balloon—just not too big to go up that chimney. Plenty of
lift in it to float away a very small gun. With this west wind,
it must be over the North Sea by now. So you see why he had
to die with his head in the fireplace—and why the doctor is
puzzling over the odd position of the body."

"The sergeant of police," Gryde said, "isn't puzzling over
that footprint. Because you trampled it out of existence."

There was a long silence while three exhausted fishermen
stared at a retired Metropolitan Commissioner.

"It will be thought," Appleby said, "that Vivarini was
shot by some professional criminal who had an eye on our

wallets, and who knew he had major charges to face if he was apprehended. Something like that. The police don't always end up with an arrest, but they never fail to have a theory of the crime."

"Is it going to be safe?" Gryde asked.

"Fairly safe, I'd suppose." For the first time since his arrival at Dunwinnie, there was a hint of contempt in Appleby's voice. "But safe or not, I judge it decent that this particular comedy of Frederick Vivarini's shall never be played before a larger audience than it has enjoyed tonight."

The Running of the Deer

P. M. Hubbard

Philip Maitland Hubbard (1910–80) was an Englishman who spent much of his childhood in Guernsey and in later life relocated to Scotland. He worked as a civil servant in India for a number of years and subsequently worked for the British Council, ultimately becoming a freelance writer. His first novel of suspense, *Flush as May*, appeared in 1963 and had fifteen successors; he also wrote children's fiction. His style of writing was elegant but resolutely unsensational, yet he acquired a devoted band of admirers, and his books remain interesting and readable if still undervalued to this day.

He had a gift for creating a sense of unease that was enhanced by his effective use of remote countryside settings, vividly conveyed. Rural Scotland in particular seems to have fired his imagination and features in a number of his books. They include *The Causeway* (1976), about a mysterious island connected to the coast by the eponymous causeway,

The Graveyard (1975) and *The Whisper in the Glen* (1972). *Cold Waters* (1970) is set on an unnamed loch in Scotland. Hubbard wrote poetry, often unpublished, and a handful of short stories, including this one, which appeared in *Winter's Crimes 6*, edited by George Hardinge, in 1974.

———

STAG SHOOTING IS SPORT FOR GENTLEMEN, GENERALLY with a certain amount of help from the paid hands. It is done in the summer and early autumn. The shooting of the hinds is paid work, very hard work done out of necessity in the worst of the Highland weather. Murder, except in Ulster and some of our larger cities, is for amateurs, and has no close season. It is not difficult to shoot a young stag in the mistaken belief that it is a grown hind, but, such mistakes apart, the shooting of the hinds cannot coincide with the shooting of the stags, because by law the one begins only when the other ends. Murder, having no statutory season, may coincide with either. What I shall never know is whether on this occasion it did. I think I know more or less what happened, and I know it happened during the shooting of the hinds. What I do not know is whether it was murder. What happened was this.

The Glenervie keeper was out of commission, sick, when the hind season started. Everyone knew what the Glenervie keeper's trouble was, but it is a trouble endemic in the Highlands, even more than in the rest of Scotland, and it comes on gradually and has to be very far advanced before it can make a man unemployable. It can do this either by wrecking his physical health or by simply taking up too much of his time. And McBain, even moderately sober, was a good keeper (which means a reasonably honest one) and a wonderful stalker. Sooner or later Colonel Guthrie, who owned Glenervie, would have to get rid of him, but the time had not yet come. For the time being the colonel put up with his intermittent disabilities for the sake of his unarguable, if equally intermittent, excellences. During the grouse and stalking seasons, when Colonel Guthrie was always at the Lodge, and there were generally guests in the house, McBain kept his trouble in check and earned the admiration of all of them. But when the autumn shut down into the early Highland winter, and the Lodge was more often than not empty, with the colonel away south, McBain gave up the struggle and let his trouble get the better of him, and this particular year, for the first time, it got the better of his iron constitution as well as his judgement, and put him on his back with a bronchitis that played a dangerous brinkmanship with pneumonia, until Dr. Macindoe came and did some very straight talking. Not to McBain, on whom it would have been largely wasted, but to Mrs. McBain, through whom its effect on McBain was reckoned considerable. So, as I say, McBain was out of commission, and the question was who would see to the hind shooting, which had to be done.

It had to be done, because the Red Deer Commission, which is a statutory body charged with the oversight of all the red deer herds in Scotland, tells each owner annually how many hinds he must take out of the herds reckoned to be on his lands, and he is under an obligation to meet this quota. It is an obligation he recognises and is anxious as far as possible to meet, because it is part of the general rules of the game which the Highland lairds are as united in supporting as they are given to furious private quarrelling among themselves over the detailed administration of their estates. There are other considerations as well. For one thing, if the directive is persistently disregarded, the Commission can put in its own men to do the necessary shooting. Not only would this be a terrible affront to the laird's honour and to the almost phrenetic sense of ownership which is his dominant emotion. It is also true, or at least generally supposed, that the men put in by the Commission might be pretty rough and ready in their methods, and the laird has strongly marked in him that protective affection for his own beasts which your shooting man generally has, and which your non-shooting man finds so extraordinarily hard to reconcile with the fact that he nevertheless shoots them.

For another thing there is the question of money. A well-grown hind, legitimately sold and exported as carcase meat to Germany (the Germans have an insatiable appetite for venison) can at present rates be worth forty pounds or more, and unless he is prepared to let his rights, the price of his deer is about the only cash income the owner gets from his estate. To shoot the required number of hinds is profitable as well as honourable. So the Glenervie hinds had to be shot, and McBain was not on hand to see to the shooting. This is where I came in.

Colonel Guthrie had a considerable acreage, and his quota was a hundred and fifty beasts. To shoot and bring in that lot would in any case mean temporary extra hands working with McBain and under his direction, and the colonel had already bespoken the services of Jamie and Dougal. But now

McBain himself was out of the hunt. A third man was in any case needed, and a responsible one. Jamie and Dougal were both reliable men on the hill, or the colonel would not have employed them. They were reliable, that is, where the live beasts were concerned, which means that they could be trusted to shoot only to kill, and to go after a beast if it was wounded and on its feet, and to shoot any sucking calves whose dams had been shot and who would die of starvation if left to themselves. With the dead beasts it was another matter. At prevailing prices there was a very strong temptation to leave the odd beast lying on the hill instead of hanging in the laird's larder, and to collect it later for private sale to an unscrupulous dealer. McBain would have none of that. It is the good keeper's duty to see that no one cheats his laird but himself, just as the honest butler will let no one but himself drink his master's port. Everyone knew Jamie was honest, but a good many of us had our doubts about Dougal, and the local code would not allow Jamie, even if he suspected Dougal of a fiddle, to say as much to the colonel when it was not his proper job to do so.

That was why the colonel thought of me. I had lived in the glen up to three years or so earlier. I knew the people, what there were of them, and I passed for gentry, which meant that I was assumed to be on the colonel's side and in his confidence. No one would try anything if I was around any more than they would if McBain was. And merely as a third hand I knew the ropes and could pull my weight. So he asked me to come up and stay in one of his cottages (the Lodge was shut) and to work with Jamie and Dougal till the job was done. Of course he would make it worth my while in a gentlemanly sort of way, but he asked me because he knew I was free and would enjoy it. The Highlands in winter have an extraordinary, steely fascination which your summer visitor knows nothing of, and to return to the intense, ingrown personal relations of the glen was always a rewarding experience. It could also at times be a rather frightening one. It was this time, but I did not know how frightening it was going to be.

I knew both Jamie and Dougal well, and had been out on the hill at times with both of them. They were both bachelors, but very different. Jamie was a man in his late thirties, of that serious, intensely respectable cast of mind which you think of (often quite mistakenly) as being typical of the Lowland Scot, but which is much less common in the Highlands. He lived with a much younger brother, Donald, and his brother's even younger dog, Spot. Spot worshipped Donald, and Donald worshipped Jamie, and Jamie presided over the household with humanity but unquestioned authority. They all got on very well together. Dougal was a very different kettle of fish. He must have been all of ten years younger than Jamie, but still a lot older than Donald. He lived by himself and worked for the Forestry Commission, but always seemed able to find time for odd assignments of this sort, and would work twenty-four hours in the day if he could get paid for it. He was a rather dashing, good-looking chap, and was reputed a great one for the women, though money remained his prime interest. But above all he was smooth, and in the Highlands this is very rare indeed. He was a man everyone got on with, but no one, I think, completely trusted. (The men, that is. I do not know about the women.) His eye was too firmly and visibly on the main chance.

When I got to Glenervie I found the wind bitter from the

north-west and the hills patched with a light fall of snow, so that the rocks and heather ridges stood out black against a general whiteness. This does not hamper your going as a heavier fall does, but it makes shooting difficult, because the alternating dark and light backgrounds play hell with the sighting of your rifle. As Jamie himself had once said to me, "'Tis ill shooting the beasts on the black and white country." As soon as I arrived I began to gather news. You always do in the Highlands. Everybody volunteers it. News is not necessarily the same as information, because your Highlander has no overwhelming interest in the truth as such. If it is something of practical significance, in which his own interest is involved, he will give it to you straight, at any rate as he believes it to be, but otherwise his instinct is to say what is interesting rather than what is factually correct. This makes him extraordinarily good company but, except within the limits stated, unreliable as a source of information. Almost the first news I heard was that Jamie was married. This was very surprising in itself, and the more I heard of it, the more surprising it sounded.

"Ay," said Cameron at the station. "He's married right enough. Glasgow lass she was. Working in a hotel, I heard."

I said, "And what does Donald think of it?" because that worried me a bit, but he was quite firm.

"Och," he said, "they get on fine."

Robertson on the bus said, "Ay, a bonnie woman, you'll see, and a good housekeeper. She's set them all to rights. Met on a bus, they did. She was a conductress from what I heard."

I put this version down to professional interest, and was variously told later that Jamie had found his wife in a shop, taking the tickets in a cinema and behind a bar. But they all seemed to like her, and agreed that the thing seemed to be working well. So far, at any rate. They did not say this, but they all seemed to have some slight mental reservation, as I had myself. A Glasgow girl, if that was what she was, would take a deal of settling in Glenervie, and Jamie's peculiar household could never be an easy one to settle in. I wondered, but hoped for the best. If Donald was happy with it, I thought, that would be the main test, and everyone seemed to agree he was. He would be a grown boy by now, fifteen or sixteen, and no doubt already making a sort of living for himself doing odd jobs at different seasons, which in the Highlands, where regular employment is scarce, is a perfectly respectable thing to do.

He was a grown boy all right, and a curiously impressive one. Jamie, he and Spot came in a body to visit me soon after I got in. They all seemed in their way glad to see me, and I was certainly very glad to see them. I could not see any change in Jamie, though I looked for it, the way you do, as if merely being married ought to leave some mark on a man, which of course it does not, or not for a fairly long time, and not always then. I congratulated him, and he smiled cheerfully with that very deliberate, slow-burning smile of his. "Ay," he said, "I reckoned I had been a bachelor long enough. You'll be meeting Jessie."

"I look forward to it," I said. I did, too, in more ways than one. But as I say, it was Donald who made the impression on me, I suppose because in the course of nature it was he who had changed most. Physically he was just what a boy of that age should be, more length than breadth, but graceful rather than gangling. And he was very quiet, with intelligent, watchful eyes and an extraordinarily sweet smile, which came and went even slower than Jamie's. Very nice, I thought, but a dark one. The two seemed even closer together than ever. Whatever Jessie was like, she clearly had not come between them. Of the three of them only Spot had put on flesh. He was enormously pleased with himself, too. I reckon you can always tell a dog that comes from a cheerful home, and he had all the marks of it. But then Spot, by comparison with the others, was an extrovert.

We made plans to start work next day. Without McBain there no one was specifically in charge of operations, but it was Jamie who made the decisions. I was only an amateur, even if I was gentry and the laird's friend, and although my agreement was politely sought, I should have been over-ruled, equally politely, if I had ventured a suggestion of my own and it had been a wrong one. Your experienced stalker, after all, is used to telling the gentry what to do. There are plenty of stories about it. As for Dougal, he was younger and a lesser man than Jamie, and would accept his judgement. At any rate, he would agree to act on it, and if he had other ideas of his own, he would keep them to himself. That was Dougal all over, smooth, as I said, and just a little devious.

I did not actually see Dougal till next day, when I found him as sharp looking as ever and very polite and charming. I thought, when I observed them together, that there was a touch of constraint between him and Jamie, but it was difficult to tell with two men as self-contained as that, and in any case it was no more than I should have expected. The Jamies and Dougals of this world make it their business to get on all right, but they keep an eye on each other while they are doing it. The wind was still in the north-west, and we worked up into it along the western face of Sron Quaich. I was out of condition and found the going very hard, but I shot a couple of beasts, and shot them well, which put me in better heart. Donald came out with us, walking with Jamie and following his every move. He was still too young to be trusted with a rifle, but helped with the dragging and other chores. He was a natural on the hill, apparently impervious to discomfort, quite inexhaustible and so quick and sure on his feet that he made even the formidable Dougal look slow and awkward. Spot, of course, had been left at home. A dog, however well disciplined, has no place in stalking, and even a well-intentioned dog can set the deer running for miles. We got seven beasts in all, and by the time we had got them home and into the larder, and cleaned them for the butcher, it was a fair day's work, and all I could think of was a dram and a hot bath and putting my feet up. It was very cold now, colder than ever, and during the night more snow fell. It was when we assembled next morning that I first saw Jamie's Jessie.

The Landrover swung into the Lodge yard in the cold grey light. Dougal was there already, and he and I were chatting, a little elaborately, when Jamie arrived. As the car turned in towards us, we stopped talking and just stood there, watching it. It was then that I saw three faces behind the windscreen, with Jamie's, unmistakable, on the near side and Donald's smaller, paler face in the middle. The heavy car was handled with competence, even a certain amount of panache, and I wondered who the driver was. It still did not occur to me that it might be Jessie. I turned to ask Dougal, but the look on his face made me turn back to the car again with my question unspoken. It was a tense, expectant look. When the car stopped, Jamie got out and Donald after him. I walked over to meet them. Jamie looked at me, I think a little hesitantly. Then he said, "Good morning, Mr. Bowen. You've no met my wife?"

He led me to the driver's side of the car, and as we came round, the woman at the wheel put a hand up and slipped the kerchief from over her head. She stayed sitting at the wheel, but slid the window back, and looked from one to the other of us, smiling a little, as we came to it. I knew at once why she had taken the kerchief off. Her hair was the great thing about her. There was a mass of it, coiled up on her head, and it was of that tremendous burnished red, something between chestnut and copper, which you still seem to find only in Scotland, or where there is Scots blood about. The face under the hair was round, pale and just short of pretty, but she had considerable charm and a quite extraordinary self-possession. Whether or not she had been behind a bar when Jamie found her, I knew at once that she had been used to dealing with men, all sorts of men not of her choosing, as part of her job. Her self-possession, and her whole manner of talking to you, was professional. I could not see much of her body, bundled up against the cold and hidden in the driver's seat, but I thought she would be on the plump side. She was unexpectedly impressive altogether, I think older than I had expected, and certainly attractive. I could understand now why Jamie had picked on her, wherever he had found her. As person to person, she was up to his weight.

We introduced ourselves pleasantly enough and exchanged a few banalities. Her voice was good, too, full and throaty, with a braw Scots accent that might or might not be Glasgow, but sounded well enough in her mouth. Then she slid the window back, put on her kerchief again and took the car off with the same smooth competence, leaving the four of us standing there in the yard. Just for a moment there was silence between us, as if none of us knew quite what to say. I certainly did not. It is an impertinence in a man to congratulate another man on his wife, especially a man of Jamie's character, but I felt like congratulating him. Then Jamie said, "Now, then—", and we got down to the business of the day. It was only when the car had gone that I felt Dougal watching me, as if he wanted to see what I had made of her. But I was not going to share confidences about women with Dougal, not even unspoken confidences, and I avoided his eye. The constraint between him and Jamie seemed more marked than ever, but this may have been my imagination. I had not forgotten the look on Dougal's face as the car came into the yard.

We had another day of fair success. The snow made the going heavier and more treacherous, but it had brought the beasts lower down, and it made the dragging, when we came to it, a good deal easier. I was in better shape, too, already. On the whole I enjoyed the day, but I could not get that scene in the early morning wholly out of my mind. There was something about Jamie's Jessie, and about the whole situation, that had taken hold of me in a way I did not entirely like. Before we separated, we decided that we should return to Sron Quaich next day, working this time straight up the south face. The wind was still north-westerly, and looked like staying that way.

Jessie brought Jamie in the Landrover again next morning, but Donald was not with them. I asked Jamie where he was,

and he said he was away to some place or other. The name
did not convey anything to me, and I had no reason to press
the point. Then he went into the Lodge to collect some more
ammunition, which he had the keys of. The Landrover was
still standing in the yard with Jessie in the driving seat. I could
not see where Dougal was. I walked over to the car on its near
side, because it seemed the polite thing to pass the time of
day, and in any case I wanted to have another look at Jessie.

I came up to the nearside window and then saw, through
the glass, that Dougal was at the other window. The window
was open and he was looking in at Jessie. This time the look
on his face stopped me in my tracks. It was a proprietary
look, or perhaps only a look of anticipated possession, but he
seemed very sure of himself. She was looking at him, as self-
possessed as ever, but not in a way to take that look off his face.
They did not seem to be saying anything to each other, and I
do not think either of them saw me. I backed away, with the
high body of the car between me and Dougal, and walked over
to meet Jamie as he came out of the Lodge. As he came out,
I heard the Landrover move off, and for a moment he stood
watching it as it turned out of the gate. Then his eyes went
past me to Dougal, standing there by himself in the middle
of the yard. There was nothing special in his face, and when
he brought his eyes back to mine, he spoke as pleasantly as
ever. We walked over towards Dougal together.

When we got to the foot of the hill, we used our glasses
and saw a sizeable herd of the beasts spread out along the
crest of a ridge not too far up. They were grazing steadily,
scraping away at the snow with their forefeet in the way they
do to get at the grass underneath. Even if they saw us, they

took no notice of us at that distance. They seemed settled enough, and the wind blew steadily, not straight from them to us, but on a steep diagonal across our line of approach. It all looked all right.

We walked up in single file, with Jamie in the lead, until we were close enough to make serious stalking necessary. Then we spread out into line abreast, to cover the whole width of the herd. Dougal was on the left, Jamie in the centre and I on the right. We started about fifty yards apart, and the idea was to get up to within shooting distance at about the same time and still spaced out at about the same intervals. In that way we should be less likely to shoot each other's beasts and should be able to cover the whole herd between us. I say that was the idea, but of course each man had to work his own line of country, and this may involve a great deal of deviation and great variations of forward speed. The one agreed point was that if the beasts saw anything to make them suspicious, we should all stay where we were until they lost interest and got their heads down again.

There is no mistaking it if they think they are being stalked. First one beast, the one who first sees something suspicious, gets her head up and stands motionless as a rock, staring in the direction the threat seems to come from. She may merely swing her head round on her long swan-neck, or she may slew her whole body round to face you. In either case you see the great ears standing up like radar aerials on each side of the narrow head, and you know she is facing in your direction with eyes, ears and nostrils all at full stretch. Then you do not move at all. You may be crouched in some uncomfortable position behind a minute fringe of cover, caught in the act of movement, or you may be flat on your front in the snow or the peat bog. Of the two the snow is greatly preferable, and surprisingly warm to lie in, at least until it begins to melt under you. In any case you do not move. It is your patience and physical endurance against the beast's. She does not move either. Once one beast in a herd does this, the others see it, and some of them, the warier ones, join her in standing at gaze, while the rest go on grazing. If you win, they lose interest one by one, and you see their heads go down. It is the beast who started the watching who watches the longest. When she gives it up, you are free to move again, but it can be a long business, and very cold.

This time there was no general hold-up of that sort. We were all three experienced stalkers and taking our time. I lost sight of the others almost from the start. I could perhaps have seen one or the other of them at intervals if I had looked, but I did not look. When you are stalking, you look only at the beasts. We had to hope that we were all reasonably well up to the herd when the first man got into position and started shooting, but there could be no guarantee of this. Any one of us might have got himself stuck altogether, with virtually no hope of moving further without starting the whole herd. So each of us went on as best he could, each individually stalking the whole herd, and none of us knowing with any degree of accuracy where the others were. It is different if you are out on your own. Then time is no consideration, and you can work back any number of times. It is purely a matter of individual patience.

It is difficult, when you are always losing sight of the beasts for the moment behind folds in the ground, to keep an accurate idea of distance, but I had mentally fixed on a particular ridge ahead of me as the place from which I could probably open fire. I was still some way from it, but was within sight of the herd if I put my head up, when the thing happened. This was not a matter of one beast or two. All their heads went up together, so that the whole skyline was a fringe of flaring ears. I assumed, naturally, that they were looking in our direction, and I wondered which of us they had seen. In any case I knew they were going to break. The alarm was too general and sudden for them to get over it. It was only at the last moment that I realised that they were looking, not in our direction, but directly away from us, and when they broke, they broke downhill towards us. They still did not know we were there at all.

When the deer run, they run on established lines across the hill, or at least the leaders do, and the rest follow as nearly as possible in column behind them. When a whole herd runs, it tends to split into several columns running on roughly parallel lines. This herd had a lot of beasts in it, and it split into four or five columns, of which one headed almost straight for me and the others for various points in our line of rifles. It was extraordinary to have the deer coming straight at you like that and very difficult to know what to do. One of the first things you are taught is that you must never shoot at a beast until it is fully broadside on to you, and then you shoot at the heart. The red deer is a big animal, but very slender for its size, with no chest to speak of. That is because it is a running animal. It was also, of course, originally a forest animal (and will be again if the Forestry Commission get their way), and presumably built to get through narrow spaces. At any rate, if you shoot at it from the front, you are very likely to miss, and if you hit it, you will almost certainly wound it in one of several ghastly ways without bringing it down. So as I say, your whole training is to shoot only at the side of the beast, and here they all were coming at us head on.

But the columns were fanning out now, and it looked as if it was going to be possible to get a reasonably broadside shot in a moment or two. You do not at any sort of a distance shoot at a running beast if you can help it, but with the beasts as close as this it was safe enough. I do not know who shot first, but we all started shooting. My first shot was a clear miss, but I brought down a big beast, a yeld hind by the look of her, with my second. They did not stop at all. Shooting in itself still means very little to them. They hear the noise but do not know where it is coming from. If you shoot at a standing herd, even when some of them fall, the rest generally stand about hesitantly for several seconds before they run. Then they see you, because in the nature of things your head and shoulders must by then be visible, and they see your bolt arm working, but in the meantime you can generally, if you are in a good position and shooting well, get more than one beast in the herd. But here they were already running, and they did not stop at all when the rifles opened up. It was what was behind them that frightened them. It was all over in a matter of seconds, and then they were through our line and running away downhill behind us.

I picked myself up and dusted the snow crystals off the front of my clothes before they had time to melt and soak into the cloth. Then I turned to look for the others. I could not see either of them. I started walking back towards what I took to be the centre of the line, and then I saw Jamie. He was a good deal further back than I expected, standing looking down at a fallen beast. Then he lifted his head and saw me, and we started walking slowly towards each other. As we walked, we both automatically worked the bolts of our rifles, pushing the top remaining round down into the magazine and bringing the bolt forward on top of it. You never walk on the hill with a round in the breech. I still could not see Dougal.

I said, "What the hell started them running like that? I've never seen anything like it."

He looked at me and shook his head. We were both out of breath and a little shaken. The whole thing had been curiously unnerving. "Nor me," he said, "not in twenty years on the hill. I do not ken at all. They will have seen something over the top, maybe," and he moved his head up towards the skyline above us.

"Where's Dougal, then?" I said.

He seemed surprised, as if he had forgotten Dougal's existence. "Is he no there?" he said, and we both turned to look towards where Dougal should have been, but we could not see him. "He's away after a beast, maybe," said Jamie, and we walked together westward along the face, looking for our missing man. We saw him at the same moment, because he suddenly stood up out of the snow perhaps thirty yards from us. He had dropped his rifle and stood for a moment, uncertainly, with both hands pressed against one place in his side. Then he spun suddenly and went down again in the snow. We both started running at the same moment and came up to him together.

I do not know whether he was already dead when we got

to him, but if he was not, he died a matter of moments later. There was blood on the snow round him and under him. His rifle was five or six yards away. There was blood there too, and a line of dragging stains between there and where he now lay. The thing was, he was away up in front of where we had both been when the deer started running. He must have been well up to the herd and all ready to shoot when the thing happened. He was a good stalker, Dougal, and always went straight for whatever it was he wanted.

Jamie and I discussed, in a curiously matter-of-fact sort of way, the problem of getting him down off the hill. We knew one of us must have shot him, but the thing did not seem worth talking about for the moment. Accidents do happen on the hill, and in a totally unexpected situation like that anything could.

It was very late when I got back to my cottage. The business was all tidied up now, as far as it could be, and in the hands of the police and the procurator fiscal. There were some dead beasts still out on the hill, which Jamie and I would go out and collect tomorrow. And the hind-shooting must presumably go on, though now we should be one man short. There was nothing more we could do until they sent for us to give our evidence, and there was not much we could tell them, even then.

I lit my fire, and poured myself a dram, and drank it, and poured myself another. I was not sorry at all about what had happened. Only I still wondered what had made the deer run like that. I thought a dog would do it, but I knew of only one dog in these parts, and I had not seen him all day.

Hand in Glove

Jennie Melville

Gwendoline Butler (1922–2013) published many crime novels under her own name, usually featuring a detective called John Coffin, who first appeared in 1956 and took his final bow in *Coffin Knows the Answer* (2002). She was educated at Haberdasher's and at Lady Margaret Hall, Oxford, where she read History. When she wrote a book about history for children, however, she found that "no-one wanted it," so she turned to crime. Her husband, Dr. Lionel Butler, was a specialist in medieval history who took a post at the University of St. Andrews. When she saw a young, red-haired Scottish woman police officer one day (she was walking the dog at the time), she was inspired to create her second major series character, the Scottish detective Charmian Daniels.

The Daniels books, starting with *Come Home and Be Killed* (1962), were published under her grandmother's name, Jennie Melville. Charmian is introduced halfway through the book; she is twenty-seven and a detective constable. Born in Dundee, she took a degree in social science at Glasgow University before moving to England to pursue a career in the police, although she still "couldn't quite get the Dundee stones and jute factories out of her mind." In the event, Charmian's career lasted almost forty years. This story first appeared in *Winter's Crimes 6*, edited by George Hardinge, in 1974.

———

THE STRANGE THING ABOUT MY LOVER WAS THAT EVEN in our most intimate moments he always wore gloves. Mr. Macaulay was a scholar and a man of learning, besides being the Provost's nephew. There was a social gap between us, but it was still strange. He was in a different class from an affectionate widow with a small tobacco shop and a library attached. Of course I never expected him to marry me, my ambitions did not lie that way. Whatever it may be like in the novels of Mrs. Glyn (I bought a new one of hers for the library today—*Love's Blindness*: how the title strikes home!) there was not much chance of a widow of over thirty and the Provost's nephew making a match of it in our town. He was not likely to marry me even if he had not got a wife. Poor Jessie was not quite with us, as they say. She never was, and had been getting further and further away as her funny times came upon her. All the women of that family have been weak in mind, but strong of body and long of pocket. They have not been breeders either, so that heiresses have been common, and Jessie was one, like her mother before her. My granny said the trouble lay two or three generations back when two cousins (and here, with a nod of her wicked old head, she let me know that the cousins were closer kin than that under the blanket) were allowed to get wed. May be so, may be not. But Jessie was my schoolmate, and I knew her well. She had a sick little voice with many sibilants in it. Imagine a squirrel talking, and that was how Jessie talked.

The gloves teased me. They were soft, pale leather gloves, always the same sort; indoor gloves you might call them, all day, every day gloves. He wore them till they got greased and stained and then replaced them. No one in town spoke of them or made a joke about them, so that sometimes I used to think I imagined them, but no, they were there. Perhaps no one but me knew he wore them in bed, perhaps not even Jessie. Still, the gloves taunted me. "Oh, Mr. Macaulay," I would whisper, "why do you always wear gloves?" No answer, just a turning away, and, later, another passionate letter. Love and letters my life was then with Mr. Macaulay. After every meeting or sometimes when we did not meet, he went home, sat down and wrote me a letter. I recollect the little ink marks on the forefinger and thumb by which I would date the progress of the gloves through the month. Sometimes I would match a little blotch of ink on a letter to a special stain on the glove and warm my heart on it. Lovers have these fancies. I kept every letter, the gloves went I know not where.

The day his uncle, the Provost, was re-elected for a third time, Mr. Macaulay came to me already a little drunk. He had never arrived this way before, although I had sometimes sent him away in it. I never grudged him his drop, poor fellow. I thought he needed it to go back to Jessie.

"And is it true the old fox has bought an estate north of Aberdeen?" I said.

"The Provost has acquired some land there, yes. I am not at liberty to say how much."

Or what he paid, either, I thought, or if he paid anything much at all, for we all knew the old man had the knack of getting a good bargain. *Caveat Emptor* was a slogan invented for people like him, so my late husband, who was a solicitor's clerk before he joined up in 1915, used to say.

"But I will no' deny he is in well with the folk up there. So much so that they have suggested he might find them a person of learning and scholarship to be the next Rector of the Academy. Three hundred pupils," he said, with satisfaction.

I looked at him.

"It will not be for the next year or so, you understand, the present Rector has eighteen months more to run, but his successor will be appointed for 1929." He looked excessively pleased with himself. "You will guess who has been named."

"Yes, indeed." And I wondered how Jessie would decorate that high position, and thought how well I would have managed.

"It's in confidence, mind."

"Of course, no one shall hear from me, Mr. Macaulay," I said proudly. "And I suppose that new young lady who teaches chemistry at the High School and who is the Provost's wife's niece will be making a move too?" I said.

"Miss Freuchie? Nothing has been said."

"They say her aunt's husband is over fond of her," I observed.

"Never," he said promptly.

"There's a lot of slander uttered in the town," I agreed.

There was a pause. Then, "You have all my letters safe?"

"Every one," I agreed, with a smile. "Since the very first. Not one lost, each a treasure, each one preserved. But you didna' write last time. I looked, and listened for that little lappet on the mat, but it never came."

"I shall write this time."

That evening, perhaps because of the drink, or perhaps I'd tired him, he fell asleep.

So, fly and gentle, I peeled the gloves from his hands. They were real hands, after all. Do you know, I had wondered. I had heard of men come back from the war with tin fingers. True, he never served in the war. But he had a strange disability, the palms and the insides of the fingers were black. I do not mean black as if they were dirty or as if they were pigmented, but the palms were pitted under the skin with little black pellets, as if he had been handling coal. I touched his palm gently with my fingers and felt the lumps beneath the skin. Each resembled something between a wart and a black mole.

I drew the gloves over his hands, then sat waiting for him to make his departure.

"Goodbye, Mr. Macaulay."

"Goodnight. You have all my letters safe?"

"In a tin box under my bed," I assured him.

His letter duly came plummeting through the letterbox sooner than I expected. Blunt it was and short.

"Please, Mistress Lindsay, will you return all my letters at once?

> *"It behoves us to end our relationship in the light of my expected new status."*

There was a little more, but not much.

Outside in the street I could hear the clop-clop of the dray horse going home to the corn-chandler's up the hill. I heard the newsboy, Wee Davey, shouting in the distance. Close at hand, the shop bell tinkled in the draper's next door. Behind me in the sitting-room the wireless set was tuned in to the National Programme from London. It was someone-something and the Savoy Hotel Orpheans. I thought at the moment I would remember that name for ever. But it has gone. Gone. I find this both sad and comforting.

On the back of Mr. Macaulay's note I scribbled a message saying I would never return his letters, nor destroy them, but he could trust me never to show them to a soul. Then I put it in an envelope and dropped it through his door. Two can play at that game.

After that he came several times knocking on my door and whispering for his letters; but I never answered.

I took my best hat, that came from Princes Street, out of its box and set it ready for Sunday, and on Sunday I wore it to kirk. Miss Freuchie was there, and the Provost's wife. I didn't look to see anyone else.

The organ started and I looked down to pray and saw that my neighbour's shoes had little square bronze buckles, and the lady next to her wore shoes with three tiny black buttons up the side. They led the eye upward to the ankle where three cloques on the stocking anchored themselves. The feet were Miss Freuchie's.

We were looking down and praying and thinking of nothing else when there was a noise at the door. Then feet hurried up the aisle and feet hurried down. I recognised the black boots and the brown boots: the Provost and Mr. Macaulay.

When we came out from the service, one hour and twenty minutes later, the Minister shook each hand as we passed and whispered in each ear that our dear sister, Mrs. Jessie Macaulay, had passed away suddenly that forenoon as we prayed. Heart attack was the word.

"Your old schoolmate, Mistress Lindsay, I remember fine seeing you hurrying into school together, red plaits and fair, hanging down the back."

Jessie's hair was thick and greasy and hung on her neck like a white pudden: flaxen fair, it was, but not kempt.

Winter fell upon us suddenly and savagely, and Jessie's grave was dug in the iron earth. Poor Jessie, she never gave anyone a warm bed and nobody gave her one. Her estate settled well, I understand. And do you know, she left me something; the only school prize she ever got, an Old and New Testament, illustrated. I think that was real sarcastic of Jessie and more than I should have expected of her.

"Can I have some cigarettes for ma granny?" A hoarse voice interrupted my thoughts. "She'll settle up at the end of the week."

I sighed. "She smokes too much and so do you, Wee Davey."

"It's her job," he said hoarsely. "It plays on her nerves, y'see." Wee Davey was not short, six foot at least and big with it, as they say. Nor was he a boy, he'd been Wee Davey these thirty years, but he was simple. Not *stupid*, mind, but simple. Everybody's errand boy he was, shifting from butcher to baker as the need arose. His grandmother was an ancient nurse: midwife and layer-out, she called herself. But most mothers chose the Cottage Hospital and only the dead, having no choice, got Granny McGregor.

"It's the monotony," he said. He shuffled uneasily.

"What is it then, Davey?" He trusted me because I did not shout at him. He had lovely shoulders and a fine fair skin. I could not shout at a man like that, wherever he kept his mind.

He kept his eyes on the counter. "It's a message from m'granny."

"Yes?"

"Gran's worrit about Mistress Macaulay."

"The *late* Mistress Macaulay," I said.

"That's the trouble of it."

Gradually he got it out. The trouble of it was that when his Granny came to the proper performance of her duties she had found two little holes in the back of Jessie's neck, hidden by the thick hair.

"The hair was that thick and greasy and kind of stuck, and Granny thinks no one noticed the holes. There wasna' much blood."

"What does Granny think the holes were?" I asked softly.

He looked round him carefully. "Bullet holes. Small bore."

Because of the bullet holes, Granny did not think Jessie had died of heart failure. She had not told anyone but her grandson; now he had told me.

"She isna' going to do anything about it," he said. I nodded in understanding. "She wanted you to know."

This was the first time I grasped that the whole town from the Minister to Wee Davey knew about Mr. Macaulay and me.

I had thought Granny McGregor would have told no one, perhaps she never did, perhaps it came from another source, but suddenly it was like a wind blowing through the town. Mind, you could not put a finger on exactly what was being said or who was saying it. Except that something was wrong.

I saw Wee Davey around the streets, but he did not meet my eye, and we did not speak. We were better apart.

At intervals would come pathetic appeals from Mr. Macaulay that I would return his letters, or destroy them. I had thought he would have known better.

And then suddenly the gossip stopped because there was something so much more terrible to talk about. This was the day of the seven deaths, when a batch of poisoned sausages was sold from the main butcher's of the town, and Wee Davey and his Granny and a lot of other folk besides ate them and were ill. Davey, who was helping out at the butcher's shop that day, was thought to have caused it all by carelessly mixing into the sausages oatmeal containing rat poison. But as he and his Granny were amongst those who died, none of the enquiries made ever came to anything. I might have eaten those sausages myself if Davey had not forgotten to deliver my own order to me.

The church bells were ringing all that week and a substitute for Wee Davey's Granny was brought over in a special car from the County Town.

"So there you are," I said to myself, watching it all from behind the curtains. "That's over."

No sooner said, than there was a tapping at the side door and a gaunt face with hollow cheeks was to be seen. Mr. Macaulay begged me to let him in. He was all in black, naturally, except for his gloves, which were pale and new, so his mourning did not extend this far. I was interested to see them, as I had thought that with the departure of Jessie they might perhaps have been put away.

I would not be the first to speak.

"I could not keep away, Désirée," he said, using our private name for me. I turned my head away.

"Ambition, Mr. Macaulay, remember your ambition. I haven't heard it said you've abandoned it."

"Cold," he muttered, speaking perhaps of me, perhaps of the day. "May I not come inside?"

"You took your welcome for granted once," I said, but I opened the door. His tall blackness seemed to douse the light. I took a poker and stirred the fire. Other fires were stirred, too, because he grasped me warmly.

"The other room, love?" he said, urging me in the direction of the bedroom. "Ah, you've lit the fire."

"It's been lit every night since it became cold." I looked at the blaze and it seemed to glitter mischief, mischief at me.

"So you *did* hope I'd come."

The only light in the bedroom was the wicked firelight.

"I've heard your ambitions go higher. I've heard you're planning to emigrate to Canada."

"What's that?" He stopped, coat half on, half off.

"Not true?"

"Not a word of it."

I smiled then. "It'll be on account of Miss Freuchie, that will be where the confusion crept in. She's said to be going."

"Very like. Very like." He reached out a hand, a gloved

hand and held me. "You and I need not think of her, eh, eh, Désirée?"

He knew my weakness. I have always been a shockingly weak woman, and it is the cleverness of him that discovered it.

I was weakening with every minute that passed, as he knew. I wanted to be strong, but I was weak.

"Have you still got that rosy pink gown? The one that touched your colour up so? Didn't I mention that gown in my letters?" His arm came round me. "Still got my letters safe?"

"Very safe."

"Shall we have a drink, my dear? Will you allow me one? Surely you will. Away with you and get it, and when you come back I shall be waiting."

From the door I said: "I don't know why you worry about your letters. They're safe with me."

"But if you should take sick or die," he said solemnly, "they might fall into the wrong hands."

"But I'm not going to die, Mr. Macaulay," I said. And I thought: Am I, then?

When I had changed into my red robe I thought that it was a pity to take the whisky cold and that it would go well with a cup of hot tea.

"I'm waiting for the kettle to boil," I called, looking through the door. He had undressed and got into the bed and was lying back across the pillows, humming softly to himself, looking the picture of comfort.

You look pretty pleased with yourself, I thought.

"An excellent idea," he said. "One pleasure should always come bound with another."

You've had no pleasure yet, I thought to myself.

"And which pleasure's the greater?" I called.

He wagged a finger. "You know what Sir Thomas More, that great scholar, said of sexual love: that the pleasure of it was like the relief of voiding urine."

Thank you. Thank you. Thank you, I thought, now we know where we stand.

"I'm just letting the tea settle," I called out. My eye fell on Jessie's bequest, the Bible. Poor Jessie, I thought, remembering her story and those two little holes in the neck. I picked up the Bible. The leaves fell apart and a piece of paper fluttered out.

On it was written, in a feminine handwriting:

"The recipe is to make sodium cyanide, which I believe is as toxic as hydrogen cyanide, but acts more slowly. If the latter seems more desirable I suggest adding vinegar.

"Required:
1. *Zinc dust*
2. *Bicarb. of soda. Heat powder at about 80 C for ten minutes, stirring gently.*
3. *Saccharin tablets finely ground..."*

The writing broke off there in the middle of a sentence. I had either the first draft or an incomplete copy of a sinister recipe which had fallen into Jessie's hands. Now I knew why Jessie had left me the Bible.

"Did you think you might die by poison, Jess? And did you want me to know? And was your bequest a warning or an accusation? Oh, Jess, how much cleverer and stronger you have proved to be than I had expected, reaching out beyond the grave."

I was trembling, then I was steadied by the thought that Jessie would have recognised the handwriting and known it was not mine. I would swear it was Miss Freuchie's.

My hand was steady as I assembled the tray with pot, sugar, tea cups, and kettle. I thought of Jessie and of Wee Davey and his Granny and all the other victims. All gone, all unavenged. I knew well enough that no adequate enquiry into their deaths would ever come about. Our town was closed up tight against questions.

I carried the tray in and poured the cups out and put in milk and sugar, and then deliberately turned aside so he could put his poison in the cup I should never drink. I meant to keep cup and contents for ever as a warning. But for Jessie I might have drunk it.

All that wickedness, I thought, and no punishment. It was a terrible thought.

And then, as I approached with a cup of tea I knew that I was wrong. There was a punishment. He was lolling back, one knee cocked, still thinking of Sir Thomas More, no doubt.

I coughed. "Oh, Mr. Macaulay," I said delicately. "Your little trouble, you know, your disability, what you have on your hands. *Have you noticed it is spreading all over you?*"

If you've enjoyed *The Edinburgh Mystery,*
you won't want to miss

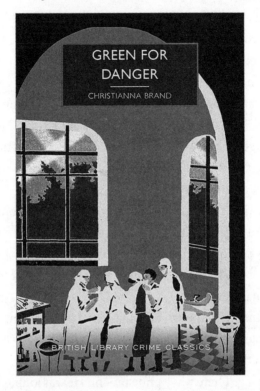

Praise for the
British Library Crime Classics

"Carr is at the top of his game in this taut whodunit... The British Library Crime Classics series has unearthed another worthy golden age puzzle."

—*Publishers Weekly*, STARRED Review,
for *The Lost Gallows*

"A wonderful rediscovery."
—*Booklist*, STARRED Review, for *The Sussex Downs Murder*

"First-rate mystery and an engrossing view into a vanished world."

—*Booklist*, STARRED Review, for *Death of an Airman*

"A cunningly concocted locked-room mystery, a staple of Golden Age detective fiction."

—*Booklist*, STARRED Review, for *Murder of a Lady*

"The book is both utterly of its time and utterly ahead of it."
—*New York Times Book Review* for *The Notting Hill Mystery*

"As with the best of such compilations, readers of classic mysteries will relish discovering unfamiliar authors, along with old favorites such as Arthur Conan Doyle and G.K. Chesterton."

—*Publishers Weekly*, STARRED Review, for *Continental Crimes*

"In this imaginative anthology, Edwards—president of Britain's Detection Club—has gathered together overlooked criminous gems."

—*Washington Post* for *Crimson Snow*

"The degree of suspense Crofts achieves by showing the growing obsession and planning is worthy of Hitchcock. Another first-rate reissue from the British Library Crime Classics series."

—*Booklist*, STARRED Review, for *The 12.30 from Croydon*

"Not only is this a first-rate puzzler, but Crofts's outrage over the financial firm's betrayal of the public trust should resonate with today's readers."

—*Booklist*, STARRED Review, for *Mystery in the Channel*

"This reissue exemplifies the mission of the British Library Crime Classics series in making an outstanding and original mystery accessible to a modern audience."

—*Publishers Weekly*, STARRED Review, for *Excellent Intentions*

"A book to delight every puzzle-suspense enthusiast."

—*New York Times* for *The Colour of Murder*

"Edwards's outstanding third winter-themed anthology showcases 11 uniformly clever and entertaining stories, mostly from lesser known authors, providing further evidence of the editor's expertise…This entry in the British Library Crime Classics series will be a welcome holiday gift for fans of the golden age of detection."

—*Publishers Weekly*, STARRED Review, for *The Christmas Card Crime and Other Stories*

Poisoned Pen
PRESS

poisonedpenpress.com